Olivia

By the Author

My Date with a Wendigo

Olivia

Olivia

by

Genevieve McCluer

2020

OLIVIA

ISBN 13: 978-1-63555-701-5

This Trade Paperback Original Is Published By
Bold Strokes Books, Inc.
P.O. Box 249
Valley Falls, NY 12185

First Edition: July 2020

Credits
Editor: Barbara Ann Wright
Production Design: Stacia Seaman
Cover Design by Tammy Seidick

Acknowledgments

Thank you to Cristina for being an indispensable resource for Toronto. Thank you to Jessica, Danny, Alexandra, and Kassandra for all of your support and help. And a special thanks to my editor, Barbara. This definitely wouldn't have happened without you.

Prologue

Elizabeth: The New Client

My office is finally clean. It's taken over an hour to get out the smell of the mapinguary, but I suppose I knew what I was in for when I started working with fiends. They can't all be as conscious of their odors as my wife is. Tossing the empty bottle of Febreze into the trash can, I holler for Ashley to send in my next client. A tall woman, who looks to be in her thirties—though who knows for how long—with her hair in long dreadlocks, walks in and glances at the beaten-up couch across from me. This must be my two o'clock appointment. I believe her name is Olivia Crocetti. I rise to greet her, extending my hand. "Ms. Crocetti, it's a pleasure to meet you."

She recoils, leaping back to the door. "You're Elizabeth Rosseau-Lester?" She looks skeptical, but more like she's terrified that it is true than that it's not. I've had a lot of strange reactions since I started working here, but this is a new one. Usually, it's more the clients trying to eat me and a lot less acting like I'm trying to eat them. Maybe it's my hair?

"I am. Why don't you have a seat? You don't have to shake my hand if that makes you uncomfortable." I sit as a demonstration. "Why don't you tell me what brings you here?"

Her gaze shifts between me and the door. She looks like she wants to bolt. "If you cancel last minute, you still have to pay full price." Obviously, if there are extenuating circumstances as to why she can't see me, I'd waive that, but since she seems incapable of making up her mind, it might give her that last bit of encouragement she needs to stay to work on her problems. She only made the appointment a few hours ago and didn't leave a message, so I have no idea what she might be here for. Here's hoping it's not anthrophobia, cause I'm doubting I can help with a fear of humans.

"Your receptionist…I assumed you'd be another ghoul."

I'd hired Ashley a few months back. It actually cost less than my original method of giving her a percentage every time she stood guard during an appointment, plus she seems to enjoy it. The only downside has been that sometimes, her spinning desk chair gets a little too loud in the middle of my appointments. "I'm afraid I'm not. Is that going to be an issue?"

She hesitates, looking for words. It's clear that this isn't a comfortable subject for her. "You're human."

It's anthrophobia. This will be complicated. It's like going to a spider for help with arachnophobia. Although I should keep that in mind. I may have to invite Penelope over for some exposure therapy once Roland reaches that point. "I assure you, fiend problems are no stranger to me. I've been working with you all for over a year. You can talk to me. I can help."

"I'm sure Bram Stoker said the same thing."

She's a vampire. I've heard about the baggage they have with him. She's both more and less pale than I would have expected. Definitely nothing like Blade. "You're not my only vampire client. Please, let me help. Let me show you that humans aren't all bad. What brings you here today?" And please say it's not just to learn how to deal with humans. Talk about diving in headfirst if she has a human therapist.

She seriously considers the doorway. All she has to do is walk out. It's not like Ashley or I will chase her. I'd be out a hundred bucks, but that's not her problem. She takes one step and hesitates. I think she's looking at Ashley, but there's a wall blocking my view, so I can't be sure. It took me ages to get used to Ashley's eyes. They don't look like they should be able to see, as gray and milky as they are.

I let her take her time. I've put enough pressure on her already. I don't want to add any more. She'll decide eventually.

"My parrot's sick," she finally says.

I'll admit, this is not a response I was ready for. It raises way more questions. Is it nocturnal? Does she have a bright colorful parrot that squawks all over her ancient castle, manor, or lair? Does it sit on her shoulder? Was she ever a pirate? "That's not really my area of expertise."

"I'm aware of that," she grumbles, finally closing the door. She makes no effort to move to the couch or even face me. "There's no fiend vet. I have to see that one we all see. I think I heard her name was Sun."

"Yes, Amelia Sun. I refer a lot of my patients to her."

Her body is still, gaze locked on the closed door. She doesn't even need to breathe. It took Dennis quite a while to grow used to that. He was still trying to breathe for months. "I thought you'd be able to help, but you're just another human. I don't know what I was thinking. You can't magic years of abuse away. I need to take Harvey in tomorrow. He's quite ill. I'm not sure what's wrong with him, and I can't make it go away. I'm not losing him."

It's all starting to make sense. It is anthrophobia, and it sounds like for good reason, but if she can't get over it, her pet bird might die. That gives me a specific goal to work toward, even if it's flatly impossible in a single session, no matter how good I am. Being the object she's afraid of will only make it that much harder. "Then let's get to work. Your parrot's name is Harvey?" Build a bond, make her trust you. She needs to see me as…well, not human, so a vampire?

"There's no point." Her hand flies to the doorknob. I don't even see the motion. It's a neat trick, but being married to a wendigo has given me plenty of time to grow accustomed to it. "I'm not dealing with a human therapist."

As the knob starts to move, I say, "Then turn me." She stops, turning toward me, the door still closed. I may have saved the appointment. I want to get turned anyway. My wife's immortal. It makes things easier for me.

For only the second time since she walked in, Olivia faces me. Her eyes lock on mine. I find myself falling. I've never dealt with a vampire who is more than a few decades old. It's like staring into a bottomless void. Wow, I thought being under a siren's song was bad.

Her mouth opens, revealing sharp fangs as she takes a step. I'm not sure if I'm incapable of moving or if I've actually stepped toward her, but she's growing closer and closer. The last time one bit me wasn't anything like this. My scar itches thinking about it, and it's enough to lure me back to reality. I still don't move, but I regain my senses, righting myself. I'm not sure when I stepped out of my chair.

"That's unusual," she says.

"I told you, you aren't my first vampire."

Her gaze travels up and down my body as if she's checking out a piece of succulent meat. God, I haven't had a good steak in ages. Abby's been having a rough time of late, so I've been trying to avoid keeping meat around the house. "I'm not sure making you like me would help."

"It means you won't be afraid of me. Besides, you're endangered. Right? Think of it as conservation."

She closes her mouth and steps back. Great, why is it so hard to find someone willing to make me into a fiend? Ever since Abby pulled that vampire off me, it seems like it can't happen. Maybe I should suck it up and ask Dennis. I'll give him a discount on his next session. She takes a few more steps back at human speed. If she wanted to leave, she'd already be gone.

"You've already made a lot of big steps. You approached a human all on your own. If you have to see her tomorrow, let's get you to that point."

"I was planning on biting you," she growls, teeth glinting in the fluorescent light. "If I bite her, it won't exactly help me, will it?"

"It would probably make her day job a little difficult."

"Among other things." She groans, falling gracefully into the couch. I guess she's staying. She tries to meet my eyes again, but her gaze returns to the floor. "Maybe I should turn you."

"I'd certainly prefer it."

"Eventually, you'd change your mind."

"I doubt that. There's no way I could ever be tired of eternity with my wife." That's not exactly a professional thing to say, but if she realizes that I'm part of the community, maybe that'll help.

She pauses, not looking at me as she takes in this information. There aren't that many queer people in the community. Hopefully, her being however old she is doesn't make that an issue. I knew I shouldn't have said anything. "I ate my wife."

Well, there are all of Abby's anxieties. I can never let them meet.

She smirks at my gobsmacked expression. I hate letting my clients get to me. I need to be professional about this.

"Well, why don't we start there? It sounds like there's a lot for us to work through." I cross my legs, attempting to meet her eyes. She turns away, the smirk vanishing.

"If you think irritating me will help, then I'm more than happy to demonstrate otherwise. My past is mine and mine alone. Your job is to make it so that I can see Dr. Sun tomorrow. If you decide that any other area is relevant, I will show you the full extent of what I can do. That little parlor trick earlier was a little nothing I learned from an old enemy."

I try my best to gulp as quietly as possible. Looking afraid of a client is never a great plan, especially when they're an immortal predator. "It's all part of who you are. I can't work on this without addressing what causes it."

"I'm certain you've read Wolpe's work. Desensitize me."

I've always preferred a holistic approach. Behavioralism seems a bit silly, and Wolpe's work is a little outdated at this point. Not that his methods don't work, they're just never what I use. If my focus was on addiction or phobias, maybe I'd feel otherwise. "If you want, we can work on exposure therapy, but I don't think we can get you over your issues without addressing the root cause."

"I don't need to be over them. All I need is to be able to be near that vet."

"Well, you're near me, talking to me, why is that any different?"

"Because I was tricked into it."

"Olivia—"

"Ms. Crocetti is fine."

"Well, Ms. Crocetti, I didn't trick you. You've managed to talk to me this whole time. We've already started exposure therapy."

Those fangs glint at me again. She manages to meet my eyes for only a second. "You expect me to what, set his cage on a table and hide? You're a therapist. It's one thing around you. It's quite another with her."

"From what I've seen of her, Dr. Sun is pretty accepting." Okay, she just doesn't care, but the difference is semantics. "If that's what you need to do, then I don't think it'll be an issue. It's more important that you get Harvey help than that you avoid looking foolish, right?"

I didn't know vampires growled. It's terrifying. "We'll see who's the fool."

"That's not—"

"I'll see her tomorrow," she announces, cutting me off. "I won't be a fool of any sort."

Abby's right. Vampires are so moody. "Then let's keep working on it. You still have forty minutes left. Let's make it so you don't have to run away." Because that's totally doable in forty minutes. I know better than to make promises to clients that I can't keep. Why would I do it to one who already wants to kill me? "Pretend I'm her."

"No. This is ridiculous."

"You wanted Wolpe. You're getting him. Pretend I'm her."

Her eyes narrow. I was never this confrontational with my old clients, but eventually, I had to stop showing fiends my belly. If I don't stand up for myself, they'll rip out my throat and drink my blood.

"Dr. Sun," she begins, snarling, "I need your help."

Chapter One

Dr. Sun

"How can I help you?" The vet is smaller than I expected, though perhaps I always expect humans to be as imposing as—nope, not going down that path. I swear, Ms. Rosseau-Lester has me thinking far too much about my past. I knew therapy was a bad idea. It better have actually helped.

"My parrot is sick," I manage, focused on the counter, on his cage as I place it before her. The deed done, I take a few steps back. She's right, I'm never this uncomfortable around humans when I'm eating them. I need to think of her as food. I lock my eyes on her neck, the pale skin covering powerful veins and arteries. Great, now I'm hungry.

"You know you could come in during my normal hours?" She giggles, running a hand through her shoulder-length black hair before tossing it over the vein. "My late-night hours are more for horrifying monsters with a few bullet wounds."

"Fiends," I correct. I don't care that much, and it's a pointless difference that I never heard anywhere until I moved to Canada, but I'd rather no one get pissed and eat her before Harvey's better.

"Whatever." She sighs, leaning against the counter as she peers into the cage. "What seems to be the problem? You're still paying the black-market rate."

"That's fine. He had a little bit of a cold a month ago, but I thought it had gone away. Now he's having trouble breathing, he's more standoffish, and he's losing weight. He's barely even talking, when normally, he never shuts up." I avert my gaze again. Maybe I'm just too tense. I shouldn't be cowering from a filthy human. But she's the only one who can help Harvey. There's no other vet I could deal with anywhere near here. I looked her up. She's pretty well trained in aviary medicine on top of being my only option. I'll suck it up. I don't have a choice.

She glances up, attempting but failing to meet my gaze. "I'm glad you brought him in. There're a few things this could be, but we need to get him X-rayed right away. You shouldn't have waited. This is an emergency, and his life could depend on it."

A human is scolding me. That's a new one. I know she's right. I can't believe I let my fear control me for this long. I shouldn't have expected him to get better on his own.

"You brought him in now. It shouldn't be too late." Her gaze softens as she turns back to Harvey, concern clear on her face. I guess I took him to the right person. "How old is he?"

"He's fifty."

Letting out a slow breath, she nods, eyes locked on him. "I'll do my best. Has he been yours the whole time?"

I nod. "Yeah. I bought him back in 1969."

"Well, you've both aged amazingly." She snorts, lifting the cage.

I start to walk away. I've had far beyond my maximum tolerance of humanity for the day. Maybe I'll grab a bite on the way home.

"Wait. I need to get a history from you. Since he's been in your care this whole time, you should know everything. It's a lot better than I usually have access to. Vampire, I take it? Never mind, I don't care. Come on, you can fill me in while I run these X-rays." She gestures over her shoulder for me to follow as she walks into a back room.

My feet don't seem to want to move at first, but I force them. He's worth it. I'll deal with whatever I must if it'll make him better. She motions for me to wait in a little room with a large window into a bigger room while she heads in there with Harvey. I hate leaving him alone with her. "Normally I'd put him under, but at this old, it might not be a great idea. Could you come in"—she falters as she finds me already before her—"here."

"What do you need me to do?"

"Get him to hold still while I set this up. Actually, does radiation hurt you?"

I blink. "I'm not sure. I would assume that it doesn't."

"Well, I'll keep it in mind if he won't stay still."

"Harvey, stay still for me, okay? There will be some scary lights and sounds, but it'll be okay, and I'll be right there." I point at the window I'd been looking through. "Okay?"

He doesn't say or do anything to demonstrate that he understands, but he's a very smart bird. We head back to the other room where she takes a few pictures. He holds still each time she needs to make an adjustment. "Obvious question first, has he ever been sick before? Anything at all?"

"He's had a couple colds, and he had a vitamin D deficiency in the seventies. I was still new at this, but I changed his lighting setup and got him some calcium pills. It took care of it almost immediately."

I try my best not to notice her surprisingly warm smile. I don't need a goddamned human feeling bad for me. "Anything else?"

"Not really. He hasn't had anything too bad until this."

"That's good. It seems like you really care about him."

Of course I do. He's my best friend. Hell, he's my only friend. "I do."

"I'm glad he's in such good hands. You should see some of the horror stories that come in here during my normal hours. Humans are a lot worse at looking after animals than you are. I swear, sometimes it seems like they don't care at all. If all they want is something cute to hang around, they should get a stuffed animal."

I manage to meet her eyes. "Humans are terrible."

"Yeah. They certainly are."

I was not prepared for this. I'm not particularly keen on most vampires for a number of reasons, but hearing a human talk like that just sounds wrong. "You're one too, you know. Or are you trying to claim that you're the exception? Humans are disgusting things ruled by fear and their own pitiful desires." I bare my fangs, maintaining eye contact. I'll not have her try to escape from being the monster she is. We're all doomed by our fates.

She shrugs. "Sounds like me."

"You admit that you're just like them."

"You were one too, right? I'm sure it's been a few decades, but it's not like that makes you some saint or anything. Humans are monsters, and you're both."

If she wasn't looking after Harvey, I'd rip out her throat where she stands.

Leaning against the wall, she smirks. She pulls a bottle of pills out of her pocket and pops one, swallowing it without a drink. Her playfully bitter expression falls as she stares at the computer, taking a step toward it. A few button-presses later, she swallows, staring at the ceiling, popping another pill. "I thought it might be. He has signs of aspergillosis. I'd like to run a couple more tests, but I should be able to fix him. At his age, it can be pretty risky. Depending on how he responds to the medication, he may need surgery."

"Whatever it takes."

"It won't be cheap."

"Like I said, whatever it takes."

She gives an appreciative nod. "Glad to hear it. I think I still have some of the right antibiotics in my pharmacy. I just need to make sure it's the right kind for him. He's a Congo African gray, right?"

"He is."

"All right. Get out of my hair for an hour while I check up on a few things. I'll have the medication when you get back."

I grit my teeth, doing my best to glare. "You want me to leave him alone with you?"

"It's only an hour. I need to run my tests, and it'll be easier without someone asking questions the entire time. I promise I'll take good care of him." Her gaze never leaves Harvey. She's watching him through the window, all but ignoring me. I'm glad she has the right priorities.

"He'll listen to me," I insist. "He can be an ornery old bastard. I don't want him struggling and ending up hurt because you didn't feel like dealing with me for a little while."

With a shrug, she drops the bottle back in her pocket and gestures toward Harvey. "Fine. You can stay. Go grab him. The machine's in another room."

I do as she says. The goddamn indignity of having to obey this pitiful creature. I really might eat her when this is all done. Nevertheless, I comply the entire time, and we run through all the tests that she needs to be satisfied. Whether she's testing to make sure she gives him the right medication or just that we run enough tests to run up my bill, I can't say for sure. When we're done, she hands me a bottle of pills to give him once a day, and I give her the four hundred for her time and medication. This better work. I don't want to have to deal with her again anytime soon.

❖

The door slams shut behind me, blocking out the outside world. Setting his travel cage on its stand by the door, I let Harvey out, hoping he'll spread his wings for a little while. He only offers a pitiful squawk and hops onto my forearm. All right, I could do with the company. That vet gave him his first pill while we were there, so I won't need to worry about that until tomorrow.

We walk to the kitchen where I put the kettle on for a cup of tea. I don't need to drink, but after years in England, it became an unavoidable habit. I wish I could make it as good as Oscar always did. Maybe it was just the absinthe. I'll have to look into that sometime now that it's legal. Not that that's ever stopped me, but it makes it cheaper.

I sit at the little table in the corner of my kitchen. My dining room sees so little use. Perhaps I should take someone here to eat sometime or maybe buy one of those delightful blood pastries I've seen in the market. Then I'd have an excuse to break out the fine china.

Harvey hops off my arm to wander around the table. I stand, and he starts to hop back toward me, stretching his wings to glide onto my arm. "It's okay," I tell him. "I'm just going to the fridge."

"Come back," he manages to say. I'm so relieved I can almost feel my heartbeat. He hasn't said a word in weeks. There's no way the medication is already working, but perhaps it's the placebo effect. I only hope it's not him managing a second wind before he grows worse.

I return with a few carrots. There's a bag of blood in the fridge for emergencies, but I need something fresh tonight. I'll eat later. "Would you eat for me?" I ask. He's had so little appetite of late. He barely even touched an apple yesterday when they're normally one of his favorite foods.

"Carrots," he states firmly, diving for the snack. I can barely contain my joy as I beam at him. He's eating. All right, Dr. Sun, maybe I'll let you live after all. He makes quick work of the first carrot but seems to think better of it and only half-heartedly pecks at the second. It's not a miracle. I wasn't expecting one, but it's still an improvement.

"Was that good?"

"Carrots good."

Sometimes I worry for my mental health when the only person I ever talk to is a parrot, but then I remember how awful everyone else is. The kettle sings its song, and I rise again. I can feel Harvey's eyes on me as I walk over, taking my time. Normally, if he was this desperate for attention, he would fly over. I scoop some loose tea leaves into my old tin teapot and pour the boiling water in after it.

I grab a lemon and some cucumbers from the fridge and start chopping. Harvey squawks impatiently from his spot on the table. If he wants me that badly, he can fly over here. When I'm done, I take the two little cucumber sandwiches and carry them over with my teapot. He complains again as I grab my second favorite teacup—my favorite is still in the sink from earlier—but I don't make him wait long.

I take a bite of the cucumber sandwich while I wait. It does nothing for my hunger, but I'm feeling particularly nostalgic today, and it seems appropriate. Plus, if I'm lucky… Harvey snatches a cucumber from one of my sandwiches. Setting it on the table, he munches on it, looking up at me between bites. That's what I was hoping for.

When the tea's done steeping, I pour a cup and add a slice of lemon and some honey. Harvey watches me patiently. "Tea?" he asks.

"Yes." I take a sip. It's far too hot, but it hardly matters. Ever since I found out that tea's safe for parrots, I've been buying the caffeine-free variety. Caffeine doesn't do anything for me either way, but the taste is a bit off. It's worth it to not risk poisoning him. There's no way he'd not drink my tea just because it's bad for him.

"Tea?" he asks. Maybe he really is dying. He's actually being polite.

"It's still too hot for you."

He cocks his head, staring with those little yellow-brown eyes.

"Beg all you want. You're not getting any until it's cool."

He kicks his cucumber and flaps his wings at me. I take another slice of cucumber from one of my sandwiches and hand it to him, taking a bite of the sandwich myself. I was never the best cook in life—I left that to my wife—but sometime over the years, either I've improved or I've adapted to my meager skills. He bites into the slice, more attacking it than eating it, but I'm pretty sure he swallows a few bites. I'll deal with the mess later.

When I've almost finished the cup, I blow on it and right his cup where it lies on the table. I pour the last few drops into it and top off my cup. He leaps upon the shallow cup and shoves his face in it, tilting his head back to drink. His happy little dance is gratitude enough for me. He'd never be so proper as to actually thank me. I scratch his head when he's done, and he gives me a merry squawk before taking a second sip. I decide to join him, and we enjoy our tea in peace.

Once he's done, I let him hop back on me, and we walk around the house. The parlor has grown grander in recent years since I replaced my old rabbit-eared television with one of the newfangled flat ones. The same brown leather couch still manages, somehow, despite Harvey's best efforts. He makes me happy I have tile floors. We pass my bedroom and head toward his, the massive cage and pile of toys standing against their own walls. The doctor said he needs his sleep, and while I'm certain he'll fight me, I intend to make sure it happens.

"Not bedtime," he mutters. He sounds like a petulant child, yet he's older than that vet.

"You're sick, and it is bedtime."

He bites my finger.

I'm too strong to give him any response without crippling him, so I ignore him. I set him in the cage, turning off the automatic light attached to it. I try to keep him on a consistent schedule, but not if it might impact his recovery. He begrudgingly jumps off my finger onto his perch, turning back and fixing me with the most pitiful expression he can manage. It's almost enough to get me to leave his door open.

"Get some sleep," I say, draping the cover over his cage. I hate using it if I don't have to. It feels oddly rude. His curtains are normally enough.

He lets out an annoyed chirp but offers no further protests. Perfect. Now I can go have an actual meal.

❖

I take a seat at the bar, leaning back on the torn leather stool as I sip my mai tai. I hate this. It's not what a bar is meant to be like. Even when I let my men have shore leave it was never this bad. It is, however, the easiest way to find a meal that's as unappetizing as it is morally unquestionable to eat. It'll only take a few minutes. Someone always gives me cause before long.

"You know, you're kinda hot for a black girl," a man behind me slurs, stumbling into the stool next to me.

Ask and ye shall receive. “Well, that’s just the nicest thing I’ve heard all night.”

He leans against the counter, leering, his putrid breath puffing on my neck. I’d be doing the world a favor if I killed him. “How’s abouts I buy you a drink?”

That is what I’m here for. “Sure, another mai tai sounds great.”

“Two whiskeys,” he shouts over me, waving for the bartender’s attention.

Him raising his arm almost sends me hurling. He smells like he washed up from the sea after a few days of rotting. I’ve been in battlefields that didn’t smell this bad. Granted, I was human then, so my nose wasn’t quite as strong, but it still hardly speaks well of him. I’m not entirely certain that his blood won’t corrode my stomach.

The bartender, Carl, returns to glower at him. He’s a tall thin man with a bushy beard, who must suspect something of me by now—though perhaps just that I’ve a thing for terrible men. That would’ve solved so many of my issues. “You said two whiskeys?” He picks up a bottle from under the bar, looking to me for approval.

It hardly matters to me. I give him a nod.

He pours the two drinks and slides them over to us. “That’ll be eight bucks.”

“You’re a damn thief. I don’t know why I come here,” my prey grumbles, ripping his wallet from his coat. “These prices for the swill you serve.” With a heavy groan, he tosses a ten at the bartender, who snatches it out of the air without a word. Normally, I’d have to really work to find someone quite this reprehensible. It’s far from necessary. I’ve eaten plenty of good people, but it’s easy, and I have some aggression to work off. I wish he would put up a fight.

Giving me an apologetic look, Carl walks back to the other end of the bar, leaving me alone with this bag of filth. “Drink up,” the drunk insists.

What a gentleman. I throw back the shot and give him the most lascivious grin I can manage without throwing up. It takes some work, but I’ve had centuries of practice. “You want to get out of here?” I ask, throwing my hair over my shoulder. Hell, it’d probably work on me. He doesn’t have a chance. I don’t even have to use my powers.

“Do I? With a—” His face contorts into an ecstatic expression, as if I’ve made all of his debauched fantasies come true at once. “Hell yeah." His yellowed teeth show in what must be a smile before he downs his own drink, wincing at the flavor, and leaps off his chair. He seems perfectly capable of walking now as he grabs at my hand, trying to lead me to the front door.

I gesture to the back, and we head out into a narrow alley that smells of urine and garbage. He smirks, already ripping off his belt. He holds it like a garrote as he turns to me. Was he hunting me too, or is he expecting something far more depraved than I'd led him to believe?

I pin his hands to the filthy wall, holding him in place as the belt slips from his fingers. "The hell you doing?" he asks.

Bless us, O Lord, and these, thy gifts, which we are about to receive from thy bounty. Through Christ our Lord, Amen. My teeth sink into his neck, my hand muffling his scream as he struggles against me. I was right, he does taste rancid. It is what's on the inside that counts after all, and his insides are vile.

I manage a couple liters before I can't stomach it anymore. He sinks bonelessly to the ground, his eyes slowly closing and opening, peering up at me in confusion. "Wha—"

"Go back inside and get some food and juice. What happened here was exactly what you wished." I stare into his eyes, dragging him away from the truth into a world of my creation. "You came out here and had your way with me, and now you need a drink. So you're going to go back inside and not say a word of the woman you met today. You wouldn't want them to think that you'd been with a black woman, would you?"

He shakes his head, his eyes staring unblinking into mine.

"That's what I thought. Now stand up, walk inside, and never bother me again."

He rises as shakily as he collapsed, but his feet seem determined to carry his load. He turns without a word, opening the door we'd left through and shambling back inside. I used to kill them, but eventually, if exsanguinated bodies start piling up, people begin to grow suspicious. It's far easier having a few confused drunks with bite marks they'd never be willing to show anyone.

I turn on my heel, alive again as I saunter through the dark alley back to my car. I needed this. I had to tolerate far too many humans for my liking today and yesterday. If I didn't fill my belly with one, I would feel supremely robbed. Now I'm sated, and Harvey seems to be on the mend, so I'd say the day turned out pretty well. I pull out of the narrow parking spot in my Mercedes, flying back to my house. The streets are all but empty. The bars won't let out for another half an hour. Yesterday, I was terrified that my world would fall apart. Now everything seems to be coming up roses. Maybe I'll order a new toy for Harvey when I get home.

Chapter Two

The Hunt

Thatch roofs burn unimaginably quickly. Between the smell and the handful of us who are already on fire, the air is thick with smoke and the stench of death. There's nowhere to run. They'd claimed there was safety in numbers, that we could hide together, and we'd all be safe. One by one, they fall before me.

Sara is the first to go. In the light of the sun, bearing crosses, crossbows, stakes, and torches, they set upon us, destroying the roof and setting the place ablaze. They find her still sleeping. She screams as the shaft of wood pierces her heart, rousing the rest of us from our barely begun slumber. There is only one door. All they have to do is wait for us to burn up or run out to them, but it's not enough. They want to satisfy their sick pleasure by shedding our blood with their own two hands.

I can give far better than I'll receive. I rush them, trying to buy time for my friends, but the wretched curs invoke the God I've fallen so far from. As his word is a sword, they've made a bludgeon of the cross. Literally. It's large, wooden, and sharpened at the bottom, but it's full of their faith and fear and of every wretched sin he drove me to.

It burns, but I do my best to shrug it off, scrambling to my feet, my cheek still sizzling as I leap at one of them, fangs and claws bared. I rip out the throat of the man who hit me, but a crossbow bolt to the back sends me reeling again. A few inches to the left and it would've been my life.

Leonard collapses without a word as his head is cleaved from his body. I don't see Mara anywhere, but it's possible she escaped. Lord, I hope she did. Reginald and Arthur are both still fighting for their lives. Gunshots echo throughout the small chamber, and a few hunters fall. I grab a sword from one of them and set myself on another.

He wrestles with me, his blade caught against mine, a hand on each other's arms as he attempts to use my inertia against me and I try to use my supernatural might. We fall into the sunlight. It's unpleasant but not fatal, something they know all too well from that damn book. It was far easier when they just believed the local legends. It disconcerts me so much that he manages to seize the upper hand, shoving his sword into my gut. I reply in kind by burying mine to the hilt, pinning him to the ground as he bleeds out.

The fire is spreading. The next building blazes as a volley of bolts is unleashed upon me by the waiting hunters outside. I hate to say it, but every ounce of military training, of honor, urges me to stay on, to fight to the last man. But there's no honor—no sense—in this bloodbath. This isn't a war; it's a slaughter. We're nothing but vermin to them, and they're intent on exterminating us.

I rip a bolt out of my leg and hurl it toward my attackers, taking off in the other direction. It burns. I don't know how many times they've hit me, but I've taken quite a beating. I'm not sure how long I can go on. I run for as long as my legs can take me, which isn't nearly far enough. I collapse, sprawling on the ground. The whole village is on fire now. Everything is ash and smoke and flames. The air is scorching, and the dewy grass is covered in soot.

I crawl on my belly like the worm they seem intent on making me, managing to throw myself into the bushes before the regiment reaches me. I hear the sound of marching boots, the screams of my kind and theirs, all muted by the roar of the fires.

They drag out any survivors. Their own wives, their neighbors, their children. Anyone they think could be a threat, and in this time of upheaval, that's everyone. They tie their hands and legs and leave them sitting on the ground next to their smoldering homes as the lives we've built together fall apart around us.

When every last survivor is rounded up, the man who must be the leader of this glorified militia stands at the head of the company, facing down their victims. "Give them the cross," he commands. "If they won't take it, or if it rejects them, then you know what to do."

I lie there, hidden by foliage, as every person I've known in the last decade is put to trial. I couldn't utter a sound if I wanted to. Each one is met with a cross and immediately staked. I don't know how many were really vampires. It wasn't as if we kept a list. They were supposed to see if the cross burned, but in their fervor, few of them seem to care.

When all is said and done, there are barely more than a dozen villagers left. The score of hunters leave them be, without so much as a word or a farewell, as they make their way onto the next town. Their hunt isn't over. They have more of us to put to the slaughter.

I don't know how they didn't see me. The trail of my blood should've led them right to me. I don't move an inch until the sun sets. I'm not sure I even could. I'm paralyzed by pain and fear, but just as the fear freezes me, when I have my chance, it galvanizes me. I make a run for it, eating one of the surviving villagers as they lie huddled together for warmth. The deed doesn't even rouse his companions. I'm tempted to take another. What's to stop me? Why shouldn't I? They're all the same, just like the men who did this to us. Humans can't be trusted.

I wipe the blood from my lips as I set out, away from the hunters, with no destination in mind. Nowhere can be safe, can it? Maybe I should go back home to Italy. Perhaps this craze hasn't reached there yet. Or maybe I should head to the New World. I could find someplace secluded. There's still more land than the people there know what to do with.

Either way, I'll need lodging and a port, so I head for a city that can provide both. London-bound, I make my way on foot, avoiding any other travelers. Even at full speed, it takes most of the night, but I arrive in town in time to find a familiar face, one of the few I'm happy to see.

"Vanessa," I mouth, pulling her into my arms. The coolness of her body provides me great comfort. She hugs me back, looking as shaken as I am.

"It's horrible," she says. "Patrice, he..." She shakes her head, tears falling. "Everyone is dead."

I nod. I have no words to describe the horror I've seen. I've lost so many people in my life, more than I would care to count, but never like this.

"It's that damn book," she growls, her nails digging into my hand.

"I know."

"We have to get out of here. Anyplace is better than Britain right now." She stares into my eyes, pleading with me to agree.

"You'll hear no argument from me. I came here in hopes of returning home. You're welcome to come with me."

"You think Italy is safe?" She scoffs, shaking her head in disbelief. "We need to be someplace far from here, someplace where no one will come for us. We can make a new life together. I can't be alone right now."

"I know." I squeeze her hand, doing my best to reassure her. "Okay, we'll need a ship either way. Perhaps we could head to America or maybe Africa. Anyplace where we can find some seclusion."

"Yes, that's perfect. We will."

We both glance around, our eyes never staying in a single place. I wish I'd bothered to scrounge up weapons before I left. I wouldn't feel naked. No one seems to be coming. There's no blood on her at all, and the dirt and mud has covered up what was visible on me. I need a bath and a way out of here. "We should rest," I say. "We need to map out our journey and figure out how we're getting there." There may be a few other things I'd like to do with her, but they're hardly worth mentioning. "We can't do anything until we have a plan."

"We'll steal a ship."

"We'd need a crew." I can sail just fine, but anything large enough to take us that far would be more than the two of us could manage.

She shakes her head, baring her teeth in frustration. "We can't trust a crew."

"I know." I hate this hesitation. I never used to be like this. I was a man of action. I made decisions and damned anyone who stood in my way. Now look at me. "Let's rest, clean up, get some new clothes for me, and figure out how we're doing this. We can't stay out in the open. We're too exposed."

Wanting for any better plan, Vanessa and I head to the inn and buy a room for the night. We've known each other for most of a century. I don't love her, and she doesn't love me, but her embrace does me a world of comfort in a time when I desperately need it.

The next evening, I awake to find her missing from our bed. Assuming that she must have gone to book us passage, I step outside. In the alley, I find her—her body, at least. Her head is gone. There's blood, both human and her own. She must've gone out to feed in the night. Someone found her. England isn't safe. Perhaps nowhere is at this point.

Maybe it's the sentimentality in me, but I find my feet not taking me toward the docks. I'm following her scent trail. They still have her head. I've sacrificed my honor and everything good about me, but she was a dear friend, and I can't allow anyone to live with a piece of her like that. She deserves better.

By the time I find the warehouse, I'm seeing red. I will end whoever dared to harm her and anyone who gets in my way. I don't take the door. It's too obvious, and I've little doubt they're expecting someone, if not exactly me. I find a weak plank in the roof and climb in. I regret that decision.

I expected to find her as a trophy, perhaps already pinned to the wall. Instead, these monsters have dozens of us, carcasses rotting, putridly stinking from whatever foul deeds they did with them. If my vision was red, then at this point, it's black. Someone's blood pounds in my ears. I've already forgotten their name. Humans don't deserve names. They're no better than animals if they're capable of this.

I add their bodies to the pile. They fall with little fight, too weak from their ale and debauchery. The sick bastards deserve it.

With a stir, I awake, not cold with sweat, but shaking and nauseous. The dream isn't normally quite as detailed. Usually, it's only the bloodshed, all of it, all at once. It's strange to relive the whole thing. Perhaps that alley brought back some bad memories, or perhaps it's simply that time of year. I wrap my arms around myself, quivering under my down comforter. I'm safe. The hunt's over. It was all dismissed as a cholera epidemic. Mankind no longer believes in us, let alone sets about eradicating us.

I rise from my bed, dragging the comforter with me. Harvey sleepily squawks from his room, but I don't want to wake him. Instead, I go to the kitchen.

The tea does nothing to soothe my nerves. I know there's no way I'll get back to sleep. I still see their blood on my hands, and I still see my kind falling before them.

I need to go out.

❖

My car grinds to a stop in the gravel parking lot. It's around nine a.m., and the sun decides to poke out past some clouds. I'm glad I thought to grab my sunglasses. I hide under my jacket, throwing up the hood as I leave the car.

I leisurely walk through the brightly lit garden, simultaneously smelling the fourteen different types of flowers they planted a few months ago. I linger, letting the scents cling to me as if bathing in it could somehow purify my mind of all the vile scenes I just relived.

Singing floats out from the church, the scent of the candles wafting in the breeze. It's all comforting. So little of it has changed over the centuries. I do miss the Latin, though. Everything sounds profane in English; it's not right.

I take a seat on a bench out back, letting the building shade me from the sun. Birds chirp from a nearby tree, and I can hear the sermon inside. I half listen to his words, letting the scene take me. I don't think I fall asleep, but I lose track of time as I sit there. When I look up, there's no more talking inside, and the shadow has moved a good distance. This was exactly what I needed.

"Olivia," a warm basso voice calls from behind me.

I turn to see Father Gregory walking toward me, the gravel crunching under his feet. "Good morning, Father."

"Good morning. What brings you out in this weather?" he asks with a wry grin as he gestures toward the bright sunny day.

Leaning back against the bench, I say, "Nothing. I just needed an escape for a few minutes."

"Sister Paula says you've been out here for almost two hours. Are you sure that all you want is to take in the scenery? You know I'm here if you need anything."

I hesitate. I hate burdening him with this knowledge. "Perhaps confession first?"

"Of course, my child."

I roll my eyes. I've given up any right to that title. God himself has thrown me out. "It's been four weeks since my last confession."

"It felt like longer. What is it, my child?"

"I'm not...I've hurt people."

"Of course. I'm glad to hear that it seems to all be people who deserve it these days." His big meaty hand pats my shoulder as he offers a warm smile. "Did you kill them?"

"No, Father."

"Then I don't see what the harm is."

"I'm still hurting God's children. Clearly, he doesn't approve."

"You do what you have to in order to survive. You're one of his children too."

I huff, turning on him, narrowing my eyes as my hand instinctively flies to my chest. The old scar reminds me of how untrue his statement is. I don't know why it's lasted all these years, no other burn has, but after all this time, I still carry that reminder. "He has cast me out, Father. You know that as well as I do. It's why we have to meet out here rather than in the confessional. I can't enter his ground."

"All of this is his ground, Olivia. The whole world is, but even where you're sitting, you're in the backyard of a church. It's consecrated ground. If you were as unwelcome as you claim, you couldn't even be here. I think—"

"The last time I tried to enter a church, it burned so much, I thought I was going to die. I know exactly how he feels about me. I'm a monster."

"No one is beyond forgiveness. Not even a monster."

I bare my fangs. To his credit, he doesn't even flinch. "Perhaps we should all burn. He could start over again."

"Why do you say that?"

I grit my teeth, digging my nails into the metal bench beneath me. It groans under the strain. "Never mind."

"Olivia, it's eleven a.m. on a Sunday. You're a vampire out and about at a church. Why aren't you asleep? What's going on with you? You're acting even more cynical than usual."

I shake my head, staring at the ground.

"Is Harvey okay? He hasn't—"

"No. I took him to the vet yesterday, and it looks like he might be on the mend."

"That's wonderful. I'm glad to hear it." He gives my shoulder an affectionate squeeze before pulling away, leaning over to peer into my eyes, studying me. "Then is it the dreams again?"

I nod.

"Maybe it's time for you to see a therapist. There's only so much I can do."

"I saw one," I mutter.

I can almost hear him blink. His jaw drops open. "You...Olivia, that's amazing. Was it the one I recommended? Did she seem to help?"

"Of course not." Maybe. I managed to actually talk to Dr. Sun without panicking and running away. That's more than I've been capable of for quite a while. "She's human. She's part of the..." I hesitate. He knows about our society, but I'm always reluctant to mention anything specific around people. As much as I trust him, that way lies nothing but trouble. "I can't work with a human. They're disgusting. They'll all betray me in the end."

"Olivia, I'm a human."

"You don't count. You serve God."

"A lot of people have done terrible things in his name. I'm not sure that gives me any extra credibility. In fact, given your nature, that should make you more suspicious of me."

I sigh, giving him an appraising look. He's unarmed, having even left his crucifix inside. "It's Protestants I don't trust."

"I know that's not true. You don't even seem to trust any of our nuns. They'd all be willing to talk to you. They seem fascinated by you. Why do you trust me?" His voice is calm, patient, almost as if he's giving another sermon.

"I don't know." I do. It's just silly. In truth, he reminds me of my father. Both my actual one and the priest I had growing up. They were strong men but two of the kindest people I've ever known. They didn't even judge me for my decisions when I was young. They supported me all the way. I don't know what they would think of me now, but the fact that he seems to approve of me means far more than it should.

"Well then, think about it. I would love to know if you ever come up with an answer."

I shrug.

"Would you like to tell me about the dreams? Which ones were these? You said there are a few."

Shaking my head, I reply, "No. I've relived them enough for the day."

"Then how can I help? Olivia, I don't want to see you suffering like this forever, in a hell of your own making. I know you think that's what you deserve, but you're wrong. You're a good woman. I've known you for thirty years now, and there's not a thing about you that would make me think you deserve to suffer like this." He rolls his eyes as I turn to argue. "No, not even that. Fiends are welcome in my congregation."

"I believe *he* still disagrees."

"Would you like to try walking in with me? Perhaps you've been forgiven."

"I'll save myself the headache, Father." I stare at the simple wooden door standing between me and the halls of the church. It seems to mock me. If only I could step right in, but I know the pain it brings me, the toll it takes. I'm not welcome in God's domain.

"Well, you're part of my church regardless." He scratches at his close-cut beard. It's almost military standard, and I've always wondered if he served. It always seems wrong to ask. Though I suppose that's not as common anymore. I don't think the Canadian army even allows beards.

"I should go." I move to stand, but he stops me, placing his hand lightly on my forearm. I could easily pull away, but he only wants my attention.

"Please wait. If you're not going to talk to me about this, promise that you'll find someone else to talk to. You don't have to be alone."

"I'm not alone. I have Harvey." I pry loose, stepping away from the bench. It's been a century. If I was going to get over it on my own, I'd likely have done it by now, but I don't know what to do about it. I don't think Ms. Rosseau-Lester can help me, but there doesn't seem to be anyone more capable. "But I'll think about it."

"That's all I can ask. You know I'm here for you anytime."

Without turning back, I nod. "I know, Father. Thank you. Say a prayer for me." I still say them, but it never feels like they get through. I know God has no interest in anything I have to say.

"I always do. Are you sure you want to leave? We have some coffee brewing."

"I'm all right. You have a good day." I walk away, still shaking off the lingering remnants of my dream. I feel better, less like it's all happening again, but I still can't rid myself of those images, those smells. They're as fresh as the day they happened.

I head back to my car, admiring the flowers again on my way. The sisters always manage such beautiful displays. I wish they didn't view me as another one. I'd rather they not spare me a thought. The more people aware of me, the worse things will be. I gun the engine and set off, making a leisurely pace through traffic back toward my house.

I pull up in front of the Italianate structure, parking in the garage before heading around to the front door. My senses perk up for any sign of an intruder. There's no reason to think there would be one, but old habits die hard. The house is empty, with nothing of note save for a few dirty teacups in the sink.

I wash them and go to Harvey's room. He needs his sleep, but I want to check on him. I lift up the cover, receiving an annoyed squawk for my trouble. "Nighttime," he says.

"Not anymore."

"Good morning."

I smile at him. I don't know what I'd do without Harvey. I'd say he's the best pet I've ever owned, but calling him a pet seems insulting. I grab some seed and one of his toys from their boxes and place them both in his cage, leaving the door open.

"Scratch," he demands.

I stroke his head affectionately and gesture to the feed. "You hungry?"

"Carrots."

"Eat your seeds."

"Carrots."

I think that means he's doing better. I grab a carrot from the fridge and cut it into slices, dropping a few on top of his seeds. "Happy?"

"Happy," he agrees, attacking the carrot. After a few pieces, he gobbles down some seeds and attacks the toy I brought him. He spins the little puzzle box, nicking it in a few spots as he works at the colorful sides. It's good to see him having energy again. It's probably too early to give him the next pill. I wish we could get them all over with, so I didn't have to worry anymore.

I sit there, watching him play until he grows bored and hops on my shoulder. "TV," he insists.

"You don't even like watching TV. You sit with me for five minutes and fly off."

"TV."

"Fine, but I told you." I carefully sit in the well-worn couch to avoid disturbing him from his seat on my shoulder and find something to watch. I can tolerate humanity from a distance like this, though I do wish there was an alternative. We settle on a bright and colorful kids' show that seems to capture his attention, and he manages to sit through an entire episode. I guess I shouldn't doubt him. He knows what he wants. He even flies a few feet excitedly at one point, but I have to help him back up on my shoulder. I really hope this medicine is actually helping. I need him to be healthy again.

When he finally grows too restless, I help him back into his cage and turn the lights back off. I don't put the cover on, so he can stay awake and spend some time with me if he wants, but I hope he'll get some sleep. I know he needs it.

For my part, I return to the couch and try to find something decent to watch. I wish I could find sleep myself. If only all it took was a curtain.

Chapter Three

The Reunion

Something falling on my stomach rouses me from a fitful sleep. I don't remember the dreams, only that they were bad, which is to say typical. I look down, ready to rip whatever has stirred me limb from limb, only to find Harvey. He flew here. He's flying!

"Morning," he squawks, a cheeky little grin in his eyes.

I can barely contain my glee. It's all I can do not to hug him. He doesn't like hugs. I instead affectionately scratch his head. "Good morning to you as well, Harvey."

"Morning," he repeats, playfully flapping his wings and hopping on my belly. "Morning."

I reach my arms to the ceiling, stretching. I'm not sure my body really needs it, but it just seems like part of waking up. He hops off of me and flies over to my desk chair. It's wonderful to see him flying again. I could almost cry.

When I walk over to him, he flies onto my shoulder. "Treat?"

"All right. Want a grape?"

"Grape."

I take that as a yes and procure a couple from the fridge. He attacks them, ripping them apart and eating pieces. So much energy this morning. We're halfway through his course of medication, so I'd expected him to be even more lethargic after everything it was putting his little body through, but this is a welcome surprise. "I'm going to go shower. Enjoy your grapes."

"Play."

"No, shower."

"Play!" He hops toward me, kicking a piece of grape.

"Want to come shower? Will that make you feel better? Then we can play with your new toy." It arrived the other day, but I've been waiting to open it. He already has too many toys. I need to stop spoiling him. This is why he has no manners.

"Shower."

"That's what I thought." He flies after me and plays in the water as I shower. It's nice and refreshing, even if I have to keep the temperature a bit more reasonable for him. I might actually have to thank that vet. The way she was acting, I was a little worried, but she seems to really care about the animals she looks after.

When we're both dried off, I show him the confetti-tree thing. He glares at it and gives it an experimental peck, squawking happily when a piece of it falls to the floor. I hang it from his cage, and he menaces it, flapping his wings in a display of his prowess before diving on it, scouring the little toy. Confetti after confetti falls before his might, littering the bottom of his cage. My little warrior, just like his mama.

After a fruitful day's work attacking the thing, he proudly looks up at me from its half-ravaged carcass. I pet his head and reach for the toy only for him to bite my finger. "Play."

"You want to keep playing with it?"

"Play," he repeats.

"Okay. I'll leave you to it."

He tilts his head, staring up at me as I move away. "Where?"

"There's something I've been putting off for too long. I told Father Gregory I'd consider it, and I'm running out of excuses not to give it another try."

"Try?"

"Don't worry about it." I give him another quick pet, and he hops toward me and gives me a little kiss good-bye, his beak softly striking my cheek.

"Be good," he says.

Giggling, I walk out of the room, leaving the door open so he can fly around the house. It's worth having to clean up after him if it means he can get his exercise. I think he's putting on weight again, but that's hardly a bad thing when he's been looking this gaunt. I leave a few bits of carrots around the kitchen for him to find if he feels up for exploring.

With that done, I throw on a pair of slacks and a nice blouse and fight back a brief bout of cowardice. I want to stay here, to hide away from the world forever, but it's growing clearer by the day that that isn't always an option.

Grabbing the keys from their hook by the door, I climb into my car, and take a deep breath. I don't want to do this. Ever the soldier, I suck it up and drive to the Community Center just in time for my appointment.

❖

"Ms. Rosseau-Lester," I manage, taking the seat across from her, my eyes locked on the floor. Why is this so difficult? Hunting humans is easy. I could kill her in an instant. Is it because I have to be vulnerable around her? Christ, what am I even thinking being here? I wince as I cross myself for using the Lord's name in vain.

"What was that?" she asks, stifling a chuckle.

"Nothing."

"Was that vampiric self-harm?"

"What? No. That's ridiculous." It did hurt, though. A lot.

"Are you Catholic?" she asks, adjusting her laptop as she crosses her legs.

"I am. What of it?"

"Seems unusual for a vampire. Do crosses still hurt you? I know I should know these things, but I've heard very inconsistent information on it. I've known one vampire who wore a cross with no issue and another who was burned just by touching one."

This is why humans shouldn't be therapists for fiends. It doesn't matter how much they're part of the community or if they're married to one of us; they'll never really understand. Maybe I should go ahead and turn her. It'd certainly make this easier for me. "Vampire is a bit of a catch-all for a number of…" Would we call them species or races? Science has progressed so much since I last bothered doing any substantial biological research. Perhaps I should catch up on that sometime. Maybe I'll buy a little lab and look over their results. "Species," I decide. "I believe striga is the closest to my ilk, though even that seems somewhat wrong. I suspect there's been some miscegenation over the years."

“Oh. That explains a few things. I’d looked over all the varying myths—”

“Yes. That would be why. We’re a queer hodgepodge of several strangely compatible creatures.”

“You’re one whom the cross doesn’t hurt? Or is that some sort of placebo effect based on the vampire’s belief?”

“I’ve heard a few takes, though I’m not terribly able to test it myself. The most common claim seems to be that it’s heavily faith-based, going both ways.” Why am I teaching her this? Do I want to expose my weaknesses?

“Interesting. Since you have faith, that means it doesn’t hurt you?”

I wish. “Not quite.” My scar burns as if to remind me of how untrue that claim is. “It still hurts me.” Am I possessed? Why would I possibly share such a thing with a human? This is precisely what led to the Hunt in the first place. Stoker shared all of our secrets and led to one of the greatest genocides the world had ever known.

“So that *was* self-harm. What, is it your version of self-flagellation?”

She doesn’t even understand Catholicism. “No, I took the Lord’s name in vain, so I crossed myself.” I would probably sound less mad had I actually done it out loud in the first place. “I do it less than I should due to the pain, but sometimes, it’s necessary. Even if I’ll never actually earn his forgiveness.”

Ms. Rosseau-Lester purses her lips, considering me. I swear, everything I say she takes as an admission of some other mental defect. “Are you able to go to church?”

Here we go. “No. I can’t enter a sacred place. I just meet with my priest sometimes.”

“Well, if you’d like, there’s a chapel on the second floor. I know it’s not Catholic, but the holy symbols have been removed. I think there’re even a couple fiends who hold congregations there from time to time. It’s really quite lovely. It won’t be quite the same, but it might help you feel better if you ever really need to go to church.”

I open and close my mouth, narrowing my eyes as I stare. That’s actually not that terrible an idea. It would feel wrong, going to a different sort of church, but I suppose beggars can’t exactly be choosers. “I’ll keep it in mind.”

"Thank you, that's all I ask. Your priest, is he human?"

"Yes."

"And you have no issue talking with him?"

Groaning, I lean back, my eyes falling back to the floor. "He's a man of the cloth. It's not the same."

"He's still human."

"Well, it wasn't Catholics who were hunting us, and he's a servant of God. He's as removed from his humanity as I am from mine."

The keyboard clacks as she jots down a note. No doubt calling me out for some imagined hypocrisy. "Last time we talked, you were trying to take your bird to the vet. Did you manage to do that?"

"I did."

"That's fantastic. How is he doing?"

"He seems to be a lot better."

She smiles, looking far too proud of herself. To think I made a human feel this contented…it makes my blood run cold. There's probably still some coursing in me from last night. "Do you think the exercises helped?"

I want to say no. I want to insist that they were a stupid little waste of time and nothing more than play. It's not the real world, and it doesn't make a difference. I was able to overcome it on my own because I'm strong enough to manage anything, but whether or not that's true, there's a reason I'm back here. If it wasn't for her, I don't know if I could've talked to Dr. Sun. Granted, I wouldn't have been able to talk to Ms. Rosseau-Lester in the first place if I had known she was a human, but there was no way I could've expected the same to work for the vet. I knew she was human. "Maybe."

"Perfect. Would you like to try more?"

"I don't see how it could be necessary."

"Just having to talk to a human at all is enough, then?"

I bare my fangs. Cheeky little human, taunting her betters. "I don't even know what I'm doing here. This was a mistake."

"Olivia—"

"That's Ms. Crocetti." I almost said General Crocetti. Old habits truly do die hard. How long has it been since anyone has called me that? I'll not have a human act so familiar with me. I'd sooner be friends with a snail.

"Ms. Crocetti, you came back here for a reason. Clearly, this is still bothering you. Why don't you sit back down and tell me why you're here rather than making me guess?"

I didn't even realize I'd stood up. The door is only a couple paces away. I could walk out and never see her again. I compromise, leaning against the couch, my gaze still on the door. I've put up with a human disgracing my sight long enough. "The dreams are getting worse," I admit. "I haven't been sleeping. I can't. Every time I close my eyes…" I shudder, not letting the images invade my waking mind. It's too much. We should have wiped them all out when we had the chance. Humans are a plague on this world, and we'd all be better off if they were gone. "I just keep reliving it."

"The Hunt?" she asks, as if she knows a thing. She wasn't there. She can't imagine what it was like. Being hunted by the very people you'd called your friends. Life keeps teaching me that I can't have any.

"Mostly."

"What else?"

I snarl, turning on her. "You keep pushing, don't you? You expect me to spill my guts to the very kind that want me dead. I've seen thousands of you, killing us, hunting us." And not just then. No matter the reason, her people always find an excuse to persecute me and mine.

"I've said that you're welcome to turn me. You'd be doing me a favor. You were once human. I feel as little relation to them at this point as you do. My life is here."

"Then you're a bigger fool than I thought. You're still one of them. You'll never have gone through what I've gone through, and you'll never rid yourself of their stench." Shaking, I dig my fingers into the back of the couch. For centuries, I'd let myself trust humans. I'd seen the things vampires were capable of, and it seemed that humans were the lesser of two evils. Never again. I won't repeat that mistake.

"My wife is a wendigo, one of my best friends is a ghoul, and I only see about a dozen human clients, as opposed to my massive fiend practice. I've chosen my side. For you, it's clear that the war never ended, and you're welcome to view me as a traitor, but I'm not your enemy, and I never will be."

Never? Not even if I set upon you, draining you of every drop of blood and leaving your lifeless husk on the floor? Even then. you'll still be on my side? "I've heard it all before. I'm old. Nothing ever really changes."

"Yet you're still here."

I resist glaring at her again. She's made her point. As far as I'm aware, there's no other therapist anywhere who deals with us, and certainly none in Toronto or likely all of Canada. I need the help. Maybe it's worth it to suck it up and talk to her. With a derisive snort, I make my way back around the couch, taking my seat again, my eyes locked on the clock above her head. I still have over half an hour. I take in a deep breath. Am I really doing this?

She sits patiently, waiting for me to make the first move.

"I ran," I say, more to myself than to her, my voice scarcely louder than a whisper. "My friends, people I'd known for decades, if not longer, were all murdered, and I ran."

She nods, letting out a heavy sigh. I can feel the sympathetic look she's giving me, even without meeting her gaze. "You did what you had to in order to survive. There's nothing wrong with that."

"Of course you'd say that. You married a wendigo. I know how they happen. I don't even have half as good an excuse. I could've fought. I could've won. I'm a soldier, a warrior, and instead I made a coward of myself. I'm a disgrace to Venice."

The clicking of her computer keys is the only sound in the room. "If you had the chance to do it again, would you do it differently?"

I pause, trying not to let myself imagine it. Would I? Of course I would. I'd stay and fight. I'd die with my comrades. I don't care how despicable vampires are. I'd not let that happen. I couldn't. I wouldn't. "If I could do it all over again?" Wouldn't I? It was all I could do to survive. I don't want to die, not anymore. I had that choice taken from me long ago, and now I keep living with all of my guilt. Am I so afraid of the fate that I know awaits me? "I don't know," I admit, my voice shaking as I try to blink away tears. "I don't. I really don't."

Handing me a box of tissues, she says, "That's okay. But it also means that you shouldn't regret it. There was no good option there. You did what you had to."

Aren't therapists supposed to let you come to your own conclusions? I know there are many schools of thought, and I'm fifty years out of date, but it seems strange having one tell me something.

Perhaps she's saying this not as a therapist but…as what? I've made it quite clear we're not friends. "I've done countless horrible things in my life. I only regret two of them, and that will always be one. I don't care if it was my only option. I don't care if I'm just as much of a coward now. It was the wrong one. I should have fought."

The silence builds as she stares, waiting for me to go on or perhaps for me to meet her eyes. I don't give her the satisfaction.

I wipe my eyes and blow my nose, tossing the tissue into the nearby rubbish bin. Maybe I'm simply too broken for therapy.

"I'm going to recommend some medication for PTSD. There's a dealer on the other side of the mall who usually has them in stock. Prazosin should help with the dreams. With vampiric tolerance, I'd recommend starting with about four pills before bed and working your way up if that's not enough. I'm not a psychiatrist, and this is not a prescription, but I've had a prior client who it helped a lot, and I think it might let you sleep."

Now that's a surprise. I was expecting more of a fight. She had been so insistent on going over my history with a fine-toothed comb and resolving each and every issue at the root of this. "And the…" I gesture at her and her humanity.

"Lamotrigine has been effective from what I've read, but I haven't had any clients who liked it. They might have some in stock, though, so take a look at it, but please try the two pills separately so you know how they each affect you rather than trying both together and hoping for the best."

I nod, almost annoyed by how much I appreciate this. I need to sleep. I don't know why it set me off that badly the other day, but it won't stop. "Thank you."

She blinks. "Uh, you're welcome," she sputters, a look of sheer surprise on her face. "Medication on its own isn't as effective as pairing it with therapy. We've already made some progress. You've even managed to meet my eyes a few times. I really do think this is good for you."

"Maybe."

"How about we finish this session and you think about it?"

Was I that obvious? I suppose she's earned that much. She's done far more than any human has for me in over a century. "Okay. I can do that."

"Thank you. Do you have any friends? Anyone you talk to other than your priest?"

"Harvey…my parrot."

She nods, swallowing audibly as her eyebrows crease. Is she worried about me? Her heart rate even increased. That's novel. "Do you have a job? Anything that would put you around other people? Not even necessarily humans."

"I don't trust fiends much more than I trust humans. I haven't had to work since the thirties. I invested wisely during the Depression, picking a few businesses I was fairly confident would pick up when the economy did and keeping them afloat. They paid dividends, as have the few after."

"That must be very lonely."

"I have Harvey." Am I lonely? "I have books. I prefer being alone."

"Any lovers? I know you'd mentioned a wife—"

"Drop it right now." I bare my fangs and stiffen, ready to pounce. "She is off the table for this discussion."

"Okay." She gulps, shuddering as she moves back in her seat. It's the first time she's seemed that scared. The girl has some grit; most humans would be out of the room. Or on the floor. "I know that it's part of the whole vampire aesthetic, and perhaps after however many years you've lived, you're beyond these needs, but most people require some companionship from time to time. I think things would be a lot easier for you if you had a friend." She scratches a scar on her neck.

"Why, are you offering?"

She chuckles. "I don't think you'd have me."

"Wow, you really are a good therapist."

It's weird seeing her smile. "Glad I can help."

I adjust in my seat, not quite comfortable being on this good of terms with a human.

"Well, what is it you want to change in your life? You first came to see me because you wanted to be able to approach a human, and now it's the dreams, but you don't seem to want to work on the source of your PTSD. I know that it can be hard, but I need to know what it is that you want to work on if you want my help."

I sigh, staring at the back wall for lack of a window. "Maybe I'll have an answer for you if I come back. For now, hopefully, the medication will take care of it."

"All right. That's perfectly reasonable. There's no rush to figure things out. I'm just glad you're reaching out."

Twiddling my thumbs in my lap, I consider her words. Is that what I'm doing? Do I really need help? I know that that's what Father Gregory wanted me to do. Wow, I'm failing my priest. Why is it this hard to talk about? I have to relive it every night. What's one more time? It's not as if I haven't had enough time to deal with it—it's been more than a century—so what am I waiting for? I just don't trust her. "Reaching out to a human certainly doesn't make it easier."

"I'm sorry. I'm sure that's tough. But it gives you exposure in a controlled environment, where there are hundreds of fiends right outside those doors and only one of me. I promise I don't want to hurt you, but I can also guarantee that I can't."

She has a point. "No, you certainly can't."

"Great." She grins, her teeth showing. "Well, let's work from there. Is there anything I can do to make you more comfortable with me? More comfortable interacting with a human?"

What would help with that? Other than her being dead. That would absolutely make things easier. "I'm not sure."

"Would phone sessions be any easier for you? You wouldn't have to see my face."

Fuck. That might actually work. I hate the idea of giving her my phone number—who knows what she could manage to do with that—but it might be the best idea. Maybe if I turn my GPS off it won't be an issue? Modern technology can be so intimidating. Even rotary phones are such a new invention. "Okay. Yes. We can try that."

I give her my number. I guess I'm really doing this. Now I really need that medication. I pay for the session and thank her again. As loath as I am to admit it, she seems to actually know what she's doing. I hope this will help.

❖

It takes some searching. I pass a stand carrying all sorts of weapons, another with an excessive collection of venison, and a few that seem to be offering more exotic affairs, but I finally find the right place. At least, I think it's the right place. They seem to be selling a wide variety of medications, if you can call some of it medication. The cannabis I can understand, but some of these things seem like they'd do far more harm than good.

"The hell do you mean two hundred?" A woman to my right almost screams. "This is barely even a hundred dollars' worth. You want two hundred for it?"

"That's the price, take it or leave it," a masculine voice replies. "My last shipment never came in, so I'm running a little short. I can't part with it for less than that."

"Oh, give me a break." She scoffs, her grip tightening on the bottles. "The hell kind of scam are you running? You sure don't seem to be light. You have just as much stock as usual. Where's Claire? Is she here? She knows me. She'll give me the right price."

I sift through the various bottles and packages, not all of which are labeled, trying to find the pills that Ms. Rosseau-Lester suggested. Prazosin, Prazosin…I don't see it.

"She's not in. She should be back next week, but I'm telling you, it's two hundred."

Her fist slams on the table, "Call her up."

"She said she's not to be disturbed," he snarls back.

She's grinding her teeth loud enough that I can barely concentrate. I turn to her, giving her a dirty look, only to find Amelia Sun holding a couple bottles and looking ready to murder the poor demon. She doesn't seem to notice me. "I'll give you one fifty for it, fucking scalper."

He sucks on his teeth but eventually nods. "All right. One fifty and you get out of my hair."

She throws the money on the table and begins to storm off. I'm tempted to stop her, but I think I'm well past my limit for dealing with humans. Why are there so many here? This is supposed to be a place for fiends, and yet there're two of them running about like they own the place. It's a veritable infestation. "Do you have any Prazosin?" I ask. "I'm also looking for Lamotrigine if you have it."

He looks me up and down, chewing on his cheek as he considers me. Does he even run this stand? "You don't need that shit," he mutters, shaking his head. He pulls a vial from somewhere on the table. "Try this. Prazosin's for bad dreams, right? You'll have never slept as well."

"I knew it," Dr. Sun calls, storming back, her eyes ablaze as she spins on him. "This fucking charlatan. This isn't even your stand, is it?" She snatches the vial from him, examining it with an expert eye.

"Okay, it's not snake oil, I'll give you that. What with those horns, I thought you might still be behind the times on grifting." She pops the cork, sniffing it. "Really?" She turns to me, recognition finally dawning on her face. "Oh, it's you. This is just ether. I suppose it'll knock you out, maybe. Not sure it'd work on a vampire, but if that's what you're going for, I'd advise some vodka or maybe heroin." She glares at him. "Who the fuck *are* you?"

"Claire's out of town," he mumbles, quietly enough that she likely can't even hear him. "I said I'd take over for her."

"Right, and does she know you're trying to ruin her business? I've been a customer of hers for the last three years, and I'm telling her exactly how you handled this."

"What?" His eyes widen, the glowing red orbs flashing in surprise. "No." His voice cracks as he takes a step back from us.

"So, you were trying to rip me off?" I let my fangs show, meeting his eyes, making my murderous intent abundantly clear. I'm no demon, but I can look plenty intimidating. "Do you know what I do to people who betray me?" Mostly let them get away with it, honestly. I'm zero for three there. "Do you have what I'm looking for or not?"

His eyes shift between the two of us, finally settling on me. He clearly thinks I'm the bigger threat. I guess he's never known a human. "I don't know. Maybe."

"Give her money back, all of it," I say.

"Okay." He throws the wadded bills on the table, his eyes never leaving mine. I think he may be entranced. I hadn't realized that worked on demons. "Now give me what I'm looking for, and for her trouble, give this nice lady anything else she wants for free. If you think Claire will be pissed at you for that, just wait until she finds out what you were doing to her customers." I have absolutely no idea who Claire is.

"Take whatever you want. It's yours."

I smile. After all the power I had to give up over the last hour, it feels good to be in control again. I needed this. "Good boy."

He doesn't run. He doesn't even move. He stands there, waiting for us to take whatever we want and be on our way. I wish more of these stands offered this kind of service. I'd shop here more often.

Dr. Sun sifts through the bottles, looking like she has far more of an idea of what she's looking for than I do. She tosses me a couple packages filled with bubble sheets and grabs a few wads of something in wax paper, stuffing it in her pocket. We walk away from the pitiful demon as he looks on. I wonder if I could've actually taken him in a fight. I'm no slouch, but some demons are in a whole other league. My age and experience mean nothing to someone who predates the first crusade. If it wasn't my powers that made him behave like that, it was Claire. Whoever she is, she must be one hell of a terrifying woman.

"Thank you," Dr. Sun says, breaking the silence when we make it to the door.

"You're the one that came to my rescue," I reply. This feels weird. Maybe my therapy session is already paying off, but I can't believe I'm being nice to a human. No matter how much she's done, or how attractive she may be—which is something I definitely hadn't noticed before, when Harvey was my only concern—she's still a human.

"Yeah, but I was mostly bullshitting him. Claire would charge one seventy-five."

I chuckle, surprised to find a smile spreading across my face. "Well, I'm glad I could help you rip him off."

She pockets the pill bottles, smiling up at me. "Is Harvey doing okay? That was your parrot's name, right?"

Nodding, I reply, "Yeah, he seems to be doing a lot better. I've been meaning to thank you."

"Just doing my job. You paid a more-than-fair price for it."

"You do love ripping people off."

"Well, after today, how about when you finish the medication, bring him back in, and I can make sure it's all cleared up, and I won't even charge you? I'd say you already paid for it, getting me all this."

"I don't recall it being quite as much as those pills are worth. One seventy-five, plus whatever else you took—"

"All right," she interrupts, holding up her hands in surrender. "I'll owe you."

"You sure you want to be in debt to a vampire?" I smirk, as threatening as I can manage with how broadly I'm still grinning. "Who knows what I might ask you to do."

She shrugs. "Nothing worth more than about eighty bucks."

Leaning against the wall, I sigh. Why am I bantering with her? I was terrified of her the other day. I've done far more interesting things with humans than rip off a drug dealer before, and I certainly didn't start bonding with them. It's not like I'm not afraid, I still think that having humans at the Community Center—anywhere other than the slave market or on the menu—is the worst idea we've ever had. Maybe it's just because she saved Harvey's life. My opinion of her has been far more charitable since. "Here I was, planning on having you help me kidnap young maidens to feed off of."

"See, I've been to the market. I know that they go for way more than eighty dollars. You'd owe me."

"I guess I'll have to find something else for you to do." I need to get out of here. With Ms. Rosseau-Lester, it's professional, and with Father Gregory, it's religious. I have no desire to have a human friend. Hell, I have no desire to have any friends besides Harvey. "I should get going. Thanks again, Dr. Sun."

"Call me Mia. We're partners in crime now. I'd say that earns you a first name basis."

That sounds almost exactly like friends. Unfortunately, my parents would never forgive me for being so rude as to not respond in kind. "You can call me Olivia."

"Was I not already?" She leans against the wall near me, grabbing one of the bottles from her jacket. She takes a pill before offering another to me. "Want one?"

"Like I said, I'm leaving. Have a good night." Fortunately, no one stole or dismantled my car while I was inside. I hate leaving it out here. I give her a half-hearted wave and walk back to it as casually as I can manage. What the hell was that? I shouldn't even bother getting over my fears if it's going to result in more of that behavior. Humans can't be trusted, and I certainly shouldn't be flirting with them. I blink, staring at my key in the ignition. Is that what I was doing? Damn it all.

Chapter Four

Prazosin

I'm so hungry. Hungrier than I've ever been in my entire life. I don't know how long I was asleep. It feels like years. I need to eat. I need to drink. I push myself to my feet. Every inch is a mile. My body doesn't want to cooperate. Did I really swoon on the day bed? What happened? I remember...what was it? All I recall is blood. My own? I look down at myself, but I don't see blood anywhere. Why does that sound appealing? I must be even hungrier than I thought.

Wait, where did he go? I wasn't alone. Was I? My head hurts, everything hurts, and I feel like my stomach is trying to devour itself. My chest feels as if there's molten metal being poured onto it again and again. I don't even have it in me to scream. Maybe I should just lie back down. I don't know if I can. I'm starving. If I don't eat something I might die.

Outside, I hear cannons, clashing steel. I need to get out there. We're under attack. I have to help my men.

I finally manage to stand without falling back down. Staying on my feet takes all of my will. I have to drag myself to the door. My limbs seem to have been replaced by iron bars. I ignore it, pressing on. I've only managed a few feet. If I only had a bite, I'd have the strength to go on.

I push open the door, shielding my eyes from the sudden light from the window. My wife is sitting up in bed, looking out at the sea. She's waiting there. She looks delicious...beautiful, she looks beautiful.

"My love, are you all right?" she asks, noticing me as I catch myself on the bed. The battle outside is so loud, it's no wonder she

couldn't hear me. Everything is so loud. Her voice is booming in my ears. I can hear her heart racing. I can hear the blood pumping through her veins. I close my eyes, trying to shut everything out. "Are you unwell? Should I fetch Emilia? Perhaps she could bring you a wet cloth or some water?"

I groan, trying to support myself as I fall against the bed. I'm stronger than this. It couldn't have been that long, so why am I so weak? Have I been poisoned?

She places a warm hand against my forehead. "You feel cold."

That smell. I can smell him on her. He was right. More than that, she smells like food. Why do I keep thinking that? "You did do it," I breathe.

"I'm sorry?"

"Spare me your apologies. He told me all I need know." Why would she? She loves me. He can't be right. I can't think clearly! I need to eat. I need to eat her. I shake my head, trying to rid myself of that horrid thought. I need to think this through. I still don't have proof. Where is it? I know it was missing, what was it? Nothing is coming clearly.

"Whatever do you mean?"

I snatch her wrist away, my nails biting into her skin. I feel blood on my fingers. That's unlike me. I'd never let my nails grow that long. I stare at them, releasing her. My hands don't look any different than usual. But there's blood, sharp and red and tempting. The smell of it calls to me. I bring my finger to my lips, slowly, hesitantly, fighting against these base instincts. My tongue reaches out, unbidden, snatching the droplet of blood. It tastes like heaven. My mind is clearer, but it's still fuzzy. I need more. If I just had more blood, I could figure out what to do.

She clutches her hand to her chest, staring at me in confusion. Blood trickles down, staining her dress. I need it.

I tackle her to the bed. The act is familiar, intimate, and yet violent. I don't want her, not for who she is, not for the woman I love. I'm eyeing her like a piece of meat. I know she betrayed me, but is this what it's come to? "What are you—"

I sink my teeth into her neck, ignoring her inquiries. They're meaningless words now. We're well past that. All that matters is the blood. Why am I biting her? I thought I was going to lick more of it off her arm. That would make more sense. It's like my body is moving of its own will.

She convulses under me, fighting back. "Stop. That hurts."

Her pleas fall on deaf ears. The words don't even register until sometime later. All I see, all I taste, all I need is her blood. I hold her there, feasting on her, taking her for every last drop.

When it's all gone, I stand up in a state of utter bliss. It feels amazing. This must be ambrosia. How could I have ever eaten anything else? This was all I needed. Oh, but I can think again. The fog is gone.

My own deeds finally strike me. Her body lies before me. I want to vomit. God, what have I done?

I grab her, shaking her, willing life back into her. She can't be dead! She can't. I won't allow it. No. I can't lose her. I can't be the one who did this. Even if she was having an affair, how could I kill her? How can this be who I am...what I am? I've murdered her.

I jerk awake, panting, my eyes wide. It's been years since I last had that dream. It's almost always the Hunt. Even my subconscious isn't so cruel as to make me relive that. Why now? These pills were supposed to help. I swipe at the table beside me, knocking the packets of pills onto the floor along with the glass of water. It shatters against the wall, shards of glass scattering about the newly formed puddle. The pill containers bounce off, unfazed.

I climb out of bed, the image of her lifeless body burned into my retinas. She's all I see, everywhere I look. I did that. I killed her, and it wasn't even true. I was just so hungry. This is why I'm damned. It's not because I'm a vampire. It's not for any other reason. I murdered the love of my life. I ate her.

I truly am a monster.

It's been so long, and yet her memory still haunts me. I've never loved again. I'm not worthy of it.

That's why. That's why that dream is back. Her ghost is haunting me. She's reminding me of why I can never be with anyone again. I don't deserve it. It's the same reason that Vanessa died, isn't it? I don't deserve love. No one who could do what I did could possibly deserve love.

I collapse in the hallway, leaning against the wall as the tears fall. I should've died that night. I wanted to. I tried to. I tried to kill myself, but he wouldn't let me. There's another mortal sin. I'm damned many times over. It's no wonder this scar never goes away.

The small cross-shaped burn on my chest shows clearly through my nightgown. Every other wound has healed. Only this one remains, to remind me of exactly how God feels about me. Even his infinite capacity for forgiveness isn't enough for me, not after all I've done. He has cast me aside.

I deserve hell. I should get it over with. I can end my life, end my suffering, and accept my fate. If only I wasn't such a blasted coward.

That night, I had the courage. Back then, I was still a soldier. I hadn't spent my life running away. I shot myself in the head, and I survived. It didn't even scar. Instead, the gun was wrestled from my hands, and I was bound and left to starve for I know not how long. Long enough that he thought I'd listen to him when he offered me blood. Long enough that it worked.

I stare at the ceiling, wishing I could stare up into heaven itself. If I could only beg for his forgiveness in person. I'm just too afraid to accept my punishment. Perhaps that's the only reason I keep living.

A squawk sounds from my shoulder. I blink away tears, trying to make out the blurry image. "Okay?" Harvey asks, perched on my shoulder, his head cocked in concern. "Okay?" How long has he been there?

I shake my head. I'm not okay. Sighing, I drag myself to my feet. I can't leave him alone. Maybe that's why I keep buying these animals, so I have an excuse to keep on living. I stumble into the kitchen, my legs yearning to collapse all over again. "Would you like some fruit?"

"Tea."

"I don't feel up to—"

"Tea."

Is he trying to look after me? If I make some for him, I'll have some myself. It won't make a difference. Maybe I'll put some blood in it.

"Tea," he repeats.

"Okay, okay." I put some water in the kettle. Looks like we're having tea.

❖

Either they wrote the same paragraph over and over again in this book, or I'm having trouble concentrating. I was hoping to bring my knowledge of biology into the twenty-first century. If I don't have some understanding of it, I won't know what to invest in, but more importantly, I'm trying to get my mind to focus on something else. I've been on this page for almost an hour.

I've tried taking half a dozen each of the pills, and nothing has happened. It's not some miraculous instantaneous cure-all, but how can I still be this bad? Her face refuses to leave my thoughts.

I'm better than this. I'm stronger than this.

What the hell is wrong with me?

Shoving the book aside, I stomp over to the fridge. I drink the blood cold. I need something to help me focus.

It doesn't seem to make a difference. Tastes good, though.

Dr. Rosseau-Lester and I had a session yesterday. I don't care how good she is, I'm not weak enough to need to see a therapist two days in a row. I can deal with this myself. I've been dealing with it on my own for hundreds of years. She thinks I need exposure therapy? She thinks I need to be around people? Fine. I'll go be around people. I am a general in the Venetian army, I am a centuries-old and powerful vampire, and I am stronger than any fucking issue I might have.

I slam the door behind me, keys in hand, and climb into my car. Where do humans spend time?

I go to the mall. The actual one. The one that isn't a façade used as a black market.

In the massive parking lot, row upon row upon row of cars surround me as the sun blares down. I swallow a lump in my throat and park. There are so many people here. Why would any place need this many people? This is ridiculous. Why would they all come to the same place?

I've been in big cities. I spent a lot of time in London in the 1800s, but this is absurd. This is far too many people.

Reaching for the keys, I fumble, not even able to turn off the ignition on my first try. If I could sweat, I would be a mess right now. I should go home. This is a stupid idea.

No. I can't. I can't keep dealing with these dreams. If desensitization is what I'm after, I'll get it. Ms. Rosseau-Lester wants me to take it slow, build my way up, just keep having little chats with her until I can consistently handle meeting her eyes and being in a room with her, but that's too inefficient. I won't keep being a coward. I can do this. I will face my fears, and I will overcome them. That's all there is to it.

I successfully snatch the keys from the ignition, slam the door behind me, and stomp out onto the hot pavement. Even through my sunglasses, it's far too bright. How do people stand this?

I saunter over to the entrance as casually as I can manage, grit my teeth, take a deep breath, wonder if my lungs have atrophied over the years, grip the door handle, and start to pull. I just need to open it. The door isn't that heavy. I could fling it off its hinges without a thought. Why isn't it moving?

Grasping my wrist with my other hand, I give it a tug, almost falling on my ass as the door flies open. I manage to stay on my feet because I am a vampire and not some pitiful puppy and stride right in without a fear in the world.

There are too many people.

I swear I can count a hundred right here.

There are children running about, climbing on some plastic and metal monstrosities atop a bouncy green floor. Their parents, I presume, are watching them from benches against the wall. All around, shoppers wander between stores, carrying bags of various spoils.

I still haven't taken a step. My feet have forgotten how to move. How is everyone else able to simply walk around? Don't they know the monsters that surround them? These humans are capable of anything. They could set upon each other at any point, they're killers, merciless machinations of… I sigh. Of God. They're his creation, as I am. Even as flawed as they are, they aren't wrong. They're just as they're meant to be. I'm the one who isn't. I'm the one who's a monster.

Wow. Did I really have a Nietzschean moment of realizing that I'm the real monster? I'm a vampire, a murderer. Of course I'm the real monster.

Humans are too, though.

I steel my nerves and take a step, walking past his favorite creations. I have to think of them like that. Don't think of them as the reactionary fools, hunting down your entire species because a book told them we were bad. Think of them as children of God.

I cross myself, barely noticing the pain as I walk. It makes me feel a little better. Since I'm already here, I decide to step into a clothing shop. I haven't updated my wardrobe in a few decades, and after the moths found one of my closets, I'm sure I could use some new outfits. I've already replaced most of it online, but it's always better when you can try things on. It was far easier when I could have people sew garments to my measurements, but I couldn't have a human touch me like that without killing them.

I find a dress that appeals to me, a cute top, a nice skirt, and some jeans. The last time I bought jeans, bell bottoms were still in fashion. I take my meager selections and approach the changing rooms. "Did you find everything okay?" a woman asks, approaching me.

The air seems thicker. I try to swallow and can't. My breathing starts and quickens.

She stares at me. "Was there something you were looking for?"

I blink. I should just kill her.

An unconvincing smile slowly appears on her face as her eyebrows knit together. "Hello?"

Say something before she gets suspicious. She might figure out what I am, then she'll round up everyone here, they'll find every piece of wood and sharp object they can scrounge up, and they'll all chase me down and shove a stake through my heart. If I don't act quickly, I'll die. "Sorry," I mutter. "I'm fine." I want to drop the clothes where I stand and flee, but that would be too strange, too suspicious. "Just want to try these on." My voice shakes as I sputter the words, dashing into the changing room before she can ask me anything more.

I collapse on the little bench behind the red curtain, clutching my knees to my chest, trying to get myself to stop breathing. This is too much. I'm not ready. I can't take it.

My cheek stings, I stare at my own hand to find that I've slapped myself. I have to beat the sense back into me. Letting out the last of my breaths, I lean back, staring up at the ceiling, past the thin rod holding up the curtain at the dotted rectangles of drywall and plaster. I don't even care about the clothes anymore, but I must keep up the charade. No, more than that, I have to make myself do this. I'm sick of being afraid all the time.

I try on the outfits. Apparently, I still have a better eye for clothing than I'd expected as they all fit. Back in my tan button-up blouse and gray skirt, I grab the new articles of clothing and take them to the counter.

Managing to smile and nod at whatever she says, I hand over the cash, reluctantly take my change when she offers it, and walk out of the store. The bag slams against my calf as I stop dead. I was heading toward the exit, but I already decided what I'm doing. I won't give up.

I turn around and proceed deeper into this horrific labyrinth, shutting my eyes as I pass through a throng of people. I can almost feel them stabbing at me.

When I open them again, I find myself surrounded. There are humans everywhere, on every side of me. There are table after table filled with them eating, there're some women testing out a perfume to my right, a few children playing with a remote-control helicopter to my left, and behind me, there's a wedge of hunters, heading right toward me.

I turn back around, my eyes wide, to see more of them walking through the field, straight at me, crossbows in hand. My grip on the bag tightens as I look for any means of egress. I can't take them all. Even if I manage to, it'll cause more to come, looking for me, out for blood. This was a terrible idea. I'm going to die. I can't. I can't. I can't.

Doubling over, my hands covering my eyes, I wait for death. It doesn't come. I don't feel their bolts skewering me or their flames devouring me. No blade comes for my head. I look up. I'm still in the mall. People are staring at me but only a few. Most of them are still going about their business. Where did those hunters go?

I scan the crowd, looking for any sign of them, and I swear I see a familiar face. It's only for an instant. Someone walks in front of her, and she seems to disappear, but I swear it was her. Was that all a hallucination?

Shaking my head, I shove through the small crowd of concerned onlookers, looking for any sign of her. She was real, wasn't she? Bianca?

There's no sign of her anywhere. I can't smell her either.

With a heavy sigh, I throw myself into a nearby chair. The table seems to be empty, so I'm not drawing any extra attention to myself. I pinch the bridge of my nose, shutting my eyes, focusing on my other senses. I'm not looking for her anymore. She was just part of my delusion. I'm trying to center myself, to calm down enough that I can leave without leaving a pile of bodies behind me.

After a few moments, I stand up, my eyes still closed, and walk back to the entrance, using my other senses to avoid walking into anyone else. When I'm finally back in my car, the tears begin to fall.

That's never happened before. The flashbacks have only ever been in my dreams. It's never made me hallucinate. Maybe the pills only made me worse. I'm not taking any more of them. I can't handle that again. It felt real. I was certain I was going to die. And I was sure I saw Bianca.

Chapter Five

Depression

I'm not quite sure how long I've been on this couch. I know that *The Great British Bake Off* was on at some point, but I couldn't tell what happened. I don't particularly care, either. I know I made it home from the mall. Well, I must have. I'm here. I don't remember the drive at all.

It was dark a minute ago, why is the sun up? Oh, well. I can deal with it. It's not worth the effort to draw the blinds. It's not like I'll spontaneously combust or anything. I just have a bit of a headache. I close my eyes. I'm not sure if I've actually slept yet.

I wake up to a beak poking repeatedly against my head. Did he slap me with his wing? "Harvey?" I mutter. My voice is hoarse. It sounds strange to my ears.

He squawks, flapping indignantly.

"What?"

He squawks again.

If only parrots could talk. "You're hungry, aren't you?"

"Carrots?"

It takes all of the strength I have, but I force myself to my feet and shamble to his cage, tossing some feed into the dish before giving him his medication. He squawks again, looking curiously at me before flying into his cage and taking a bite of the food.

Yawning, I wander back to the couch.

I must've fallen asleep again since the sun is now down, and phaser noises are coming from the TV. Lying there, I can't quite summon up the energy to put anything else on. I stare, only able to use one eye as the other is pressed against the armrest of the couch. There's a spot on the floor. Where did that come from? It's not blood, and it doesn't look like parrot droppings or shedding. I watch it for hours. What could it be?

The sun rises, and I realize that it was a trick of the light. That was exciting.

I turn over, burying my face against the couch cushions.

At some point, I wake up and feed Harvey. That reminds me, how long has it been since I've eaten? What day is it?

Rather than checking, I return to the couch. There's already an outline in the shape of my body, and it would be rude not to fill it. Someone made a cake roll on television. I don't think I'd have the appetite to eat even if I needed people food.

Talons touch down on my chest. I blink, staring into Harvey's golden eyes. He stares back, tilting his head back and forth as he examines me.

"I'm not dead." Well, I guess I am, but that's hardly relevant to his question.

"Dead."

I blink. "Thanks."

He flaps once. "Tea?"

Something vaguely resembling a smile forms on my face. I do have the sweetest little parrot. None of my cats or dogs ever cared about me half as much as he does. "I love you, Harvey." I let my eyes drift closed again. Was there something I was supposed to do?

"Tea."

I wave a hand vaguely at him. "In a little while."

The sound of my phone ringing wakes me up. I pat my pocket and don't see it. I look at the coffee table and at the floor around me. It's only then that I realize the sound is coming from behind me. Am I so out of it that I can't even use my damn superhuman senses?

I snatch the phone from its charger on the counter and answer the call. When did I plug it in? There's no way Harvey would have known to do that. "Hello?" I ask, yawning.

"Ms. Crocetti," I recognize the voice, but I can't quite place it, "Did you forget about our appointment?"

Harvey's not scheduled for a few more days, I'm pretty sure. He still has a couple pills left. That doesn't sound like Mia, anyway. I mean Dr. Sun. Damn it.

"You there?"

"Sorry."

"You said you wanted to do therapy by phone, remember? Now's your appointment."

"Oh." It's Ms. Rosseau-Lester. I guess that makes sense. "Yes, sorry." I collapse back on the couch, the phone still clutched to my ear.

"Are you doing okay? You sound really out of it."

"I'm fine."

She sighs, her chair turning beneath her. She sounds genuinely concerned. Great, I've worried my bird and my therapist. I must be worse than I thought. "I'm generally not too big on pushing a client who doesn't want to talk, but you sound like you might need it. Did you try the medications?"

"They don't work."

"How long did you try them for?"

"I tried the Prazosin once."

"And the Lamotrigine?"

I shrug.

Somehow, she seems to catch my meaning. I can almost hear her roll her eyes. "They don't work instantly. You need to give them more of a shot."

"No, I'm done with them. I'm done with trying to fix me. All it does is make things worse." That's the most words I've said in days. I need a drink.

"What do you mean it made it worse? What happened?"

"Nothing, just more bad dreams." Can I go back to sleep? I haven't even been dreaming. It's been amazing. It's like there's nothing in my head, when normally, there's far too much in there to deal with. I love the silence.

"About the Hunt?"

No. It wasn't about the Hunt, was it? What was it about again? My eyes widen. Oh. Right. "No."

"Then what was it about?"

"I don't want to talk about it."

Her fingers tap her armrest. "I think you might need to. I don't know you that well, but you sound like you're in a really bad place right now. In order for me to help you, you need to tell me what's going on."

Gnashing my teeth, I glare at the TV, finally finding the energy to turn it off. I can still see the look on her face, the pain in her eyes, the fear. Fuck, I want to be numb again. "I can't."

"Ms. Crocetti—"

"I killed my wife. Because of…" I shake my head. No one else is to blame. It was my fangs in her neck. "I'd just been turned, and I ate her. I thought she was having an affair, and she smelled like food, and I didn't know what was happening."

Her teeth grind, and her chair stops swiveling. "It happens. You don't have to hate yourself for it."

I want to spit back that she hasn't done it or that it shouldn't happen, but even in my current state, I'm aware enough to know that her wife likely did something similar. It's not as much to spare her feelings as my own that I bite my tongue. I don't want to have it rubbed in my face that other people deal with this shit too. Let me suffer alone. "Well, it still shouldn't have happened. I still have to live with it."

"When was this?"

I sigh. "You want the exact date?"

"Sure."

"March 29th, 1508."

"Oh." She pauses, taking a deep breath.

"Yeah, I know that was a long time ago."

"I wasn't going to say that."

"I'm old. I get it." I stare up at the stucco ceiling. Her death has haunted me for over five centuries. I don't know how humans do it. Some of them move past their loves so quickly. I can't even imagine it. "She's the only woman I've ever loved, and I killed her."

"It's not your fault. I've talked to a lot of vampires. When you're first turned, those cravings, that hunger…it's more than anyone can resist."

"Then I should've found someone else to eat. Someone who deserved it." Or eaten myself if I was so damn hungry. I'm the one who deserved to die.

"You didn't know what was happening. Did you want to be a vampire?"

"No," I admit.

"Someone turned you, without your consent, and when you were so desperately hungry that you couldn't think clearly, you found someone and ate her? I'm sorry for your loss, but that wasn't your fault. It was the fault of whoever turned you."

"It is my fault. I shouldn't have trusted him."

"You knew the man—"

"I've relived quite enough without having to think of him. Forgive me, but we can talk about him another time. I've little desire to picture that smug mug of his anymore than I have to."

She falters. "Okay." She seems to be searching for words, her lips smack as she opens and closes her mouth. "You've really never loved anyone since her?"

"Not a soul."

"I can certainly relate, but I mean, it's been five hundred years. Don't you think you deserve to find someone new?"

"No. No one who would kill her own wife deserves someone new." Shaking, I wrap my arms about myself, scrutinizing my knees. "I can't do that to her…to anyone." It's a stupid little crush. I barely know the girl. What is going through my mind?

"You make it sound like you have a particular woman in mind."

"No. I don't."

"Maybe that's why you had that dream. You're trying to guilt yourself out of moving past your ex-wife."

Is that what this is? Is that the only reason I'm feeling like this? "No. It's not just that. Maybe this dream, but that was days ago. I'm fine. I'm over it. I don't want to be with anyone."

"Then what is it?"

I hesitate, but if it will get her to drop the subject of my finding a new paramour, perhaps it's worth discussing what brought on this recent bout of depression and dissociation. "Fine." She'll think I'm such a fool. "I took those pills, and I still had that dream, and I decided I couldn't take it anymore."

"You—"

"No. Not like that. Never like that, not since the night I killed her. I decided I needed a more drastic take at desensitization." Merely thinking about it again is almost too much. "I went to the mall. Not the Honeydale Mall, the real one. I decided that if I made it through, I'd be fine. It's been one hundred and twenty-one years, and I am sick of it. I can't deal with being afraid anymore. I went where I thought the most people would be. I walked past them. I tried shopping. I even talked to someone. I thought I was managing it…well, almost."

"What happened?"

I sigh. I don't know why I let myself do it. I've read enough books on psychology to know that it doesn't work like that. Why am I so damn stubborn? "I had a bit of a breakdown."

She sighs. Now she must think I'm even more in need of her care. "I'm sorry."

"I really thought I would be okay. Now I'm not even sure how many days it's been. What's today?"

"Tuesday."

"Shit. I went out on Wednesday."

"Do you have any memory of the past week?"

I shake my head, staring at the floor. "Flashes here and there. I wasn't out killing people, if that's what you're worried about. I think I was just on the couch watching television. That might be why I have the strange urge to bake a cake."

"Well, I'm glad you didn't hurt anyone. Is Harvey okay?"

I nod. "Yeah. I made sure to feed him. At least I remember that."

"You care a lot about him. Not a question…you've made it abundantly clear."

"I do. I don't know what I'd do without him." If I miss a single day of his pills, I'll never forgive myself. He's been doing so much better. I wonder if he's asleep right now. I haven't heard him squawking.

"How are you doing now?"

Leaning back in the couch, I let out a low groan. I'm glad I'm already dead, or else this couch would reek to hell right now. "I don't know."

"You're feeling a bit more present?"

"I think I am. I remember this conversation."

"That's a good sign."

I hesitate. I know it's what she's there for, but my life has taught me to never admit weakness. It's also taught me that I should never trust, and I seem to be starting to do that with her. Even if she is a human. Maybe we'll change that at some point, as badly as she seems to want it.

She seems to pick up on my hesitation. "Is there something on your mind?"

Grinding my teeth, I reply, "I think I may have set myself back another few decades. I don't know if I'll even be able to go to Harvey's follow-up appointment."

"If there's one thing I can say about you, it's that you'll do whatever you have to for him."

Or maybe so I can see her again. I still can't believe we were flirting. Maybe I'm simply desperate after such a long time without a partner. "I hope you're right."

"Do you think you'll be able to leave for any other reason?"

"To feed. I'm absolutely starving." Have I eaten in the last week? There wasn't much blood left in the fridge. I should buy more next time I'm at the Community Center.

"What about to see your priest?"

I bite my lip, trying to think if that'd be too much for me. It would involve both sun and people, even if I'd be able to avoid the latter. "Probably."

"Please try. If it's too much for you, I understand. I don't want you to force yourself to do anything you're not ready to do—especially after what happened the last time—but I don't want you to lose all of the progress you've been making. You were able to talk to two different people who you weren't viewing as food and without running away. That sounds like a massive change from where you had been, and it's very impressive. You're stronger than you know, Ms. Crocetti, and I don't want you to let yourself think otherwise."

"Olivia," I correct her. I'm already letting one human call me that. What's the harm in another?

"Olivia, then." She pauses. "I normally like to have my clients refer to me as Ms. Rosseau-Lester, but I don't want you to think your trust isn't being reciprocated. It sounds like that's a big thing for you. If you'd like, you can call me Elizabeth. Or Liz. Either's fine."

"Thank you, Elizabeth." Yeah, that doesn't feel at all weird, whereas it absolutely does with Mia. Great, I do have a crush. I will have to do something about that.

"How about we work on some more practice conversations? I'm still human, last time I checked."

"You needn't sound so pained about it."

"I know last week was a setback, a bad one, but you can get through it, and I'll help you the best I can."

I'm surprised to find myself smiling. Here I am, trusting my fate to a human once again. With considerable luck, it'll go better this time. "All right, sure. Let's do this."

We spend the next half hour going over practice conversations with her as Mia. I almost let it slip that she and I had been flirting the other day, but I manage to keep it to myself. Elizabeth suggested also trying with her as Father Gregory, but it would feel wrong. I can still talk to him fine, so it shouldn't be an issue. It's smelling and hearing the rest of the congregation that may be difficult, but I'll manage.

When we're done, I head over to Harvey's room to check on him. Please say I didn't hallucinate feeding him.

He blinks, waking up in the darkened room. I guess I haven't had the lights on much. I wonder how much he's been sleeping. Hopefully, that'll help him fight off the last of the infection. "Morning," he says, flapping at me from his perch.

"Good morning."

"Feel better?"

With a faint smile, I nod. I still can't believe he actually worries about me. When I was researching buying an African gray, I read how selfish and jerkish they were, and that even if they showed affection, it would only be on their terms. Clearly, they haven't been spending time with the right parrots. "I do. I'm going to give you your food and medicine, and I'll make some tea. How's that sound?"

"Tea!"

Apparently it sounds good. I give him his feed, as well as a nice treat for him to attack and tear apart for more food, and he takes his pill. Then I go to fix some tea, and a few minutes later, he flies after me. That bird loves his tea.

❖

As loath as I am to admit it, I'm obviously starving for both blood and affection. I'll be taking neither from Mia. She's part of the community. We could too easily grow close. I won't risk it. Besides, she's the only vet I could have work on Harvey, and I'm not willing to compromise that.

Being around humans is far less overwhelming when I'm planning on eating one. I know it seems silly, and it still sets me off sometimes, but when they're prey, it doesn't feel like they could also be a potential predator. Perhaps I'm single-minded that way.

I don't go to my normal place. I won't find a good lay there, and that's far more of what I'm after, if I'm honest. Fortunately, there are plenty of places where you can find a girl who'll happily be eaten and eat you in return. Great, I'm making puns. I must be delirious from starvation.

Sanctuary was a tad on the nose, but at least there, I knew precisely what people were expecting. With all of the clubs I knew gone—not that I ever frequented them—I have to do some searching. Hard to believe how much things change in a decade. I was never all that big on the scene. It always seemed like a bunch of posers trying to be something I was forced to be—and not always all that friendly to black people—but I don't like using my powers if I'm going to be sharing a bed with them, and it's the easiest way to find someone amenable to my needs.

Deciding an odd game-themed place is probably my best bet, despite it catering primarily to a different audience, I do some breathing exercises to calm my nerves and grab my car keys. Once there, the noise and muddle of people exasperate my anxiety, but some steady breathing and a predatory mind-set seem to help.

Looking around, I have to resist the urge to head right back out the door. This is only partly due to the impressive crowd for a Tuesday night. The rest of it is simply because I have no idea what I'm looking at. Everything is neon, garish, and oversexualized. Why would anyone want this?

Luckily, it doesn't take long. I spot a woman wearing all black with some frills and an ankh necklace—because we all must be stereotypes—who seems to be giving me the look. With a few centuries' experience, I suppose my gaydar has become something of an exact science. I barely need do more than flash my fangs to get her out of there, which is a welcome relief. The lights were bad enough, but the place was small and full. I could feel the walls closing in. Some of the crowd even brushed against me. I take a deep breath, focusing on the night ahead as I lead her back to my car. It was for a good cause. I can have a panic attack later if I must, but more pressing matters await.

I don't have to risk letting her know where I live, as she's more than happy to return to her apartment. I circle the lot once to find guest parking. I'd rather not have to deal with my car being towed, and we make our way upstairs.

She tastes delicious, both her blood and in less wholesome activities. She seems rather fond of my taste as well, though I don't give her my blood. I've no interest in dragging more people into this life than I absolutely must. If I do Ms. Rosseau-Lester—Elizabeth—that favor, she knows what she's getting into.

We have a pleasant time, though it leaves me a bit hungry. I can't have a proper meal if I intend on having her coherent enough for some fun afterward, and I've little interest in sending someone who's done nothing wrong to the emergency room for a blood transfusion. I learned that the hard way when I first tried to give up killing. I know I could always go with pre-packaged blood, but it's not the same. I prefer mine free-range.

She tries to talk me out of leaving, to spending the night with her, even insisting that we can stay up and watch horror movies together since I'm nocturnal, but I insist. I've never been too fond of horror movies. I scare too easily. Perhaps it was because of how triggering the original *Frankenstein* movie was. I think that mob scene is actually the last time I dissociated, though I didn't know the term back then.

Back home, I sip some cold tea and contemplate my encounter. I had a set goal. I just needed her to be a good enough distraction to halt this newly blossoming crush in its tracks. She was cute. In her twenties. Far too young even if we take off a few of my centuries but sweet enough. Maybe it worked. It's not as if I've been losing my mind over Mia, but this girl—she said her name was Esmeralda, but I highly doubt it—only wanted me because I'm a vampire. It's like dealing with a whole other type of hunter. That pill-popping vet seems to have many issues, not that I even know her well enough that courting her should be anywhere near my mind, but she certainly doesn't seem to care about my fangs.

Chapter Six

A Clean Bill of Health

Harvey finished the last of his pills yesterday. Now I need to go see Mia. It's my first time seeing her since we started addressing each other by our first names. That doesn't mean as much these days, but when I was human, it was a sign of a good deal of familiarity, and that flirting she and I did only compounds this feeling. I barely know the woman, and yet she expects me to act like her friend, if not more. That's not the primary reason it's bothering me, but it's nice to pretend it is. That way, I don't have to act like it's anything more during the appointment.

I head over around 11:00. She's not that far away, and the appointment is for 11:30. The parking lot is, of course, empty, because it is a veterinary hospital at 11:30 at night, and no sane person would have any business there. When I walk through the doors, she leaps from her chair, an almost too-eager smile on her face. Harvey *is* pretty great. It makes sense. "Hey, there," she says, her voice as blasé as ever. Perhaps I'm projecting.

"Hey. Sorry for keeping you here late."

"It's fine." She shrugs, and I can hear a slight rattle from her coat. "Had a few clients come in earlier, so I wasn't waiting up for you."

"Glad to hear it." I hold up Harvey, setting him on the counter. He squawks indignantly. "He seems to be feeling a lot better. Thank you. I don't know what I would've done if you weren't here…if there wasn't a vet who could see him."

"You'd go in the day. All I'm doing is being convenient for your schedule and charging you a nice premium for it."

"What happened to this time being free?"

She falters, and I swear her cheeks color. "I do owe you, don't I? Thanks again. That guy was a real asshole."

"You helped me out too."

Her teeth flash in a quick smile before she turns to Harvey, who is looking between the two of us. "How you feeling, Harvey? The meds seem to have helped?"

He flaps at her and just has to open his big beak. "Pretty."

I fumble for any sort of clarification.

"You're very pretty too, Harvey. I love your feathers."

Satisfied with that answer, he preens.

"Let's go get him tested. I'm sure he'll hate me, and you can go back to being the only pretty woman in his life."

I blink. I swear I used to be far better at handling people flirting with me. My wife was quite forward, and it didn't bother me at all. "Sounds like a plan," I manage.

We go to the same room as before. Harvey seems to understand, and she sets him up on the table. She doesn't even need my help to get him to hold still. Why does he already trust her? He's met her once. Humans can never be trusted, Harvey, you should know this by now, old man.

She leads me back to the observation room as Harvey waits patiently on the medical table, staring at us through the window. He may only be staring at Mia. After all, she is "pretty." "How is he?" I ask.

"Give me a minute," she replies, chuckling at my impatience. "How've you been doing? Seems he's a lot more talkative than the last time I saw him. He keeping you up?"

"Not really," I reply, leaving off all of the various events of the last couple weeks. "He has been more energetic, though. He'll hardly shut up and keeps demanding treats."

"That's parrots for you." She clicks a button, staring at a screen before clicking it again. "But his breathing seems to be normal now?"

"Yeah. That medication was a miracle."

"Well, I guess I'm a saint." Great, sacrilege, that ought to be a turn-off. "The X-rays look clean. The infection should be gone. Bring him back again soon. I want to make sure he's still doing better, but I'm glad we caught it in time. That could've been bad."

"I don't even want to think about it." What would I have done if

I'd lost Harvey? Other than die of loneliness. I've put up with it a lot in the past centuries, but it's never been something I handled that well. Between family and my service, I never had to until I died. "You saved him." Don't say it. You know exactly where this will lead. "Harvey's everything to me. He's the only family I have left. How can I ever thank you?" This is what I get for having a proper upbringing.

She leans against the table, a playful smile on her normally languid face as she meets my eyes. I try to keep them predatory since it makes dealing with humans much easier, but I know my gaze softens when I meet hers. Maybe it's just been too long since someone looked at me like that. "What did you have in mind?"

I will myself not to blush. I don't know if it works. I'm not even certain if I have enough blood in me to do it. "Nothing in particular. You saved the day, and it would feel wrong not to do something for you."

"Can you eat?"

"What?" My eyebrows raise. What exactly does she mean? She's another vampire hunter after all. "I didn't expect you to be the type—"

"Not blood. Please, I'm barely even into biting."

This time, I'm quite certain I blush.

"Most people are rather boring and unpleasant. Surprisingly, I've enjoyed spending time with you on the few occasions I've had the chance. You make existing seem less tiresome. If you want to thank me, let me take you out for dinner. I assume you don't need to eat, but if you can, it can be fun sometimes."

"I can eat."

"Cool. How about Saturday night? I'll close up early. It'd be nice to have something fun to do. There's a nice place not too far from here. Let me treat you."

"I'm not sure how that's me thanking you."

"Fine, you can treat me."

Did she trick me? I'm a little impressed. "All right, fine. Would you like to go to dinner with me?"

"I would love that."

This is a terrible idea. I've managed to ignore every single time I've started to grow fond of someone in the past five centuries. How the hell do I end up with a crush on a human and one who won't let me ignore it at that? I thought that girl from the club would help, but it only seems to have made me worse, if anything. "All right. It could be fun." I'm going to regret this, aren't I?

"I'll give you my number. You have a phone?" Reluctantly, I hand it over. She types in her number and name and saves it, her phone buzzing in her pocket before she hands it back. "I promise, it won't be half as bad as you fear."

"I didn't—"

"You think because you're, what, a couple hundred years older than me that I'm just gonna be a boring human?"

"I wasn't thinking that at all. You don't bore me, Mia. To be honest, you rather intrigue me. I apologize if I seemed to suggest otherwise." I'm too used to my privacy. My poker face has completely failed me. I almost wish that she'd read it correctly. If she knew that both love and humans terrify me, maybe she'd reconsider.

"Well, you intrigue me too. You might be the first monster I've ever met who didn't look like they wanted to eat me. Well, in a bad way…you looked like you wouldn't have minded the other night."

A million responses battle for my tongue. She is, of course, completely correct. I hadn't even noticed it, but I hadn't once considered her as food. What is wrong with me? Instead of acknowledging any of those points, I decide to sidestep the issue. "It's 'fiends.'"

"Fine. I suppose there's a few terms I'd rather you not call me. Can't complain about you hating that word."

"I don't mind it that much, but I'd rather you not risk being eaten for upsetting someone else. We are a significant portion of your clientele, after all."

"It's sweet that you already worry about me." Her smile grows more flirtatious. I hate to admit that it's having an effect on me. Harvey's right—she *is* pretty. "Speaking of inappropriate words, how old are you?"

"I suppose that is inappropriate."

"Tell me."

"I'm five hundred and forty-eight, if you must know."

She lets out a low whistle. "You don't look a day over two hundred. But, no, I didn't mean it like that. I just meant if you're, well, as old as you are, I wanted to make sure you wouldn't end up saying you had a date with a nice Oriental or something. That'd put a damper on the night."

I swallow. "A date? So it..." I knew it was, what am I even thinking? "Right. And that wasn't what we called you when I was growing up, but I know better either way. My most recent degree was in sociology. There was a lot of new information to take in."

"Wow. That's impressive."

"Thanks."

Smirking, she turns away from me, gesturing toward the door. "Now, let's go tell Harvey he's all right before he bores a hole through this window watching us."

When we enter the other room, Harvey looks way too pleased with himself and begins hopping about the table. The little bastard.

"It's not nice to spy on people," Mia says.

He tilts his head. "Not nice."

"Oh, don't give me that." She places her hands on her hips, staring, looking surprisingly imposing for someone who couldn't possibly be over five-six. "You little perv."

Perching on my shoulder, he ducks behind my head. "Good bird," he calls back. I suppose he's not wrong.

I scratch his head and find myself smiling. "I think he likes you." I've never really let anyone else meet him, so I don't know if he has good taste in people. He likes me, but I'm not certain what that says either.

"Of course he does. All animals love me. I'm amazing."

"Harvey, is Mia amazing?"

He peeks around my head, peering at her before he ducks back again. "Pretty."

She and I both laugh, the disturbance causing him to flap in annoyance. "I'm going to take him home. I'll see you on Saturday."

"Can't wait," she replies, and despite the snide tone, I think she may be telling the truth. I'm somewhat excited as well. Perhaps it is time to put myself out there again. Maybe five centuries of penance is enough.

As I turn my key in the ignition, he croons happily from his cage in the back seat. "Saturday," he repeats.

"Yeah," I sigh, pulling onto the road and heading home. I try to focus on the drive, but my mind seems rather set on the coming weekend. It's really happening. I feel as if I'm on a roller coaster, going down from the peaks of ecstasy to the troughs of terror and back up again. It's been a long time since I let myself care like this, and it's all happening so quickly. I barely know the first thing about the woman. Well, I suppose I'll have the chance to learn.

Back home, I try to take my mind off things by playing with Harvey. He seems to enjoy his latest puzzle box. I never had the chance to open it while I was in that near-catatonic state, so I figure it is the perfect way to celebrate his recovery. He pulls on a knob, striking the toy repeatedly with his beak. I even manage to mostly pay attention.

❖

The grounds are serene today. A few birds fly by, and the breeze is likely a bit too cold for human comfort, but it looks beautiful out, and there are enough clouds that I only have a faint headache from the sun. A wild rabbit hops along through the grass, pausing here and there to sniff the air. It leaps off into a bush as the door behind me opens. Heavy footsteps crunch the gravel, and the bench groans as someone sits next to me. "Hello, Father," I say without turning around. There's no one else it could be, but I recognize his scent and his heartbeat.

"Hello, Olivia. How are you doing today?"

I sigh, watching the bush where the rabbit vanished. I'm not even sure where to begin. "Maybe great, maybe terrible. At the very least, I'm terrified." It's easy to be honest with him. I often wonder if it's the priesthood or how much he reminds me of my father.

"What seems to be troubling you?"

I start to tap my foot, but I place my hand on my knee to still it. I've never been one for letting my anxieties show. "I've been having more of those dreams of late, but I think I'm dealing with it." Those pills are still sitting beside my bed. Maybe I should give them another chance. The dreams have not been letting up at all.

"Has that therapist been helping?"

"I think she has. There's still a long way to go, but I'm done putting it off. I'm sick of being afraid all the time."

"You shouldn't have to be."

I tap again. I grit my teeth, trying to appear as placid as I can.

"Is there something else bothering you?"

I finally turn to him, and I'm surprised to find him blurring. Am I crying? "I have a date on Saturday."

He grasps my hands, his broad grin made oddly comical by his beard. "That's wonderful. I'm really happy for you. You deserve this."

Looking away, I shake my head. "How can you say that? You know what I've done. What if it all happens again?"

"Don't be ridiculous." His strikingly calm blue eyes stare into mine. "It's been centuries, you've atoned, and you know you couldn't control yourself. You didn't deserve any of the things that happened to you, but you absolutely do deserve a new chance at happiness."

"How can I take that risk?"

"Just because I've taken a vow of chastity doesn't mean you have to. How long has it been since you let yourself live? Stop hiding away from the world. I know how hard it is, how scary, but let yourself be happy."

"She's a human."

His smile grows softer. "Are you scared of her?"

I don't know how to answer that. I should be. I think I am. She still might hurt me if things go badly. It would take almost no effort for her to gather a mob to attempt to exterminate my kind. She's had plenty of chances, though, hasn't she? After three years of working with the fiend community, she hasn't tried to hurt any of us. Even the ones who deserve it. I finally shake my head. "I'm afraid of what I might do to her."

"Clearly, she's willing to take that risk."

Choking back a sob, I wipe a tear from my eye. I still feel like I should call things off before they grow serious, but he's right. This is something she wants. She's the one who asked me out. "I feel like I'm betraying her memory. How can I move on like this? I pledged my undying love to her."

His hand rests heavily on my shoulder. "You said 'till death do us part.'"

"Just because I'm dead, that means I have the right to move on?"

"She's been dead for over five hundred years. You've mourned her long enough. I'm not saying marry this girl, though if it happens, I'd be more than happy to perform the ceremony—"

"I don't think you can do that."

"I'd like to see them try to stop me." From what I've heard, he's had more than a few confrontations with some of the higher-ups in the church. I've never been too certain of how to cope with all that. I've lived through enough of these issues that one would think I'd have an answer by now, but the closest I've come is that my faith is in the church, not the people in it. It's actually what attracted me to his church in the first place. After that scandal in Boston, he made quite an uproar. He seems an honorable man, when I'd thought they had all died out. "But let yourself have fun. Maybe it'll help you move past the other issues too."

"Maybe," I agree, leaning back as I blink away the last of the tears. A lone leaf floats by on the breeze, passing in front of…that same face. Bianca? I blink again, and she's gone. I don't think I'm having a flashback. Nothing seems to have caused one. I turn back to face Father Gregory. "Did you see her?" I ask. I'm almost certainly being crazy—I have the credentials for it—but I need to know.

"See whom?"

"Never mind." I rise, shaking my head to try to clear it. "Must've been seeing things. Maybe a tear obscured my vision."

"Olivia—"

"It's fine." I gesture for him to sit down. I don't want to worry him. It's likely nothing. "I'm going to go home. Thank you, Father."

"I'm surprised you don't want to do confession."

"Oh, right." Groaning, I sit back down. If that was her, I'd rather have as clean a soul as possible when I die. I know there's no chance I can make it into heaven, but I'd like to have as little burden to carry as I can. "Are you ready?"

"Of course, my child. What do you have to confess?"

"It's been a week and a half since my last confession. I hurt two people, but I didn't kill either of them. I did, however, have a one-night stand with one of them and run off without even giving her my number. That's not exactly great of me, is it?"

His playful smile returns, and I try not to roll my eyes. I wish I could use a confessional booth. I can see how badly he wants to tease me about it, but he takes his role as seriously as the station deserves. "Did she know that it was a one-night stand?"

"I don't know." Staring at my feet, I shrug. Clarifying it would have been best. I wasn't thinking at the time.

"You may have hurt her. I hate to say it. I know how much pain it causes you, but just do one Hail Mary."

I deserve that. I do as instructed, the pain clearing away some of the guilt. Maybe if I keep doing them until Saturday night, I won't feel like I'm betraying both my wife and Mia by going on this date. "Thank you, Father," I say again, heading back to my car.

"Oliva."

I turn back, seeing that grin returning with a twinkle in his blue eyes. I'll never get over how strange those are. "Do tell me how the date goes, all right? I'm happy for you."

Unable to hold back my own smile, I turn away from him. "I will. I'll try to be by on Sunday." He stays on the bench as I walk off. He seems to always avoid doing anything that might startle me. It's not necessary, but I appreciate it. I'd like to be able to pay him back. Maybe I'll have good news to give him after my date.

Chapter Seven

The First Date

It's taken over three hours, as I've had to look up almost every single term due to my outdated knowledge, but this article looks promising. If they had more funding, I think they could accomplish some impressive feats. They've managed to clone perfectly functioning organs that allow for transplants with a near-zero chance of rejection. The head researcher seems beyond reproach, and she's been working on this her entire life. If she'd be amenable, I'd like to be a silent partner in the study, funding the research and possibly even buying the lab if need be. This may have some fairly substantial financial returns if it's successful, but until then, I'm far more interested in what it could teach us and, perhaps, what she could teach me. I send her an email, doing my best to convince her that I'm serious, and say that I'm happy to provide an investment before we even talk.

As I type, Harvey is flying around the room, searching for the various treats I left out for him. They're supposed to keep him entertained while I'm on my date, but he's never been one for patience. I'm already dressed. I may have been a little overexcited. I tried on five outfits before settling on this simple seafoam-green dress that shows off a little more skin than I'd typically prefer. I think this is standard these days, though I may be overdressed. All I know about modern dating I've learned from fiction, and I'm not sure how helpful that really is.

It's been decades since I've worn heels. I'm glad I have superhuman grace or else I may have trouble with them. As I read over a study on gene editing, I'm surprised to hear a *ping* from my email.

Apparently, she likes the offer. *If you're serious, then yeah, I'd appreciate the hell out of that. I'd be happy to try to keep you up to date and teach you whatever I can as long as it doesn't cut in on my research. We can Skype sometime and go over everything. I'll include more later, just wanted to make sure I got back to you before you found something new to fund.*

I reply, aware of how soon I need to leave, but confirm that I'm serious and even send enough to make sure she can keep doing her work until we have the chance to talk more. The internet has made this all so easy. As much work as it has been to keep up with advancing technology, it's been incredibly worth it. I'm not sure how else I'd have found such a cute outfit. I still haven't worn the clothes I bought at that store. They seem tainted by the trauma. They're lying in a bag on the floor in my bedroom. I've barely even been in there since.

I grab my keys and a leather purse that goes with my outfit, and head out to pick up my date. I'm looking forward to seeing her reaction. When you spend all of your time locked up in your house, you rarely have the opportunity to show off your fancy toys.

❖

"Nice car," Mia says, marveling at my Mercedes. "I didn't get a good look before. She's a beauty. I can see why you wanted to drive."

I flash my fangs in a quick grin, but I cover them. They don't embarrass me, but I don't want her to want me for that. She should want me for me, not for my species. That sounds odd. I head around the vehicle, opening the passenger door for her. "I'm glad you approve."

"Such a gentleman," she teases. She has no idea how accurate that is.

"Where's this restaurant?" I ask, climbing back behind the wheel.

"It's not too far from here."

With the thought that she may actually be leading me into a trap never leaving my mind, I follow her directions and am relieved to find that we arrive at New Orleans Seafood and Steakhouse. I've driven by it a few times but never had any real inclination to go. As much as I enjoy food, it's hard to find motivation to go to a restaurant when I don't even need to eat. Especially as popular as it always is.

We shrug past a few people, and she gives her name to the hostess.

She made a reservation. I wasn't sure if that was still common. Though, again, it is nothing I have experience with either way.

For eight o'clock on a Saturday, I guess it's not that busy, but it's still far more than I'm comfortable with. I can feel eyes on us, staring, hopefully just at the lesbians and not at the vampire they were told to expect. There are no obvious weapons on them, no bulges suggesting a hidden stake or crossbow. It should be okay. I try to focus on my date.

Mia smiles back at me, barely glancing at her menu. She seems more animated than usual. She must be as nervous as I am. She's almost bouncing. "It's been a while," she admits, her words tumbling out, her cheeks coloring.

"Me too."

She blows out a breath. "Yeah? That's good to know. Must've been a couple years for me. Haven't had a serious girlfriend in around five. It's hard to find the time or the motivation." Her fingers dance across her menu, drumming a quiet beat.

"It's been five hundred and twenty years for me."

Her mouth opens and closes, and she turns her gaze back to the menu, quietly humming. Before she could've even read a single item, she turns back up, meeting my gaze with those brown eyes that seem clearer than usual. Her pupils are smaller. She seems more focused. I've never realized how beautiful her eyes are. "Really? No dates at all? Like, what, since you were turned?"

"Yeah," I admit. "Not since then."

"Why?" She shakes her head. "I'm sorry, you don't have to answer that."

"Thank you." She deserves to know the truth, but after my dream last night, I'd rather avoid the subject. I swear I've been dreaming about her almost every night of late. "I'm really not ready to talk about it yet."

"That's totally cool." She waves her hand in front of her emphatically. "I wasn't thinking. I'm sure it's a sensitive topic. Maybe I can find something a little easier to talk about. Where are you from? England, right? London? I'm not amazing with accents, but I thought I recognized it."

I shudder, thinking of my last time in London. She's clearly trying, but when you're as old as I am, every single topic can turn into a landmine. "I lived there for a long while. Not always London, but I used to love it. Less so now, but it was an amazing city once."

"Then where?"

"Venice. My family lived there for generations." I think back to the canals of my home, the stench, the beauty, the wonder. I'd loved it there. "I miss it. I haven't been back since I was turned either."

"Didn't want to see your family?" She can be blunt, but from what I understand, that's a rather common first date topic for lesbians. *So how badly did your parents react? Yeah, mine kicked me out too.*

"No. They'd died a few years before. They were wonderful parents. They never judged me for being who I was, and they adored my wife."

"You were married? She's not—"

"No, she died a long time ago."

"I'm sorry." She nods, a look of pained comprehension on her face.

"It's okay."

"I'm glad your parents approved. I'm sure that must've been difficult for fifteenth-century parents. It's still pretty tough now."

Finding my throat surprisingly dry, I take a sip of water. "They were very impressive people. We were Catholic, and that proved quite complicated."

"How did you manage to get married?"

A small smile forms on my lips as I think back on that day. She had looked beautiful in that dress. "Well, other than my parents, no one in attendance knew that I was a woman."

"Really?" She stares, rather obviously, at my cleavage. "That's hard to imagine."

I roll my eyes. "My brother died before I was born, when he was a baby. When I was sixteen, I took his name and joined the armed forces. I wanted to see the world, to make something of myself, and maybe to move away and decide who I could be. I proved myself in what's now called the First Italian War and came home a hero. No one seemed to remember the old me, and I'd earned something of a name for myself. I was already a captain, and that earned me some acclaim."

"That's impressive. And then you met your wife?"

I got a bit sidetracked there. I don't think I was showing off. "I suppose there was one other person who remembered me. We'd been friends when we were young. Well, more than friends. We had"—I blush—"explored a few things together when we were in our early teens. Though, of course, there wasn't much of a concept of teenagers. She didn't recognize me at first, but after we talked, she did. I wasn't sure what to make of it until she pinned me to the wall and kissed me." Now that's definitely too much detail for a first date.

"You like dominant women?"

Looking her up and down, I bite my lip. I've little doubt that she could and would do the same. "I courted her for a while, but we didn't have the chance to marry until after the Second Ottoman-Venetian War. I made general and was left in charge of Cyprus during the peace. I sent for her, and she came, and we were wed a couple months later."

"It didn't bother you living as a man all that time?"

With a shrug, I reply, "I was used to it. It was the easiest way to have everything I wanted. My femininity wasn't important enough for me to feel it worth sacrificing everything else."

"Do you think you might be—"

"No. I'm definitely a woman, but perhaps a little apathetic about it." I glance at the menu. At some point, I'll have to figure out what I want to eat.

"Just wanted to make sure. Had that happen to me once, though before we'd gotten serious. We don't really stay in touch, but he's a good guy."

That still takes some getting used to. "Interesting," I reply. "I'm not trying to dismiss that. I just don't know what to say. All of my understanding of trans people comes from recent schooling. I've never known one. I don't think I have any problem with them, if that's something you're worried about."

Her smile returns, and she stares down at the table or possibly at my hands. "That's good to hear. Age is no excuse for bigotry."

I've had far too much experience to disagree. "What were your parents like? Or are they still alive? Did they approve?"

"They're still alive." I can hear her foot bounce on the floor. "They don't disapprove," she says, her words substantially slower than they had been. "They're really not that bad. They're…they're quite proud of me. They just don't understand. I'm a lot more successful than they ever were, and they love what I've done with my life, but they don't like that I'm not planning on giving them grandkids, and I know they blame a lot of that on my being gay."

"I'm sorry." I consider reaching for her hand but think better of it. I really don't know what's acceptable first date behavior.

"It's okay. Maybe they'll accept it eventually." Her derisive snort seems to indicate that she believes otherwise.

Before I have time to think of a response, the waiter comes by with some bread. "Have you decided on your orders yet?"

"Sorry," Mia replies with an uncharacteristically apologetic smile. "We've barely looked at the menu yet. Could we get some wine?" She turns to me. "Red okay? I was thinking the Dom Perignon if it's not too expensive."

"That sounds great." I'm not too particular about my wine, though it does make me hungry sometimes. I'm glad I restocked the fridge.

"Of course," he says, smiling between the two of us. "Take your time. I'll be right back with that wine."

"I'm actually really hungry," she admits when he walks off. "Let me figure out what I want real quick."

We both take a moment to look over the menu. Everything sounds good, but I could go for some seafood. I've never actually had jambalaya. Maybe I'll order it and a shrimp appetizer. "Want to split the coconut shrimp?"

"Sure, that and steak sounds wonderful." She flashes a quick grin and closes her menu. "Now that we have that out of the way, what do you do for fun?"

"Trying to find a safer topic of conversation?"

"Don't want to scare you off yet."

Maybe I have good cause for this crush. She can be quite charming. "I'm pretty boring," I admit. "Mostly, I play with Harvey, invest in things, and get new degrees. I watch some television sometimes. I've been watching way too much of *The Great British Bake Off* of late." She doesn't have to know that I was dissociating during it. That's a second date topic. "What about you?"

She falters, her mouth hanging open for a second. "Damn, I should've thought up an answer if I was going to ask that question. Honestly, I don't do shit. I pretty much just work. Do drugs count as a hobby?"

There it is. "I have been wanting to ask about that, but I didn't want to push."

Shaking her head, she smiles. "It's fine. I'm not all that secretive about it. I've offered some to you a few times."

"I suppose that's true." The waiter comes by to give us our wine, leaving the bottle, and we tell him our orders.

She stares out the window for a moment, likely trying to decide how to explain this. "I'm bipolar. I normally medicate by taking downers during my manic phases and uppers during my depressive phases so I can try to stay normal and do my job."

"Oh. I never would have guessed."

"Really? I'm pretty damn manic today." She chuckles. "Thought it'd be obvious. I didn't bother to take anything, other than the wine, since I figured I'd rather use that energy and be fun on our date. After all, I think you may be the reason I've been manic all week. There's not always a cause, it can be random, but it started after I saw you at the Community Center. It's when I realized I liked you."

"That's when I realized I liked you too."

"Good. I was a little worried I was imagining that."

"I thought I was being obvious."

"I don't like to assume."

My gaze lingers on those eyes. I wonder if that's why they look different today or if it's the lighting. I swear I could fall into them. I'd never say it, of course; even I know when something's clichéd. "Why not take bipolar medication? It seems a lot easier."

"Are you kidding?" She chuckles, her lips curling upward in an adorable smile. "That shit is way too hard on you. The opiates and Ritalin are nothing in comparison. I'll take minimal side effects and lots of fun over feeling like a zombie." She pauses. "Is that bigoted? I mean, I've met a few zombies, and they seem far more alive than people on some of those bipolar meds."

"Most likely. My sociology degree would suggest that a lot of actions and beliefs are rooted in some bigotries. You'd have to ask a zombie how they feel about it."

"Can I not?"

"I wasn't going to make you."

"Good. How many degrees do you have?"

I have to think about that. As many years as I've been studying,

I didn't see much need to keep track of them. I just like to learn. "I'm not sure. Maybe around a dozen. I took a lot of correspondence courses back in the day, but it was a lot more difficult to earn a degree from that, and everything took a lot longer. Now I buy all of the books online and take as many classes as I can manage. Everything is so fascinating. Human knowledge advances incredibly quickly, and I can't keep up. I love it."

"That's cool. Learning can be a lot of fun. I actually majored in the classics in undergrad. It's why I handled the whole mo…fiend thing so well." She stares into space. "Wow, I really forgot how much I enjoy learning." Those crystal-clear eyes settle on me again. "Maybe I'll take one of those classes with you sometime. Anyway, my grades were good enough, and I loved animals, so I figured, why not be a vet? I actually really like it. It's why it's almost all I do."

"I'm glad. You're an amazing vet, and I know Harvey agrees."

"He does seem to like me."

"He's not the only one." Is that too forward?

"I'm glad to hear it." Biting her lip, she stares down, pausing for a moment on my chest. I think this date is going far better than I'd feared. Maybe this isn't such a bad idea after all.

The waiter brings out our food. "Enjoy your meals. Is there anything else I can get you?"

We both shake our heads. We seem quite content with what's at the table. Our hands touch briefly as we each grab a shrimp. Hers are softer than I'd expected. The shrimp is delicious, moist and crisp and amazing. I don't eat often enough to be the greatest judge, but this is some of the best shrimp I've had since I moved away from Italy.

"This is amazing," she mouths, her eyes half-lidded. "Oh my God. I haven't had their shrimp before. If the steak is half as good, I may die from sheer joy." He brought everything out at once rather than bringing the shrimp first, but it means fewer interruptions, so I certainly wouldn't dream of complaining.

"It is. It makes me miss Italy. The seafood and pasta were always wonderful, and of course, I actually had to eat back then, and hunger always makes food better."

"Did you have all these spices?"

"Well, no. We weren't exactly wealthy. Maybe it's just nostalgia—"

"Sorry, I didn't mean to trash your childhood meals." I startle as she grabs my hand, but I don't pull away. It's been over a century since anyone has touched me like that. It's not sexual. It's barely even romantic, but it's affectionate, sincere, and warm. "I'd love to try your favorite foods. Maybe an Italian place around here would have something similar?"

"Maybe. It wouldn't be the same, though."

"I know, but without a time machine…" She trails off, her thumb running over my knuckles. She seems to notice what she's doing and pulls back, looking both embarrassed and pleased with herself. "We'll see if we can find anything. I'm not a terrible cook, if you'd like me to give it a shot."

"I'd like that. Maybe I could cook for you sometime too."

We both fall into silence, justifying it by eating our food. We both seem to realize what we've implied. This won't be the last date we go on.

The spice of the jambalaya is surprising. It has a nice kick to it, and I feel like I deserve it. I'm really moving on. I know it's well past time, but she was the love of my life, and it will always feel like I'm dishonoring her memory.

Her eyes widen as she stares at my food. "You know there's garlic in that, right?"

I consider feigning a horrified expression. It would be fun, but I don't want to mock her concern. It's rather sweet. "I'm Italian," I remind her.

She glares.

"Garlic is fine. Well, for me. I have heard others claim that it affects them, just as I've heard others say that religious iconography doesn't affect them. I believe it's due to the fact that vampires aren't a single species but a number of different ones that crossbreed with each other."

"Wait, vampires can have kids?"

"Yes."

"Huh." She stares down at her steak and potatoes.

"In truth, I'd rather be weak to garlic. As much as I enjoy its flavor, it's rather difficult being a Catholic who can't enter a church."

"You're still Catholic?" She stares at me, her eyes narrowing. I should've thought ahead. Given the church's reputation, it's no wonder she wouldn't approve.

"I am." I swallow another bite as I try to figure out how to explain this to her. "It's a big part of who I am. I know that the church hasn't always treated us well."

"You mean ever."

I shift uncomfortably in my seat. "My current priest is wonderful." Maybe I should tell her he offered to marry us. "He's a strong opponent of a lot of the worst policies of the church and is just a good man in general. I've been through a lot in my life, and my faith has always seen me through it. I know it's hard to understand. As a gay, black vampire, the church has done a lot of things against all of my people, but I could never give it up. I hope that's not a deal breaker."

"Are you going to make me go to church with you?" she asks, staring askance at me.

"I can't enter a church."

"Well, that's a relief."

I decide to let it be. I like her, and I may even be starting to trust her. I know exactly what people think of the church and can hardly blame them for it. I need it. "Can I try a bite of your steak?"

Her expression softens, the disapproval vanishing, "Yeah, of course."

I cut off a piece and take a bite. It's perfect. I wish the red liquid was actually blood, as then it would even be filling and taste all the better, but it's still amazing. Maybe I should make some blood sausage sometime. It's been too long. "Would you like some jambalaya?"

"Sure." She helps herself, and together, we finish off both of our meals. With some hesitation, I grab my napkin and wipe a speck of food from her lips. Her eyes almost close, and she leans forward but catches herself, her cheeks turning bright red. It's a first date, and she likely expects me to be old-fashioned. She's not wrong.

Back in the car, she leans against me as I drive. She's buzzed and likely a little sleepy. It is late for humans. I stop outside her apartment. Part of me wants to see about going inside. Tonight has been absolutely wonderful, but I'm not ready for that. "I had a great time," I say.

"I did too," she agrees. "Next weekend work for you?"

"For what?"

"We both said we'd make each other dinner. We could do it together, if you'd like."

I don't have any of my family's old recipes, but maybe I can find something similar. That would be nice. "I'd love that."

"Until then." Rather than reach for the door handle, she plants a soft kiss on my cheek. I freeze, torn between seeing where this could go and my horror over how far I've already gone. "You have a good night, Liv."

"Don't call me that." It comes out harsher than I mean it to. "It just sounds ridiculous," I add quickly. "I'm not going to be an undead woman named Liv. I'd be a walking joke."

"All right then, Ollie."

I stare at her. "Ollie?" I roll it over my tongue. It's a little too masculine, but that's hardly strange. It's sort of cute. "I don't hate it."

"Well, Ollie, I'll see you next Saturday. Eight o'clock, right here? My kitchen is kind of small, but we can manage."

I want to tell her she can come to my place, that I trust her that much, but I still can't do it. I really am a coward. "I'll see you then."

Chapter Eight

Bianca

My hands are bound, and a long chain runs from them to the wall. I haven't had a drop of blood in weeks, nor seen a single soul. My body aches. The pain is unending, almost unbearable. If I had the means, I'd end it myself. Alas, I'm too weak. I can barely even raise my head. The stone floor beneath me offers little comfort. My eyes are covered, I think. It's too dark to be certain, even with my night vision. If there's no light to take in, there's nothing to see.

When the room fills with blinding light, I roll, covering my eyes with my hands, the chain ringing from the sudden movement. Footsteps fall on the hard floor, deafening in the stone room. I can't bring myself to open my eyes. It's too bright. It's too much. A soft hand touches my cheek, and I hear a woman speak. "Do you still resist?" she asks.

I can't find my voice. It hurts too much. A drop of blood lands on my cheek. I turn, opening my mouth, my tongue reaching for the droplet. I can smell it. It's my entire world. I need it. A drop lands in my open mouth, then another, and just as it's piqued my hunger, as I think I may well die if I don't have the rest, it stops. I continue trying to reach the drop on my cheek, eventually wiping it off with a finger and licking it. More goes to waste that way, but it's my only option. I need more.

"Join us. We can leave right now, and you can have all the blood you want."

I can scarcely even remember why I'm fighting. I'm starving. Give it to me, I'll do anything. I almost say it, but an image flashes in my mind. My wife. Her dead body beneath me. And him. I won't do it. I can't. Sitting up, I turn to her and open my eyes. I do my best to focus. It takes all of my willpower not to agree to any and every demand. "No."

"You know how much he loves you. He only wants you to himself. Is that truly so wrong?"

Finding the words is difficult. My throat is dry, and I haven't talked in so long. "He did. This. To me," I manage, the words coming out rough and hoarse. I want to collapse in exhaustion from the effort.

"O—"

"Bianca, the two—" I swallow, taking a deep breath to gather strength. "The two of you can go to hell."

"If that's your answer." She picks up the small canteen. I can hear, smell, almost taste the blood inside. I need it. I almost call out and beg for more, but I resist. She walks away, taking the lantern with her, and with it, the light. A door closes atop the stairs, followed by another, and I'm left alone in silence and darkness. I don't know where I am. I don't know how long I've been here. Even calling it weeks between her visits is only a guess. It could be minutes, hours, days, or even years. My only way to measure time is pain. The longer I go without blood, the more it hurts. The meager helpings they give me barely even stave off the agony.

I collapse back on the floor, unable to hold myself up any longer. I reach for my cheek, feeling for any blood I may have missed, and I suck on my finger for even the slightest bit of extra sustenance. "God," I say, my voice scarcely more than a whisper. "I know I don't deserve your aid, but please, I don't know how much longer I can last." Tears fall, wasting what little hydration I have. "Give me a way out. Let me break my chains. Please. I'll do anything. I need to get away from him. I can't serve him, I won't." I slam the shackles onto the stone floor as hard as I can. It barely even makes a sound. "Please, God. Please save me." I roll onto my back and try to stop the tears. I need every ounce of strength I can save.

Perhaps I'll never escape. Perhaps this is the fate I deserve. The restraints give me some difficulty as I cross myself. It burns, but I barely even notice amongst all the other pain. "O my God, I am heartily sorry for having offended thee, and I detest all my sins..." I strain against the pain, forcing the words out. "Because of thy just punishments, but most of all because they offend thee, my God, who art all good and deserving of all my love. I firmly resolve, with the help of thy grace, to sin no more and to avoid the near occasion of sin." One last tear streams onto the floor, and I close my eyes, waiting for death or sleep to claim me. I don't deserve his forgiveness.

I know not how many more days pass. Most of the time is spent in sleep and the rest in prayer. I lack the voice to even pray aloud, only capable of thinking. Cursed as I am, I doubt they will reach God either way. I'm beyond redemption. I should have died that night. Not her.

One day, the door opens again, the light again blinding me, and Bianca again asks me to submit. She gives me no blood. Patience never was his virtue. I must have exhausted what limited supply he had. "Stop fighting," she pleads. "It does you no good."

I don't even bother to look at her. I remain sprawled on the ground, unmoving, unwilling. The pain is too much. If I let myself respond at all, I may just give in.

"Why do you still fight? I don't. It's easier to do what he says. Please, we'll give you all the blood you need, and you can finally leave this wretched pit."

My silence is answer enough. She leaves again. This time it's worse. I can barely take it. Without even that meager meal, there's nothing to stave off the pain. I convulse, racking in agony, unable to even sleep. My entire body feels like it's trying to devour itself. I've known nothing like it. It's the worst pain I'd ever imagined. Perhaps I'm already in hell.

The next time she comes, I don't wait for the question. I don't know where I find the strength, but my lips move, and out comes the word, "Yes."

My dream weighs heavily on me as I rise. The pills seem to taunt me from my nightstand. I suppose it's hardly worth fighting it at this point. Clearly, I wasn't any worse on them. I take four of each. Then another two of each to be sure. After a far-too-long shower, trying to force myself to think of anything else and finding that my mind keeps going to Mia when I search for a distraction, I turn the light on in Harvey's room, wake him up, and give him some feed and a few snacks. "Good morning."

"Morning," he calls back, hopping to and fro as he tries to decide what to eat first.

It's almost five. My dream didn't wake me up too early. I brew some tea as I try to finish waking up, and Harvey soon comes along for his share.

"Tea!"

"Oh, you want some?" I ask, feigning surprise.

"Tea," he confirms.

I pour a helping into his little cup and sip my own. It's soothing. I need soothing. "I made English breakfast today. I know it's not your favorite."

He takes a sip. "Not tea."

"Still tea," I insist.

"Tea," he demands.

"I'm not making you a whole pot for yourself. You can have some at afternoon tea if you don't like this." It's still caffeine free. If he's not going to have any, I'll just go back to buying the normal kind. That way, I can enjoy the taste.

"Tea."

"No."

He stares at me, cocking his head. He opens his mouth as if to say it again but squawks instead, hopping back. "Carrot."

Rolling my eyes, I stroll to the fridge and grab him a carrot. He can be so demanding sometimes.

He croons happily, tearing apart the treat and eating it. My laptop starts making a noise in the other room. It takes me a moment to realize it's a call. Harvey imitates it. "Not you too."

He continues ringing at me.

"Eat your carrot." Sitting on the couch, I flip open my laptop and find an incoming call from Dr. Lange, the biologist I'm funding. Her picture pops up on my screen, and I promptly close the laptop. I'm still not dressed. One of these days, I'll learn how these things work. "Just a minute," I say, throwing on a dress as quickly as I can manage. A single article of clothing is easier. I consider a bathrobe, but it sends the wrong message. "Sorry about that," I say as I open it back up.

"It's fine. I didn't see anything." She has a very pretty smile, showing a few too many teeth. If the objects around her are to be believed, she does not live up to her name, as she's anything but tall. Her blond hair cascades down in waves. I'm not checking her out or anything, but it's hard not to notice, and she may have had an eyeful of me.

"Thought I'd clicked the voice button."

"It's fine," she repeats.

"Well, I'm Olivia Crocetti," I offer, introducing myself.

"I've gathered. I'm Hannah Lange."

"It's a pleasure to meet you, Dr. Lange."

"And you as well. Is it Dr. or Ms.?"

Being a doctor of history and psychology, both from a hundred or more years ago, is hardly relevant to this conversation. "Ms. is fine."

"All right then, Ms. Crocetti." She butchers the pronunciation. I'd like to think I did fine with hers. My German may be rusty, but I do have a master's in it. "May I ask what interested you in my work?"

"Of course. I've been interested in supporting some biology research that looked promising, and yours seemed very impressive. My knowledge on the subject is quite outdated, and it seemed a fantastic opportunity to brush up on it."

"We talking high school outdated or college?"

"Mostly independent studying."

That brings another smile to her face. "Now, that is admirable. And that led you to my work?"

"Eventually."

"Well, I'm flattered."

"Think nothing of it. You're doing good work. I just want to support you."

"And take a cut of any contracts it results in."

I shrug. "And a good portion of the risk."

With a high-pitched laugh, she replies, "You've got me there. What would you expect? That I keep you up to date on everything, or would you want to approve all of my decisions?"

"I only want information. You're the biologist. I'm only a layperson. I'll give you money, you give me results and teach me about what you've learned. It hardly seems an unfair arrangement."

"No, it certainly doesn't." She stretches, leaning back in her seat. "All right, you have my interest. I've only ever had grants before. I'll admit, I was hesitant when I first heard your offer. It sounded like selling out."

"I don't represent anyone. I'm a member of the idle rich, and I'd like to do some good with my money. Maybe I'll earn a profit in the process, but I assure you, it'll be invested again straight away."

"Well, when you put it like that, I'd be a fool not to take you up on it. What do I need to sign?"

"It should all be pretty standard." I'm glad there're a few lawyers in the Community Center. I'd hate to deal with a human for a contract. This call alone is already stressing me out. "I need to make a few adjustments to my normal contract, and I should be able to get them to you tomorrow."

"Fantastic. Anything else I should know?"

"I don't think so. Have your people look over the paperwork and get back to me."

"Thank you. I don't think I said it before."

"It's my pleasure. You have a good night. I'm going to go see about that contract."

"Sounds like a plan. You have a good night too."

I hang up as Harvey lands on my shoulder. "Doctor?" he asks.

"Yes, but not the one you're thinking of."

"Pretty?"

For a second, I think he's asking if my new business partner is pretty, making the little bird even more of a pervert than I thought, but it finally hits me. That's his name for Mia. He never learned an alternative. "No, not her. Maybe you'll see her again someday."

"Tea."

Rolling my eyes, I stand up. "Maybe later. I have some errands to run. Take care of the place while I'm gone."

He salutes me with his foot. I swear he knew how to do that when I got him.

❖

My normal lawyer is out of the office today. If I didn't want to sign this contract before someone else has time to snatch her up, I'd head out, but I check to see if anyone else is available. "Of course," a perky little selkie paralegal says. "Dovana is finishing up with another client. If you'll take a seat in there, she'll be with you in a minute." She gestures at a cubicle with a table and a chair on either side of it.

"Thank you." I take a seat, waiting as patiently as I can. I hate crowds, even if they're not human. Though a selkie barely even counts as not human.

A few minutes later, a woman sits across from me. My chair squeaks on the tile floor as I slide back. She looks human. Pale and blond but still human enough. Only, her blood doesn't smell like food. It's too tainted by the fae. A changeling?

"Hi, I'm Dovana Gudaitiene. What can I help you with?"

I collect myself enough to go over everything. She's a changeling; it's fine. No changeling has ever even bothered me in the slightest. By the time we're finished with the contract, I'm almost as comfortable as with my regular lawyer.

"I think that should be about it," she says, rubbing the bridge of her nose. "Sign here, here, and here, and I'll notarize it, and we can fax it over to her."

"Thank you." I grab a pen and sign where she pointed. I don't need to read it again for a third time. I tried taking a couple law courses once but couldn't stomach it. It's the driest reading I've ever encountered in my life, and I have a degree in economics. I sent Dr. Lange an email a few hours ago asking for a way to fax the contract, and while it sounds like it's not the easiest method for her to receive it, she found a way. We send it over, and I leave my lawyer in peace. "Have a good day, Dovana."

"You as well, Olivia. I trust I'll see you again soon."

"I'm certain of it." We shake hands, and I head back out into the main hall of the Community Center. I'm pretty well stocked on blood, but since Harvey hates my English breakfast, I may as well buy some tea while I'm here. I find the loose-leaf tea shop that I usually visit, though it's been long enough that it seems to have relocated. Online shopping is simply too convenient. "Ms. Crocetti," the young nymph greets me. "I haven't seen you around in a while."

I suppose I shouldn't be surprised that everyone knows me. I've been coming here for over a century. Well, here meaning the Community Center. It moves around once or twice a decade. "Ms. Floros, I trust you're doing well. I hope the same of your wives and husband?"

She smiles, her green teeth showing. "How kind of you to remember. Yes, we're all doing quite well. Is there anyone new in your life? I know my sister seemed quite interested when she saw you back in the 80s, if you're free."

"Interested" is putting it lightly. She was indefatigable. Even after a good helping of blood, I could hardly walk straight for a week. "I'm not actually sure right now," I admit. "Do give her my best wishes when you see her."

"Of course. I'll let you know the next time she's in town, if you'd like."

I suppose I can't guarantee I'll be more serious with Mia by then or that she'll even be alive. Crisanta rarely leaves Greece. "That would be wonderful." I look over her impressive collection of tea. They grow it all themselves and aren't great at labels, so it can be a bit of work to find exactly what you're looking for, but you can't beat the quality.

"I have some caffeine-free tea. I don't have it set out as it's rarely requested." She bends over, opening up a box under the table.

"Thank you. Yes, the usual assortments there, and a normal English breakfast if you have it. Harvey hates it, and sometimes, it's just nice to have caffeine."

"Of course." She flashes another smile at me as she stands back up, holding a few bags of loose leaves and snatching another from the table without even looking. "That should be, well, let's call it forty dollars. I'll give you a little discount."

"You don't have to—"

"It's fine. It's good to see you again."

I thank her and hand over the money. I should come here more often. It's nice being able to be around a crowd that doesn't set me off, and a lot of the shop owners are surprisingly friendly. Though there are exceptions, as Mia found out the other day. "You have a great day," I call over my shoulder as I head toward the exit, only to immediately be stopped by—

No.

No, it can't be.

"Bianca," I growl.

That same face smiles up at me, looking as innocent as ever in her white dress. "Oh, Olivia, it has been too long. I've missed you so."

If my blood was ever not, it would be running cold right now. Alas, it stays warm quite briefly out of the body. So I wasn't hallucinating. She's been following me. I look around, scouring the room for any sight of him. There's no way she's here on her own. He wouldn't let her be.

"You need not fear," she insists, grabbing my hand.

I pull free, my vision already tunneling. I need to get out of here.

"Olivia—"

"I know you've been following me."

Her blue eyes catch on mine with a pleading look I endeavor to ignore. "I wanted to make sure he wasn't with you. I managed to break free too. You don't have to worry. I promise, I'm only here as a friend." Her words sound sincere, but I know her. She's a snake and will stop at nothing to fill me with her venom. She can never be trusted. I won't make that mistake. I can't.

"You're not my friend," I spit, moving around her toward the door. What if he's waiting there? This is all a trap. Who knows how many people he may have now? I can overpower her, but I can't take all of them. What am I going to do? I should stay here where it's safe. There're more people here, they know me, and they won't let them take me. Right? What if he's gotten to all of them? I look around again, examining the faces of everyone I see. Could they all be in on this? How long has he been planning it? I won't go back. I can't. Not again.

Stepping around me, she places her hand on my shoulder. I shrug it off. "Olivia, you can trust me," she insists. She speaks only lies. "I'm sorry for all that I did. You know he made me, just as he made you. Please, you're the only other person I can turn to. You know what he's like. You know he'll find me. I need a friend. I need someone to talk to. You don't even have to help me. I want to not feel alone."

She's lying. She must be, she's talking.

"Olivia," she pleads, her voice rising in pitch.

What if she's telling the truth? Can I really doom her to his corruption again? Am I this cold? No, it's a trick, I won't let myself fall for it. "You come to me, after all this time, expecting me to be your friend? How have you even found me? This is a mere deception to bring me back to his fold, and I shall not fall for it."

Tears fall from her eyes, and she makes no move to wipe them away. "I deserve that." She sighs, shaking her head, her gaze falling to the floor. "I've done terrible things these past five hundred years. Worse than you could imagine. But they weren't my fault. If I didn't do them—"

"How did you find me?" I keep my voice as quiet as I can manage, but I can feel heads swiveling to stare at us.

"Olivia?" she asks, falling back to the weak pitiful disguise that fools so many.

"Answer me. Now."

"After the Hunt, I got away. I've been fleeing from city to city these past hundred years." She makes it sound like she has just escaped. Is this a crack in her lie? "Toronto is one of the biggest cities for us. There's so much culture here, and I haven't heard of a single fiend being persecuted since the Wendigo Trials. I knew it was a safe place and that his reach didn't stretch here. He was still in Europe the last I heard. I didn't know you'd be here, but I hoped. And I was right. I found you. I needed to make sure he wasn't here. As soon as I was certain of that, I approached you."

"How long have you been in Toronto?"

"A week, maybe," she stammers. Her eyes shift rapidly as she does the math. "Ten days, I think. It's kind of blurred together. I've been running so long, I don't even know how to feel safe, how to stop."

Closing my eyes, I try to block out her words. I won't believe them, no matter how true they sound. She suffered with him for four hundred more years than I had to; of course she'd be frightened. No, she's his. I won't fall for this. "You expect me to believe that?"

"It's the truth."

More people turn to look. I can hear someone walking toward us. Is that the plan? To make it awkward enough that I have to go outside with her, and they can grab me? I'll not fall for it. If she wants to talk, perhaps I'll listen, but I'll listen here. "Have you eaten?" I ask, my voice as calm and gracious as I can force it to be.

Faltering, she stares before finally answering, "Yes. I bought some blood over there." She points at the same stand where I purchase mine.

"Then perhaps a drink. There's a bar in the corner." It's small, overpriced, and everything is far too watered down, but for a lot of us, it's our only option, and it's always packed.

"You don't want to go—"

"Let's grab a drink." I grip her wrist and lead her away from the onlookers, settling neatly in the center of the bar even though I have to politely ask someone to move. "Two beers." They serve them in unopened bottles. It's the only thing you can trust to be what it says on the label.

"I'd rather have—"

"Two beers," I repeat.

The minotaur, who barely fits behind the counter, hands them to us. "Ten bucks." His voice is higher than one would expect, almost a soprano.

It's a small, no-name brand, and it's not terrible. I swallow half the bottle before I turn to her again, leaving a ten on the counter. Highway robbery, I swear. "How did you escape?" I ask her, still playing at affable.

"I'd earned his trust, and he was scared. There was a lot of commotion, and we were separated while running from hunters. I don't think he'd even considered the possibility that I'd leave him." Because she wouldn't. "I boarded a ship heading for Athens. I didn't even know that was where it was headed. I needed to get away. My fare wasn't free, but it was less torture than he ever gave me." She sobs, her tears splattering on the bar. I won't give in. I won't care about her. She's a conniving wretch, just like him. "There weren't hunters there, but I knew he'd follow me. I only spent a few days in town before I moved on. I found a little fishing hamlet and stayed for a week, but I was always looking over my shoulder."

That sounds all too familiar. I finish the rest of my beer. "Another, please. Make it two."

Her eyes widen, and she turns to me, reflecting my suspicion with her own. "You haven't seen him, have you?" The words tumble out slowly, as if she can scarcely believe she's even asking the question. "Has he contacted you? Has he been here?"

"I haven't seen him."

"You're sure? You know how he is, how he loves to play his games."

He's playing one right now. "I'm certain."

"Oh, thank you." She wraps her arms around me, squeezing. I can smell her on me, the stench of betrayal rubbing off. I'll have to burn this outfit. "You're the only one I can trust. You're the only person who hates him more than I do. You know the monster he is. You'd never fall for his tricks again, right? I'm safe here?"

"I won't fall for them," I agree.

She stares at the bottle before her and drains it in a single swallow. She looks terrified, I'll admit that, but she's always been a good liar. "Can I have another too?"

I slide my third bottle over to her.

"Thank you." She sips it, her gaze far-off, staring through the assortment of half-filled liquor bottles. "I haven't seen him in a hundred and twenty years, but I'm still convinced that he's always one step behind me—or maybe even ahead—that I'll round a corner and find him there, waiting for me. Olivia, what am I going to do?"

I don't know how to respond. I'm still looking for that answer myself. "It doesn't get any better," I admit.

"It doesn't?"

I shake my head.

She finishes her beer and collapses, her head resting in her hands atop the bar. Blubbering, she repeats, "What am I going to do?"

Should I help her? Can I? Screwing my eyes shut, I shake my head. I won't put myself at risk. I can't. If she finds out where I live, he will too. "There's a hostel on the second floor, I believe." Right by the church Elizabeth mentioned. Now that I think about, maybe I should take a look at that church. I don't want to lead her there, though. It could still be a trap. She could have people waiting, I could be taken again, and this time, I may never break free. "I'll give you some money. You can stay there."

"Would you show me?"

That answers that. "It's not hard to find. It's across from the stairway." I place a hundred-dollar bill in her hands and rise to my feet. "Get some sleep. I'll talk to you soon."

"Wait—"

"I'm afraid I have an appointment. I must be off."

"But—"

"Good-bye." I walk away as quickly as I can. I hear her stumbling up from the stool behind me. Rounding a corner, I find myself by Elizabeth's office. I duck inside before Bianca has the chance to see me. She may follow my scent, but there're enough other trails here that it should make that difficult at the very least.

"Olivia?" the ghoul sitting at the desk asks. "I didn't think you had an appointment."

I consider lying. "Just avoiding an old friend. I hope you don't mind."

"Not at all." She smiles, showing her yellow fangs. "I'm Ashley, by the way, not sure if I ever said. We haven't really had a conversation."

"Right. Ashley. It's nice to meet you."

I chat with her while I wait for any sign that I've been found. Bianca doesn't come in, and I leave before Elizabeth finishes with her client. I head straight to my car, and no men accost me on the way. It's possible she was telling the truth, but I can't risk it. I lock the door behind me when I return home and promptly collapse on the couch. I was hoping I'd never have the displeasure of seeing her again. He won't be far behind.

Chapter Nine

I Really Do Like Her

I knock on Mia's front door wearing black slacks and a dark blue button-up blouse and carrying a bottle of wine. I'm far more nervous than I have any right to be. We had an amazing first date, and I'm already growing fond of her. It's been a long time, and I'm still processing the guilt over finally moving on. Should I have brought drugs instead? I'm sure that would be her preference, but it seems like a faux pas, and I'm not at all sure what to buy her. I'm not necessarily against partaking, but I have little enough experience in the area that I certainly shouldn't be the one providing them.

Before I have any further time to doubt myself, the door opens, and Mia pops out, wearing a gray dress that barely covers her thighs. I'm not complaining. At all. They're lovely thighs, and if things keep going the way they seem to be, I may spend time between them eventually, but the immodesty of modern clothing catches me off guard from time to time.

"You're early," she says, hesitating as if unsure how to greet me before settling on a hug. I hug her back. She smells good and only slightly in an appetizing way.

"Is that lavender?"

"Hm?" She pulls back, looking up into my eyes.

"The perfume. I love it."

"Oh, I have lavender bodywash. That might be it. I'm not wearing perfume."

"Well it's lovely, either way."

Is perfume out of fashion now? I feel like I should know this. I don't want to ask and seem clueless.

"Come in," she says, turning around and heading inside. Hesitating, she turns back. "Can you enter without my saying that? I've always wondered what all is true, and you've only made it more confusing from everything you've said."

I step inside, smirking playfully. I'm tempted to not give an answer and let her guess, but cryptic vampires are so clichéd. "I need an invitation," I admit. "It doesn't apply to public places or the homes of other vampires, but with humans, it does. Kind of."

"Kind of?"

"How do I explain this?" I sigh, setting my purse on a nearby table. "It's not impossible to enter, but it's harder. It's…" I groan, trying to think of what I could compare it to. "Like trying to drive through heavy snow. You can make progress and likely make it through, but it's not easy, and it takes a good deal of effort. And you certainly shouldn't do it if you're drunk."

Chuckling, she leads me the rest of the way to the kitchen, and I set the bottle of wine on the table. "Would you be able to enter again now that I've invited you?"

"I would. I've never had anyone try to uninvite me, so I'm uncertain as to how that would work, but it may be possible. However, don't take this as a guarantee of safety against other vampires."

"Right, because you all have different rules and make no sense."

"You're learning." I smirk, leaning against the kitchen counter a few feet away from her. Seeing her in that dress, in the dim light of this room, looking happy and beautiful, I have an almost irresistible urge to kiss her. I don't do it, but it's disconcerting nonetheless.

She pulls herself up onto the counter by me, her arm brushing mine. "Well, Ollie, what else should I know about vampires?"

I haven't had a nickname in what must have been centuries. "I'm still getting used to that."

"What?"

"The nickname."

"What did your ex-wife call you?"

I chuckle. It sounds awful. "My Moor."

She stares for a moment. "That's super racist."

"It wasn't back then."

"Still was."

I feel like I should have a better argument against that. She wasn't racist. It was just a different time. "She married a black woman in 1498. She was one of the most progressive women ever."

"Well, if you call me your Asian, I'm staking you. Would that kill you?"

"Yes, it would."

"I'll keep it in mind."

I turn to her, staring into her eyes. "Planning on hunting me?"

She falters, averting her gaze. I wasn't trying to scare her, but it's still a bit of a sore spot. "Sorry. I know people can be asses. I was just joking."

I must have looked angrier than I thought. "No, I'm sorry. I know you were joking. Well, you told me about your issues. I have PTSD. It's very, very bad. Like, if you ever share a bed with me, I'm going to be having nightmares the entire night, though I don't think I scream or anything, but I definitely move a lot. In 1898, after *Dracula* had come out, my kind was hunted to near extinction. Particularly in England, where I was living. Almost every friend I'd ever had died before my eyes. I can barely even handle being around humans anymore."

"Fuck." Her hand squeezes mine, staying there, our fingers interlacing. "I'm so sorry. I had no idea. No wonder you seem hesitant around me."

"Honestly, you scare me less than most people, though that itself scares me a little."

"I promise, I'll never make another joke like that." Screwing her eyes shut, she leans back, her head smacking into a cabinet. She doesn't even seem to notice. "I thought I was fucked up. I never would've guessed. That's why you were looking for those pills. I'm so dumb sometimes."

"It's okay."

"No, it isn't. I was already crushing on you, and I should've cared enough to want to know what was up with you."

Instead of crying like I normally would, a massive grin takes hold. "You already had a crush on me?"

"Have you seen you?" she asks, looking me up and down. "You're fucking gorgeous, and while I hadn't realized to what degree, you already seemed like the smartest woman I'd ever met. Plus, dreads are sexy."

I run a hand through my locks. I forget about them sometimes. "Am I? I don't even remember what I look like."

"No reflection is a real thing, then?"

"Yeah." I try to remember. The closest I can recall is a painting an artist did of me back when I'd first moved to Canada. It isn't the best painting I've ever seen of me, but it is the most recent. "What do I look like?"

"I'm terrible at this," she grumbles, hopping down to have a better view. "Well, you know what your body looks like, right? You can see that?"

"Yes. Though I have a somewhat limited vantage point."

"I can see how they'd get in the way," she teases. My breasts aren't even that big. "You're absurdly fit, like I could bounce a quarter off those abs." She glances around the kitchen, finally finds a quarter, and promptly bounces it off me. There's no way she can see them through my shirt. I think she just wanted an excuse to throw something at me. "Your ass is amazing, pretty big but toned. Your legs are really long, but I'm not going to even consider believing that you can't see those. Your face, how do I describe it? Your eyes are brown but rich, almost black, and they look like they can see into my soul. Can they? Is that a vampire thing?"

"Not to my knowledge."

"You have a—I guess the word is blunt—nose, but it's cute. Your lips are…" She flushes, biting her own lip. "Is kissable a useful description?"

"Not particularly."

"Then full. Like supermodel lips. The kind I'd love wrapped around my—"

"Mia!"

"You asked." Snickering, she looks over my face again, taking a step toward me. Her scent, her eyes, everything is inviting me to give in, to let her see precisely how kissable my lips are, but I try to hold back.

"My cheeks?" I ask.

"Hm?" She shakes her head. "You have very high cheekbones, but your cheeks are sort of gaunt. I don't think it's a vampire thing, since the rest of you isn't. I think that's just what you look like. Your ears are cute. I can't see them much through your hair, but they're small and ear-shaped. I don't know how to help someone visualize an ear. It looks like an ear but smaller than usual."

"Thank you."

"Don't mention it." She takes another step, leaning in on her tiptoes. I don't move away. I don't think I could if I wanted to. "May I?" she asks. "I don't want to assume anything again. Especially with…" She trails off, not wanting to casually mention my PTSD.

Instead of answering, I slide my hand around her back, pulling her the last couple inches until our lips meet. Hers are so soft, so warm. I'd forgotten what this can feel like. I've kissed since my wife, but only as part of sex, never as a form of intimacy unto itself. I don't want it to stop. Her body presses against mine, hands running through my hair. We don't explore each other; we don't make any move to make it more than a kiss. We simply enjoy the soft caress of each other's lips and the feel of each other's…well, *her* warmth, I suppose. I don't have my own to provide.

After a long moment, she pulls away, looking up at me through half-lidded eyes. "I was right."

"Huh?" I manage.

"They are very kissable lips."

"You're one to talk."

She has an adorable smile. "As I'm assuming we're not running off to my bedroom, I'm starving. Did you find any recipes? I hope I have the ingredients. We did not plan this out well. I've just been so busy with work this week."

"I did, actually." Unfortunately, I left my purse in the foyer. "Let me go grab my phone, and I'll pull it up."

We pull out the entire contents of her pantry and fridge, looking for the best equivalents to the ingredients in any of the recipes. We have to make a few compromises and combine some traditional dinner and lunch dishes, but she has enough that we can make a decent meal. Her fridge is surprisingly well stocked for as busy a woman as she is. I think she may have bought all this for me.

She seasons a roast while I work on creaming a massive helping of mozzarella and parmesan. She didn't have enough of either for me to only use one. "What's the thing you're making called again?" she asks.

"Erbolata," I reply. "It's a sort of herb and cheese pie. It's delicious."

"Are you sure about that?"

"It is, trust me."

She doesn't quite look like she believes me, but she doesn't question me any further. She pours a small helping of cooking wine over the roast before considering it and repeating the action. "This look about right?"

"Yeah, that should be great." The erbolata won't be ready for almost an hour, and the roast for two after that, but I'm in no hurry. Now that the cheese is finally soft enough, I crack ten eggs into the pot. She only had eleven. I stir in some milk and what must look like an excessive number of herbs, primarily chard, sage, and parsley.

We let the roast sit out to marinate and reach room temperature and pour the mixture into a premade pie crust before placing it in the oven. She pours us each a glass of wine and sits at her kitchen table. "I can't even think of the last time I put this much work into a meal," she says.

Sitting down across from her, I sip at my wine. "I love cooking. The ritual of it is quite relaxing."

"Of course, you love rituals, you're Catholic."

"And I'm planning on saying grace too."

"You didn't last time."

"I didn't want to make you uncomfortable," I admit. "But it just feels wrong."

"Do you say grace before you drink someone?"

"I do, actually."

She rolls her eyes. "Okay, fine, you can say grace."

"Thank you."

I can see how badly she wants to ask more about my religion. She can't wrap her head around how I could possibly have faith, let alone how I could stand by Catholicism. She was willing to drop it before, but if she needs to talk about it, I'm not against it. I don't want to force the issue. "You really miss church, don't you?" she finally asks.

I stare for a moment, slightly taken aback. Of all the questions she could have asked, I was anticipating that one the least. I expected her to grill me or at least continue to act like it makes no sense. This is refreshingly sympathetic. I knew there was a heart somewhere in there. With a nostalgic smile, I think back to my life in Cyprus and Venice, when I could freely walk into a church and attend a service. "I do. So indescribably much. It meant everything to me. It still does."

"Does it make you hate being a vampire?"

I sigh. "It's complicated. It was forced on me and"—I choke back a lump in my throat, trying not to think about that first night—"it wasn't a fun experience. Everything about it was awful for a long while. Because of it and many other reasons, I know I'll never make it into heaven."

"As devout as you are, I doubt that."

"I wish I could believe the same. I hated it for the longest time, and I suppose I still do in a lot of ways, but because I'm a vampire, I've had the chance to learn so much and to live for so long. It wasn't what I wanted, and I'd never ask for it, but I suppose if I'd died a natural death when I should have, I'd have never met you, and that would have been quite a shame."

She tries to cover her grin by draining her glass of wine. I'm glad to see I had the desired effect. "That would suck," she says, the glass clinking on the table as she avoids my eyes.

"Most people I meet always want me to turn them. They seem to think it's some amazing thing. Immortality has its benefits, but I've always found the desire for it to be obscene. You don't want to give up your humanity, do you?"

She shakes her head. "No. Life's too long as it is. I'm glad that your being a vampire let me meet you, but I don't think I could take it."

"You're wiser than most."

Meeting my eyes, a bittersweet smile on her lips, she pours herself another glass and says, "But hey, it definitely gives you some interesting stories."

"I suppose."

"You ever meet any famous people?"

I think back, looking over all the people I've known. Some were famous when I knew them, a few became famous afterward, but most simply went through their lives, never gaining any particular renown. "Less than you'd expect, but I've known a few."

"Any you're willing to mention?"

I skip the obvious one. I don't want to go over the whole story with him, not right now. "Oscar Wilde was a lot of fun. He claimed he based *The Picture of Dorian Gray* on me, which would honestly be quite an insult if it was true, but he'd already started it by the time I met him. It was back when I could still enjoy a good party, and no one partied quite like him. I think we bonded due to my having a beautiful woman on my arm and him having a young man." I chuckle. I don't even recall her name at this point. I wonder if he knew his. "It wasn't something one could be too open about back then, of course, but all the best parties were always scandalous."

She looks almost wistful while listening to my story, as if she's remembering it too. "I'm sure that must've been amazing. I loved *The Importance of Being Earnest*."

"It is a fun play. I actually acted in it."

Her eyebrows raise, and she almost spills her wine. "Really?"

"Yes. I didn't act much, and I certainly wasn't great, but I played Algernon in a tiny little production and the priest in a bigger one. We had to make some vestments that wouldn't burn me, but it was a lot of fun."

"I wish I could've seen it."

"I'd like to think you would have enjoyed it, but I'm certainly no Ira Aldridge. He…" I stop, blinking slowly as I consider my words, not wanting to give away too much. "He was an amazing actor. Before Oscar's time, sadly, but I think he'd have loved him."

"You make immortality sound so interesting."

"It's as interesting as you make it. Same as any life."

With a soft whistle, she slumps in her chair. "Way to call me out."

"I didn't—"

"I know, but I don't do much. I mean, I'm sure most normal people would find my life fascinating—I work with fiends on an almost daily basis, I'm dating a vampire, if me using that term is okay…I mean dating, not vampire—and I just all around do lots of things that most people would never dream of. Hell, I've performed surgery on an umibōzu! He didn't even fit on my operating table. We had to find a secluded spot by the sea, and it was nowhere near sterile. His organs were unlike anything I've ever seen. But it's all work. I don't ever do things for me."

"I hope you're doing this for you."

She giggles. "Okay, I'll give you that one."

I finish the rest of my drink and check on the pie. It looks perfect. "Just like Mother used to make," I say, setting it on the table to cool. "I hope you like it. I'm not sure it's fit for modern palates."

"Well, it smells pretty damn good."

She places the roast in the oven while we wait for the erbolata to cool. It doesn't take too long, and I cut us each a slice. Hesitating for only a moment, she sinks her teeth into it. She pauses, chewing slowly, and takes another bite. After her fifth bite she says, "I still don't know if I like it."

I've almost finished my whole slice. "I love it. It's not quite my mother's recipe, but I think it's close. I can almost taste home."

"Maybe we could go sometime." Neither of us even question it when we realize what her words imply. I suppose this date must be going pretty well.

"I don't know," I say, wiping away a nonexistent tear. "I'm not sure if I could handle it." Most of the bad memories are in Cyprus, but it would still be too much. "A lot happened there, and I'm sure it's changed so much in the past five hundred years that it wouldn't even feel like home anymore. I think I'd rather leave it a memory."

"Oh." She sounds disappointed.

"Maybe we could go to England." Right, because I don't have bad memories there at all. "Once I'm further along in my therapy. I don't think I could handle it yet. It's only been a little over a hundred years since I was last there. I doubt it's changed as much. I may even recognize a few sights."

"I'd love that." She finishes her slice and considers the remaining pieces. Is she really still not sure if she likes it? "I take it you're seeing Ms. Rosseau-Lester? I've worked with a few of her clients."

"I am."

"From what I've heard, she's quite good. Does she seem to be helping?"

"I'm here, aren't I? I'm not sure I could've handled any of this without her help."

The corner of her mouth ticks up in a miniature smirk. "I'm not quite sure how to take that, but I'm glad. I just wish I could help you too."

"You are." I'm surprised to hear myself say it, but I know it's true. I'm finally starting to trust someone again. More than that, I'm letting myself be around someone, and I'm even enjoying it. It's been a long time since I had a friend and an even longer time since I had whatever this is. "Thank you."

"I don't think I did anything, but I suppose you're welcome."

We finish off the rest of the erbolata and some bread while we wait for the roast. By the time it's ready, she's full and barely touches it. So many people can't handle Italian meals.

"I had an amazing time tonight," she says, walking me to the door. "You don't have to leave if you don't want to."

"I don't want to," I admit, "but I don't want to rush into things I may not be ready for. I like you, and I'm not used to mixing affection with sex."

"Join the club."

Pulling her to me, I plant a soft kiss on her lips. "I'll see you soon," I say when we finally pull apart. I can still feel her warmth on me.

"I'll hold you to it."

She walks me the rest of the way to my car, and I drive off, far more distracted by the woman in my rearview mirror than I'd prefer. I really like that girl.

Home and feeling more relaxed and elated than I've felt in longer than I can recall, I toss my keys and bag on the table by the door and flip on the lights. It's only one, so Harvey should still be awake. His lights don't turn off until six. I check on him, eager to tell him about my day. He'll be so happy for me.

He turns when I walk in, sitting in his cage. I don't recall closing the door. I always let him have free roam. "More," he says.

"More what?" I ask.

"More."

I take another step, sinking to my knee to peer into his cage. I know I left it open.

"Othello."

I stop dead, my hand mere inches from his cage. "What?" Every drop of excitement is gone. I'm no longer looking forward, only backward. I try to focus and search through every inch of my apartment. Was it him? Did he come here? Or was it Bianca? She's been following me. She must know where I live. I knew it was a trap. I knew I was right not to trust her. There's no sign of either of them. There's no note, no footprints, and barely even a smell. I can't place it. It's familiar, and it might be him, but I can't be sure. There's no way I'd have forgotten it, even after all these years. What's going on? I pick up Harvey's cage, causing a confused squawk and some annoyed flapping, snatch my purse and keys, and head back to my car.

I'm not even sure where I'm going until I find myself back at Mia's house. I knock on her door, desperately, harder than I probably should. I don't think I damage it.

She opens it up, peering out at me with a look of confusion. "Did you forget something?"

I shake my head. I can't find my words.

"Reconsider my offer?" Her expression grows concerned as she looks past me to the cage at my side, and grows all the more so when she sees the panic that must be clear on my face. "Why do you have Harvey? Is everything okay?"

"Someone broke into my house," I manage.

"Come in," she says, rushing the two of us inside and closing the door behind us. "What happened? I know it can't just be a simple burglar. You'd have eaten them or something."

"It wasn't."

"Then what?"

I can't even process the words yet. I don't know how to say it, or perhaps I just don't want to. This is going to be a long story.

Chapter Ten

The Break-In

Having had a few moments to collect my thoughts and several glasses of wine, I begin my tale. We're in her living room, seated next to each other on the couch, but she's a couple feet away, likely scared to crowd me in my current state. I appreciate it. "I told you I took my brother's name when I was in the army. I didn't tell you what that name was. I suppose I'm a bit famous. I was Othello."

"Like the board game?"

I shake my head. There's a board game? "Like the play. I actually helped William write it. Cinthio did it first, but I'm not sure how he heard about it."

"Oh. Oh, right, I don't know why I went to the board game."

"I certainly couldn't tell you."

"Sorry." She pours us each another glass of wine. We must be on our third bottle, and yet neither of us seem at all intoxicated. "I wasn't thinking. So you were him?"

"Yes."

"Wow. Wait, you call Shakespeare William?"

"I knew him for years. It would be strange to call him by his last name."

"I guess. Sorry, I didn't mean to interrupt. Keep going."

I try to force myself to continue. It's hard. Almost impossible. But I find the strength somewhere, perhaps at the bottom of my glass. "Most of the play is accurate. Iago was a racist asshole who couldn't resist manipulating everyone, but he was in love with me, with Othello. He couldn't take being ordered around by a black man, let alone a black woman, and when he found out, his schemes turned far worse. I don't know when he became a vampire—"

"He's a vampire too? Is everyone in the play one?"

"No, just the three of us. I believe he turned Bianca and then me."

"Who was Bianca again?"

"Cassio's lover. It's not the point. He'd been trying to convince me that Desdemona, my wife, had been unfaithful. With Cassio. I didn't believe him at first, but he was very convincing, and I was very foolish. As time went on, his lies started to get to me. I swore I could smell him on her. The handkerchief was William's invention. It wasn't real, but it would have certainly done the trick. Instead, when I couldn't bring myself to kill her, he made me what I am. He left me in my parlor to awaken hungry for blood. I couldn't resist. I tried so hard, but I couldn't. I ate her. I killed the woman I loved."

"I'm so sorry." She reaches toward me but stops, setting her hand a few inches away.

"It wasn't enough for him. He wanted to own me. He was sick and tired of letting me boss him around, and for years, he'd wanted more from me. I wasn't the man he'd desired, but it didn't make his desire go away. It only made it all the worse. He wanted to destroy me, to use me, to torture me. He stopped me from killing myself over her death, he chained me up, starved me, and kept me prisoner for months. Eventually, I gave in and joined him. I did whatever he asked of me.

"It only lasted for ten years. I managed to escape. I earned his trust, convinced him that I was his loyal dog, and when he sent me out to kill someone, I never came back. I ran until I ended up in England, where I helped write my story. Will and I agreed to leave out the vampirism—it was too unrealistic—but we showed how much he'd corrupted me, how much I deserved that fate."

"You didn't—"

"I did. I killed her, no matter how much I want to believe it was him. It was still my fangs on her neck. I was still the one holding her lifeless body." Tears fall freely. I don't even bother wiping my eyes. I just accept the blurred room as it is. "I thought I'd escaped him. I thought maybe he'd died in the Hunt. Then a few days ago, Bianca showed up. I'd seen her a few times, but I thought it was a flashback. My PTSD has been bad of late, even while it was also getting better. She wanted my help. She claimed she'd escaped from him, but I knew that it had to be a trap, which seems to be the case, or I certainly hope it is. Otherwise, I left her to him. I gave her some money for the hostel and went on my way.

"Tonight, when I came home from our date, Harvey was closed in his cage. I knew I'd left it open, but I wasn't quite sure what had happened. He said Moor. I didn't realize what he meant at first until he said *Othello*. I've never said it around him, and I haven't watched any of the movies or seen the play since the 1800s. The only way he could've known it was if Bianca or Iago was in my home. I don't know which of them it was. I desperately hope that it was Bianca. If she was lying, if she's just trying to hurt me, he could still have died in the Hunt. He could really be gone. I let myself believe it for so long. It has to be true. I need it to be true." My chest heaving with my sobs, I throw my head into my hands, bawling as quietly as I can. It's too much. I can't take it. I can't go through this again. I won't be his again.

"I'm here," Mia says softly, slowly patting my shoulder. Being touched is terrifying, but feeling alone is worse.

I grab her hand, harder than I mean to. Holding it as gently as I can in my lap, I lace my fingers between hers. "I'm sorry to drag you into this."

"It's okay. You didn't mean to. And besides, they're both vampires. They can't break in here. Right?"

"He has his ways." I look up, blinking away tears. "Don't let anyone into your house. Even if you know them, don't let them inside. He could have been planning this for years. You don't know what he's like."

"How could he have possibly known we'd end up together?" Her eyes widen when she realizes what she said. "I mean, dating."

"Together doesn't sound too bad right now. I don't want to be alone."

"Well, ask me when you've had time to think about it, and I'll say yes."

That's reasonable. I'm the one who normally wouldn't jump into things. I shouldn't be doing it now. I can't stop thinking things through. That will only let me fall back into his clutches. I have to be cautious. I have to think.

"What if Bianca isn't working for him? What if she was telling the truth?" she asks.

"There's not a truthful bone in her body. You don't know the things she did to me, the things she did for him."

"It's been a while since I've seen the movie, but Iago was pretty damn manipulative. He made you do some things you didn't want to do. You don't think he could've done the same to her?"

I want to be comforted and believed, not questioned, but I can't ignore the potential truth in her words. She was weak-willed, spineless, and a coward, but then again, I was too. "Maybe."

"What if he's found her too?"

Damn it. I just wanted to feel safe, to maybe collapse in this beautiful woman's arms and pretend that a mass murdering psychopath with a hard-on for me isn't trying to hunt me down and either kill me or make me his slave again. "She can fend for herself," I try.

"Look, I don't care either way about her. From the sound of it, she deserves whatever she gets, but I have trouble believing that the insanely devout Catholic girl I'm dating would feel the same way."

"She deserves it."

"Ollie—"

"She does. But so do I. It doesn't mean we shouldn't try to help her. We're all sinners."

With a pained smirk, she looks up at me, wiping away tears from her own eyes. "'We'?"

"I didn't mean—"

"Let's go."

"Are you sure about this?" I ask, as we pile into my car. I'm not even certain myself. There's no way Bianca isn't working for him.

"I'm not letting you go alone, not after everything you just told me."

"Why? Because I'll freeze up if I see him?"

"Maybe. You'll need someone to shake you out of it if that happens."

I stop at a light. There are no cars anywhere else on the road. What would possibly trigger the light changing? "I still think it may have been her setting me up. She could've broken in and taught Harvey those words." It is still weird that he said them that quickly. I suppose I've never tried using my persuasive abilities on him. I wonder if they work on parrots.

"And if she did, what's the chance that Iago isn't far behind?" In my peripheral vision, I see her reach for the pills in her jacket pocket but think better of it, instead resting her elbow on the armrest and leaning against her hand. I wonder if she's holding it in place to stop from grabbing the pills.

"You're right. She's either working for him or she was telling the truth." Which means we're walking into a trap. "Even if I don't have a panic attack when we see them, if they want to hurt you, I don't think I can stop both of them." It takes me a moment to realize that the light has finally changed, but I slam my foot on the accelerator and make it through before it turns red again.

"I can take care of myself."

"Mia—"

"I think by now, I've been far from subtle about my feelings for you. You're not talking me out of this. I'm going with you. You need someone to watch your back. You're trying to take on a centuries-old psychopath who's hell-bent on torturing you."

"I'm not trying to take him on." That sounds like a terrible plan. "I need to know if Bianca is working for him. Either she's alive, and I'll torture her for information—"

"You'll what?" She turns, looking more shocked than outraged.

"I'm not sitting by while Iago does whatever he wants. I'm sick of letting him ruin my life. I will take back control. Maybe then I can finally have a good night's sleep."

"If that's all you're after, I think I could help with that."

That is really not helping with my righteous anger. I'd rather not think of all the various ways I could spend the night with her. I need to focus. "While I'm sure that would help me sleep, it would make no difference for the dreams. Believe me, I've tried."

"I meant oxycodone."

"Oh." I try to focus on the road, shedding the images that the misunderstanding had given me and doing my best to ignore the thoughts that have been haunting me since I first got home.

"I mean, I'd be up for your idea too."

I roll my eyes. "Are you armed?"

"I forgot my monster slaying gear at home. You don't have a gun in your glove compartment or anything? What kind of shell-shocked soldier are you?"

"Mia," I grumble. "Could you not?"

"Sorry."

"She was staying at the Community Center. We can grab weapons there."

"Sounds fun. I love shopping with you."

"Well, this time we'll actually pay." I pull into a spot in the empty parking lot. She lives so close by. I hadn't actually realized. I guess it makes her commute easy, since the vet is only a few blocks farther. "Come on." Before I can go to open her door, she climbs out, and we head inside.

Everything looks as it should. It's a little past three a.m., and the place is still crowded. I can't tell if Bianca or Iago have been, as there're too many scents. What I wouldn't give for a good bloodhound.

"How about that one?" Mia asks, pointing toward a stand stocking an archaic collection of weapons. Guns aren't too helpful against vampires anyway, though a bullet always hurts.

"Yeah, that looks fine."

"Evening, Olivia," the fext who owns the shop says. It always seems so strange when any other creature that could pass as a human runs a business here, but I suppose we are more likely to buy medieval weaponry than humans. It takes me a moment to recall his name. We hadn't even exchanged words since the center moved to the Honeydale Mall. I don't shop for weapons often. I'm surprised he remembers me.

"Good evening, Vitaly." We do have a strange concept of time, don't we? Shouldn't it be afternoon? It's only three. "I need something sharp."

He gestures toward his display. "I'll advise your human friend not to try them on me, but everything I have is battle-tested and ready. I've sharpened them all myself and can certify their quality from personal experience."

Being immortal is always so convenient when it doesn't come with a host of psychological trauma. "You don't need to tell me." Mia groans. "I still have the scar from when I had to operate on one of you and no one had bothered to tell me that."

"Sorry," he mutters. "That would be my cousin, Natalia. I heard about that story. Any way I could make it up to you?"

"Free weapons?"

"How about twenty percent off?"

She lifts up her shirt, showing off a surgical scar on her abdomen. "Thirty sounds fair."

"You drive a hard bargain. What kind of weaponry are you looking for?"

I have to say it, don't I? I've literally become my worst nightmare. "We're hunting a vampire," I admit through clenched teeth, doing my best not to see the crowd of fiends as the oncoming horde of hunters back in England. "I'm assuming you don't have stakes, so maybe some axes." It's been centuries since I've had to behead anyone.

"Do try to keep the infighting outside." He holds up one ax and a claymore. "The ax is weighted perfectly for beheading, but I'd recommend this claymore for you. It'll do the job."

"How about a cavalry saber?" If I'm to be getting into a fight, I'd rather it be with something with which I'm trained. It's not like he'll stand there while I lop his head off.

"That'd be doable." He sets the claymore back down and runs his fingers over a few more of his weapons, turning to the table to his left. "Ah, this should be perfect."

He hands the blade over. It's very top heavy. The head seems to be made of a thicker material than the rest, maybe folded. It's off from what I used in the army, but it's manageable. I give it a few practice swings in the air. "Yeah, I can handle this."

"Have any machetes?" Mia asks. "I can't use an ax, but from everything I've read about executions, they're not the most efficient way to do it."

"Fine," he grumbles. She's right. The ax would require him to be at the right angle. I'm too used to having super strength and speed. A machete is terrible for a fight, but for cutting someone's head off, if it's made well enough and sharp enough, that'd be about perfect. "Carbon steel, folded, and sharpened within an inch of its life. It should cut through bones like butter. It's just boring looking."

"Sorry," I say.

"I'm not interested in looking like a badass warrior. I'm interested in making sure that we both make it out of this alive. It's like dissecting a frog but faster, and this time, I'm cutting the spine intentionally."

"If you say so," he says. "It'll be four…right, three hundred."

I pay the man before Mia has the chance to. This is my vendetta, and I'm already uncomfortable with letting her join me, so I'm certainly not going to let her pay for it. We grab some belts from a nearby stand, as we were not prepared for this day at all, but when we're done there, I lead the way to the stairwell, my hand on the cavalry saber's hilt. I can do this. I can face him.

She doesn't say a word as we ascend. I wonder if she's ever been in a fight before. She seems the type, but it's hard to say for sure.

When we reach the second floor, it's already plainly clear that something's wrong. I knew I smelled blood. The whole place reeks of it. It's not human. I hold out my hand, signaling for Mia to wait.

She glares at me.

I don't want to say anything out loud. They doubtless heard our footsteps, but on the off chance they were dumb enough to miss them, I'd rather not make my presence obvious. However, my sign language is very rusty, and I don't think she knows it. "I smell blood, lots of it," I whisper.

"Oh." She swallows, and I hear her heart rate pick up.

"You can stay here if you want."

"Do you know how hard it is to find a cute girl I actually get along with? I'm not giving up on you that easily."

I nod. In truth, I was hoping she'd come. I don't want to face Iago alone, no matter how selfish it may be. I just hope I don't get her killed. It sounds like exactly what he'd do: let me start to develop feelings for another person, then have me cause their death all over again. No. Not this time. I won't let it happen.

Sword in hand, I push open the door to the second floor. The smell is overwhelming. Blood, viscera, feces, all mixed together and coming from—

No, *not* the hostel. It's coming from the chapel. We walk on, and I chance a look in the hostel as we pass. There're trails of blood leading away from it, but there are no bodies. There are barely even signs of a struggle. I suppose two vampires, each five hundred years old, are rather difficult to overcome. In comparison to us, a newly turned vampire is scarcely more than a human, and it makes me even more scared of Iago. I don't know how old he actually is.

I can hear bile building in Mia's throat, but she swallows it, her eyes narrowing in determination as she clutches the machete. I pull her hands farther away from her and tap her knees, trying to get her to bend them. It takes her a moment, but she follows my lead and only looks indignant for a second. What am I doing dragging an untrained human into a fight with monsters? I'm such a coward.

Leading the way, I approach the chapel. Elizabeth said that there were no actual religious items or symbols in it, so it shouldn't stop me from entering, but I'm scared to try. I hold my hand out, trying to will it to touch the door. I can do this. I need to find out.

Mia steps in front of me and pulls the door open. She promptly has to swallow her vomit again.

My eyes widen, and I almost drop my saber. I'd expected a trap, not a tableau. The bodies of half a dozen fiends decorate the space, all crucified. He's mocking me. On the altar, the lights all set to perfectly illuminate her, lies the contorted form of Bianca. She was telling the truth. I let this happen to her.

Mia takes a few steps away and hurls. I collapse to my knees, tears falling from my eyes. I hated her. I still do. But this is my fault. He was sending me a message. That sick bastard did all of this to get to me. And he killed my only lead.

Chapter Eleven

Amelia: The Crime Scene

I try to focus. I may not be finished vomiting, but it can wait. This is ridiculous. I'm used to cadavers, even if they tend to be a bit less humanoid. Besides, we were coming here to kill Bianca. I should've expected to see a dead body either way. This just means I don't have to get my hands dirty. I tuck the machete in the leather sheath slung around my waist, turning my attention to Olivia. She seems to be taking this even worse than I am. "Ollie?" I ask. "How you doing, honey?" Wow, I'm already acting like we're together. That's a great sign. Though she is too. Something bad happened to her, and she ran right to me, then my manic ass jumped to help her get some murderous vengeance. Sounds like my last relationship.

After a quick glance around the macabre scene, I kneel beside her, taking her hand. "Come on, Ollie, it's okay, I'm here." Okay, an immortal psychopath is taunting us and waiting to do who knows what. I grip her shoulders and give her a light shake, but it has no effect. Well, I guess I ought to take a look while I'm waiting, not like there's a fiend medical examiner or anything.

Trying with all my might to keep what's left in my stomach on the inside, I take a quick peek at the bodies. The food stays in my belly. I risk looking longer. The bodies are horrid, gruesome, grotesque, and about a billion other unpleasant descriptors, but they're not turning my stomach, so I elect to take a closer look.

They've all been dead—or maybe deader—for at least a day. I've had tragically few chances to examine the bodies of fiends for rates of decomposition, but none of these are at all fresh. In addition to Bianca, there's a young centaur, maybe sixteen, his rear end severed to make the crucifixion possible; a grindylow, her long green hair stuck to her neck, red and matted with blood; a goblin who may have been as old as Olivia, if not more; a redcap, his hat newly dyed; and…I have to squint, as at first, the sixth cross seems to be bare. Then I see the blood. It may be an ashray, but it could be any of a number of translucent creatures, and I don't believe ashrays can survive out of the water. I can only make out its form from the spots where the dried blood clings to it, but upon closer inspection, it seems to be a boy.

I glance over my shoulders constantly as I examine the bodies, but Iago—Christ, that's weird to say, like I'm being hunted by a parrot—doesn't leap out from behind a corner, and Ollie doesn't stir. They all have exactly the same injuries, save for the centaur. Their throats were slit with a blade, not fangs, and most of their blood seems to still be here, though it's tough to judge. I'm not sure if vampires can eat other fiends, so that doesn't tell me much. I'll have to ask Olivia when she's more coherent.

Other than that, there's not a lot I can tell. Whoever did this was strong, but that doesn't say much, and they could touch crosses, which says a lot. Either Iago has help, or Ollie is gonna be pissed. I'm sure she'd rather have whatever other weaknesses he has than not be able to go to church, though maybe that's the point.

Okay, these bodies are making me uncomfortable. "Ollie!" I shout, trying to drag her back to reality. "Can we find someplace better to go catatonic? I'll even join you."

"Huh?" she asks, her eyes still locked somewhere miles away.

"Ollie—"

"Mia?" She shakes her head, clearly still stuck wherever she was. "Sorry."

"It's okay." It's only been around an hour. That's not worrying at all. "Is there anyone we should report this to? There aren't fiend police, are there?" I'd like to think I know everything after helping the community for three years, but who knows what they might not tell a human?

"Report what?" She shakes away the last of her delirium, her eyes focusing on the gore before us. "Oh. Right. That just happened."

"Looks like it happened yesterday at the earliest."

Her eyes widen, and she finally faces me. "What? Before he

even…I'm the one that sent her here, and he immediately killed her. Was he already watching me, or was he following her? Or maybe I was right, and it was a trap, and he killed her for failing."

"Well, we know who broke in. Hopefully, that means he's the only one we have to worry about, but…" I glance back at the bodies. "Could he touch crosses?"

Narrowing her eyes, she glares at the scene arranged by her old nemesis. "Yes." She snarls, baring her fangs. "The rat bastard loved rubbing it in too. He wore my crucifix."

Well, that answers that. "I'm sorry."

"I'll kill him."

"There's my soldier." We don't have the luxury to panic right now. "We'll get him."

"I will. I'm not letting him hurt anyone else to get to me."

"Ollie, you know him better than I do, but I think it's safe to assume he knows who I am. What do you think the chances are that I'll be safer on my own?" I need to look after her. I can't let her run off to deal with this. He's already in her head.

She bares her teeth again. "He might not."

"He might not know where I live. We can stay there if you think it's all right, but he was in your house and knew when you were out, so he knows that I exist, maybe even who I am, and I'd rather have you with me. We can take him together a lot more easily than you can alone." Especially if she freezes up again.

She nods. "You're right. He'll go through you. I have to be with you at all times."

"Wait, what?"

"That's how he operates. Well, I won't give him the chance."

I guess it's what I wanted. Farewell, privacy. "Thank you." I drag her to her feet, linking my arm with hers. She's old-fashioned. I knew I had to be the damsel in distress if I wanted to look after her. "I feel safer already. Let's get back to my place."

❖

After informing the owner of the hostel as to the demise of all of his customers—he didn't take it well. I'm not sure if it was the money or the lives. It's always tough to tell with some of the people here—we head back to my apartment. It is really nice getting to ride in her car. I could get used to having a rich vampire girlfriend. I can't believe I just thought that. I don't move that quickly, and it's not happening.

We both collapse on the couch. Ollie is paler than usual, and she hasn't said a single word the entire drive back. Granted, it's not a very long drive, but it's still clear how much this is weighing on her. That asshole really did a number on her. I'll have to kill him. "Ollie," I try.

She stares at the coffee table. I really need to clean it. There're a bunch of rings on it because apparently, I've never heard of a coaster, and there's even a bit of spilled beer that I'd never noticed sticking to it. In my defense, I don't have company often, and I'm normally really high when I'm home. Hey, there's an idea. I grab the bottles from my jacket. "Something to take the edge off?"

"Huh?" She stirs, staring back at me before her gaze falls to the bottles of pills in my hand. "No. I'm okay."

"You don't seem okay."

Sighing, she leans back in the couch. "It's nothing drugs will help with. I've tried that already with the pills Elizabeth suggested." She shakes her head. "No, I should be clearheaded. We don't know what he might try next, and I will not be impaired for it."

"Honey, you're already impaired. I'm not saying get wasted, just something to help you focus."

She only shakes her head again.

Okay, I guess drugs aren't the answer to all of life's problems. I have a lot of trouble believing that, but I'm not going to force it on her. I pocket them again and take off my jacket, throwing an arm around her shoulders. She jumps but looks back at me and relaxes somewhat, leaning against me. "I'm sorry," I say. I don't know what else I can do.

A tear hits my collarbone. I ignore it. I know how proud she is. I won't draw attention to her moment of weakness. "I really thought I was rid of him," she mutters.

"I know."

She shakes her head, a lock smacking the back of my neck. "I'm sorry. For freezing up like that."

"It's okay, Ollie."

"I'm such a fucking coward."

I pull away, gripping her hand as I stare into her eyes. "You think you're a coward? No, you have PTSD. There's nothing to be ashamed of there. You've gone through far too much for me to ever believe that you're a coward."

"What if we find him, and I freeze up again?"

"That wouldn't change a thing. Your life has done a number on you, and you've gone through way more than you had any right to, including having it be extended infinitely, which sounds dreadful. I was worried about you when it happened, but I didn't think less of you in any way. You're not a coward, Ollie."

A squawk from the kitchen interrupts us. I jump and turn around. I'd forgotten Harvey was here. He stares at me from his cage on the kitchen counter. "Is it okay if we let him out?" she asks.

Fuck it, if it'll take her mind off things, he can ruin my whole apartment. Not like that would change much. "Yeah, sure."

"Thank you," she says, already at the cage and opening it. I'm never going to get used to how fast everyone around me is. I can barely even jog. "Hey, Harvey. You doing okay?"

He flaps indignantly and flutters out of his cage, making a quick loop around the kitchen and living room before landing on my shoulder. "Pretty," he says.

"You've said," she replies.

He cocks his head and looks between us. "Is your bird asking if we're together?" I did not just say that. Goddamn it. Well, if we are, I certainly won't be able to get away with saying Goddamn it anymore. Goddamn it. "Or is he perving on me again?" I say, trying to change the subject. We have been through too much today, and I'm not ready for that conversation. I tend to avoid it altogether. That's a big part of why I don't date.

"Probably a bit of both," she replies, sitting beside me again with a sigh. "You want some food?" she asks him, just as comfortable avoiding the subject as I am.

"Carrot."

"Do you have any carrots?" Her dark brown eyes turn from Harvey back to me. God…just damn it. I'm not even letting myself think any of the cliché bullshit those eyes make me feel. Not happening. Besides, it's her creepy vampire powers. Not that I'm falling for her. That would be ridiculous. She's like sixteen times my age.

"They weren't any of the things we needed to cook, and that's about the only time I've bothered grocery shopping in ages. There might be a can of mixed vegetables in a cupboard that'd have some carrots in it. My parents insist on giving me that shit."

"He's a little picky." She bites her lip. It must be the adrenaline from earlier. I'm not a horny teenager anymore. "I'll go look, if that's okay."

"Help yourself."

She breezes into the kitchen and goes through my cabinets. "I see corn, some very rotten potatoes—"

"Shit, I forgot about that."

The garbage can clunks as she tosses the bag in. "Vegetable medley," she pulls a can out from the cabinet. "It's barely expired. It still smells okay." She hasn't even opened it. Vampire senses are ridiculous. "Where's your can opener?"

"Second drawer from the fridge."

A few seconds later, she offers Harvey a plate with a few soggy carrots on it. He doesn't seem to appreciate this, but after a long while of eyeing it, he gives in and takes a bite.

"I didn't even think to bring his food. He's almost out of the stuff in his cage."

"If you want, we could go over and get it."

She glances at me for a moment, biting her lip again. "I'm not ready to go back there. Maybe when the sun's up. Not that that would stop him."

"All right."

Finished with the first of his carrots, Harvey hops around my table, pausing to examine the still beer. "Moor."

Olivia's expression hardens, her teeth clenching as she stares very intently not at Harvey.

"Moor?" he asks again, turning toward her.

"So, Mia, I'm not sure you ever said, what prompted you to start working with my kind?"

"You're gonna ignore him?"

"If he thinks he'll get attention for saying it, he'll say it all the more."

"Othello," Harvey adds.

I roll my eyes. She has a point. Parrots are contrary little bastards. "Well, I was walking home from work one night, and I heard a commotion over by the mall. Since it was both very closed down and late in the evening—I'd stayed past closing to tidy up and check on a dog that had gone through a pretty rough surgery—I assumed it was a drug deal. Personally, I love drug dealers, so I decided to go investigate." Wow, I really sound like a junkie, don't I? "Of course, when I got there, the people didn't look that peopley."

Olivia smirks. Glad I didn't offend her with that.

"Since I am quite well versed in mythology, even if I was a bit rusty, I recognized one of them as a ghoul, and the other looked to be a banshee. Though she ended up being a mavka. I still have trouble with all those ethereal women. Instead of doing what any sensible person would do and running off, I took a closer look."

"How'd that go?"

Groaning through my teeth, I reply, "Better than you'd expect. They didn't throw me in the slave market or anything, but they didn't appreciate it. When the ghoul bared his fangs, I noticed that he looked hurt. His left leg seemed weak when he adjusted to pounce. I held up my hands and said I was a doctor. I offered to help."

"Huh."

"Obviously, he was bothered by that, but it stopped him from attacking. The mavka said, through an incredibly thick Ukrainian accent, 'Let her take a look. You can eat her if she tries anything.' I remember the words exactly. I made sure that if I helped, they wouldn't eat me, which they begrudgingly agreed to. I don't think mavkas even eat, so I'm not sure what her problem was there, but I took them back to the clinic and examined the ghoul's leg."

"Othello!" Harvey insists. "Carrot." He shuts up to nibble on one of the remaining carrots.

"And you had your first customer."

"I did. They offered to pay, but I was a lot more curious than I was money grubbing. I said that I'd waive the fee this time if they'd refer me to other monsters—which they quickly corrected—and asked what was going on at the mall. Then they introduced me to that delightful market and way cheaper drugs than the dealer I was using."

"Really? Things always seemed expensive there. I prefer Amazon."

"When Amazon starts selling prescription narcotics, I'll happily buy them there. Until then, it's nice to have a black market within walking distance."

"Well, I can say firsthand that my community appreciates you." She pauses, her eyes meeting mine again. "*I* appreciate you. You saved Harvey's life, and…well, I'm very much enjoying our courtship or whatever you would like to call it."

I cannot believe that makes me blush. It's the adrenaline, I swear. "I'm glad. So, yeah, that's how I ended up as a black-market doctor. I still haven't even found any mobsters who need my work. I could double my clientele!"

"I'll keep an eye out for some."

With a brief giggle, I adjust in my seat. I wish I had a drink. "What about you? How do you have all the money to invest and buy fancy cars? Do you use your vampiric powers to make people give you money? 'Cause that's exactly what I would do and is the only reason I would ever consider being a vampire."

"I used to." She rests her arm on the back of the couch, staring behind us at the blank wall. "And I did worse for money as well. I was hardly concerned with human lives for quite a while there. Eventually, I saved up enough money that I wasn't sure what to do with it. I didn't need food, I'd already paid for my correspondence courses, and I certainly didn't want to go shopping with humans if I could avoid it. There wasn't a fiend friendly black market in town, nor was there online shopping, so I started investing. It took a while to work up the nerve to deal with the people that required, though I was able to use a phone for some of it. That helped a bit." Her gaze falls on me, but she still seems to be looking off a million miles, or perhaps a hundred years. "My fortune accumulated as I made a few smart investments, and after a while, I didn't need to worry about money anymore."

"Teach me your secrets."

"Time. A few decades and an easily refillable income makes it rather difficult to mess up. After the market crashed, I invested in everything and kept a lot of businesses afloat single-handedly. From there I gained enough power—enough freedom—that I could stop investing for money and instead do it for progress. I could find things I was interested in and make sure that they could afford to take off. It only grew easier once the internet was invented."

"That sounds incredible," I say, lightly squeezing her knee.

That seems to bring her back to me. "Immortality has its perks."

Nope. Not saying *it let me meet you.* "I'm glad."

Harvey jumps into her lap and looks up at her. "Scratch?"

"Fine." Her soft chuckle fills the room as she gently scratches her parrot's head. "I'm glad you're behaving now."

"You behave."

She rolls her eyes. "I always do."

"I'm glad that's settled," I say. He seems to make a lot fewer random annoying sounds than most parrots I've met. I guess she really is good with him. I hadn't seen them interact outside of work before. It's a little weird seeing her all tender. "He's a good bird."

"Good girl," he replies.

"Did that bird call me a good girl?"

"He *is* older than you. Respect your elders."

I glare. "I take it back. You're both awful, and I hate you."

"Really? And here I was growing so fond of you."

My cheeks heat again, and I glare at the stupid bird. "I'm not used to animals being older than me."

"He's way worse at conversation than you are, if it makes you feel any better."

I swear he looks offended. "I guess." I'm surprised to find myself yawning. What time is it? I have to close the low battery warning on my phone to find out, but it's apparently four a.m., and I've been up since six. "I'm exhausted. I should get some sleep."

"Okay." She pauses, hopefully wondering if she should join me. Now that would be worth putting off sleep for. "I should keep watch. I don't want to risk him showing up while we're both asleep."

"Can't he not enter without permission?"

"He could still burn the place down."

I consider that for a moment. I'd rather not have my apartment burn down—I live in it—but it is insured. "From what you've said, that doesn't sound like him. That could kill both of us, and he wants you alive to torture for some sick perverted reason."

"You don't know the half of it." She swallows, her eyes unfocused. "He wants me at his side, serving him. He thinks he's in love with me."

"Really?" She's said it before, but still. That hardly seems like love.

"Yes." She clenches her eyes shut, likely trying to shake a particularly unpleasant memory. "I'm so sorry for dragging you into this. I swear I wasn't expecting it."

"This all just kind of happened." I risk cupping her cheek and am pleasantly surprised when she leans into it. She did recoil for a second, but I'd expected that. "You don't have anything to be sorry for."

"Yes, I do. This is all my fault. If I'd killed him instead of running off, or if I'd at least been looking for him…there were countless ways I could've stopped this."

"You're not responsible for the actions of your psychopathic stalker."

"I am. All he wants to do is hurt me." She pulls away, moving to the edge of the couch, tears glistening in her eyes. "If he finds out about you, he'll put you through hell to remind me of my place."

"Like I said earlier, he probably already knows, and he hasn't done anything yet."

"He will." She stands up, causing Harvey to hop onto me, squawking and flapping in protest, his wing slapping my ear. "I can't let it happen."

"What are you talking about, Ollie?" I rise to join her, causing more irritated noises from the bird on my shoulder. "We already said we'd fight him together."

"I'm not letting it happen again. I can't. I'll go find him myself. If I die or if I serve him again, he'll leave you alone. I won't sit here and wait for him to burn your apartment down or turn you into another vampire or whatever else he might come up with. You saw what he did to those people. He has a penchant for creativity."

She tries to walk away, but I grab her hand. She spins on me, her eyes wide. "Does that sound like a coward?" I manage, blinking away tears of my own.

"What?"

"You call yourself a coward, but here you are, willing to give your life for me." Maybe she *is* falling for me. That makes me feel better about how crazy I seem to be for her. And I'm not even manic right now. "Does that sound like a coward?"

"Mia—"

"What's to say he won't have you attack me as a sign of your newfound loyalty if you join him? Or that he won't find some other reason to come after me?"

"Well—"

"Stay here. We'll figure out what to do, and we'll take him out together. He knows you, but he doesn't know what to expect from me."

She takes a step toward me, her gaze locking on mine, her hand squeezing mine a bit harder than it needs to. "Why are you willing to put yourself in danger for me?"

"A combination of a really bad crush and a death wish?" It seems the most likely explanation.

Surprisingly, she seems to actually like that response, as rather than chewing me out for the death wish like most people would, she kisses me. I don't know if there's a drug in vampire saliva or if it's the centuries of practice, but no one has ever kissed me like that before. I swear I melt into her arms.

Sadly, she's not willing to go any further tonight, but we cuddle for a few seconds before I pass out. It's been a long day.

Chapter Twelve

Amelia: Sunday

I wake up to the sound of something sizzling in my kitchen. I'll never get used to that, even if I live as long as Ollie. My kitchen is basically a decoration. Still in my pajamas and rubbing sleep out of my eyes, I drag myself to the kitchen to find a sexy vampire at my stove fixing bacon and eggs. "Morning," I mutter.

I'd lent her a T-shirt to sleep in, and I am not complaining about the view that it's earning me. Her ass looks amazing. "Good morning. I wanted to let you sleep as late as I could. Did I wake you?"

I shake my head, but she's not looking at me. "I don't think so. What time is it?"

"A little past noon. I only slept for a couple hours. I can't rest when he could be out there, anywhere, plotting something."

Wow, I slept in. Did she turn off my alarm? "Ollie, it's okay."

She tosses the food onto a couple plates and joins me at the table. "No. It isn't. Everyone he hurts is because I didn't stop him. I trusted him for years, and if I'd killed him then or killed him once I was a vampire instead of giving in, that wouldn't have happened. It's all on me."

I am not awake enough for this shit. "You can't put that on yourself."

"I'm the one he's trying to get back." She bites into a strip of bacon, producing an impressive crunch.

A bundle of feathers thuds onto the table in front of me, and it takes my sleep-addled brain a moment to comprehend why. Right, there's a bird in my house. "Carrot?"

"I don't have any carrots."

"Carrot," he insists, looking between our plates.

"It's not good for you. All that salt and fat."

He squawks angrily, jumping toward her plate only for her to pull it back at the last second.

"One little piece, and that's it!" She breaks off a piece of bacon and tosses it onto the table, distracting him long enough for her to eat more. I take the opportunity to take a bite, and it's amazing. Clearly, I need to marry this woman so she'll keep cooking for me. I'll even put up with more of that weird pie thing.

"Wait, I didn't have any bacon. Did you go shopping?"

The bacon falls from her lips, landing on her bare thigh. "No," she manages after a moment.

"Think it's poisoned?"

"It doesn't smell like it. Or taste like it."

"There's plenty of poisons that wouldn't," I say. Hell, I could probably grab something from work that wouldn't.

"I'd still smell it. I didn't quite trust it to still be good, since from the sound of it, you rarely buy groceries, so I inspected it quite thoroughly, even though the expiry wasn't anytime soon. It's just bacon. Same for the eggs."

"Then why?"

"He loves playing games." She sighs, gritting her teeth as she pushes her plate away. "It's a message. He knows where I am, he knows who you are, and there's nothing I can do to stop him."

I eat another piece of bacon. If the murderous psychopath is going to be nice enough to buy me a meal, it'd be rude not to eat it. Plus, Ollie made it, and it's delicious. "Why only do this? Why not try to kill me? Or you? Or do something besides leaving some food in my fridge?"

"It wouldn't be him then. Maybe he's waiting for something, but most likely, he wants to bide his time while we stew in the knowledge that he's coming."

"So let's leave."

"And go where?"

"Anywhere. How would he know?"

She shakes her head. "The same way he knows that I'm here. He's always one step ahead. He's probably watching us now."

"We can get in your car and just keep driving. Do you have a passport? We could go to the US."

"Mia—"

"Or we can kill him."

Her fingers tap on the table. "I'm not willing to keep running. I'm sick and tired of looking over my shoulder, but we don't have any way to take the fight to him. He knows where we are, and we don't know where he is."

"Then we'll wait for him to slip up."

"He doesn't slip up."

I finish my breakfast and hers as I try to process that. He's not a god, at least, I assume not. I've never met one, but he's not omniscient. "Then why did it take him this long to find you? How did you escape in the first place? He *will* slip up. We can bide our time and try to get all the information we can. How about we go to the Community Center tonight and see about hiring a few fiends? Guards, PIs, hitmen, sounds like you could afford a whole army."

"And they could all be on his payroll."

"Ollie, you can't assume that he knows everything. If you let yourself believe that there's nothing we can do, we'll never be able to kill him. We have to try something."

"And if they're in his pocket?"

I groan. "Then I guess we die. It's still better than assuming we can't do anything."

"Maybe we can get some cameras and some more weapons. Right now, you're the only person I trust with this. I'm not quite sure why I even trust you, but I do. I can't bring more people into it, but unless he's learned some impressive new tricks in the last few centuries, he can't bribe a camera or a bullet."

"What about your priest?"

She sighs, staring at our empty plates. "I trust him."

"Okay. It's Sunday, so I guess you found the only excuse in the world to take me to church. We can do that, and then we get to go shopping."

Nodding, she rises. "All right. Let's do it. I guess it beats the alternative."

So, church. Great.

❖

I swear I'll never get used to this car. It is the nicest thing I've ever seen. I bet it even offers turndown service, though I already have enough things breaking into my apartment without a car making my bed. I do want to see what kind of mint it'd leave on the pillow, though. We pull up in front of an old church. I guess it's reasonably pretty, though it's not one of those European cathedrals that you'd travel miles to see. Is it a cathedral or a church? I honestly don't know the difference.

I glance at Ollie as we get out of the car. She's said that she's fine, but I'm still a little worried she'll burst into flames when she steps into the sunlight. I worried just as much walking to the car too. I offered to bring it around, and not only so I'd have the chance to drive it, but she insisted.

"You really don't burn in the sun?" I ask.

"For the dozenth time, no. It's unpleasant, it hurts a little, but that's about it. It's sort of like walking outside with a bad sunburn but all the time."

I won't ask how she'd know. I'm not that dumb. "This is your church?" I ask.

"Yes."

It's not a cathedral, then. "How long have you been coming here?" The rocks crunch under our feet, and I can hear bees buzzing about, though I don't see any. She can probably smell them or something. I don't want to be a vampire—I barely even want to be a human—but sometimes, I have superpower envy.

"Around thirty years. It took me quite a while to work up the nerve." Eighty years definitely counts as quite a while. "I had to ask around for who'd be the most understanding. There was a djinni I knew, Akil. He was an interesting man, and he used to come here."

"A Catholic djinni?"

"What can I say? He knew the word of God when he found it."

Not worth it. "What happened to him?"

"Someone trapped him in a lamp."

"You're joking."

She smirks, taking a seat at a bench a few feet away from the back door. "Of course I'm joking. He went back home. He said it would be a short visit, maybe ten years, but time works differently there."

Can't say I know too many djinn. And anyway, I guess a Catholic djinni isn't any weirder than a Catholic vampire. No. It still is. "We're not going inside?" Maybe the sun doesn't hurt her, but it's way too hot out for me.

"I can't."

"Oh, right. Sorry." I sit down next to her, trying to avoid tripping and shoving my foot in my mouth again. I know full well she can't go in the church. What the fuck was I thinking? Before I can finish berating myself, a nun waves at Ollie through the door and runs away. "Friend of yours?"

"Sister Patricia. Can't say I know her too well. She's gone to get Father Gregory."

"I will never get used to this stuff."

"What's to get used to?"

Church. Vampires trying to kill me. Having to leave the house on a Sunday when I should be off my ass on something strong and fun. "Nothing." I sigh and cross my legs as I lean back on the uncomfortable metal bench. I get that it looks good in the garden with the little rock display and all the flowers, but couldn't we have cushions? Something waterproof maybe.

The door opens, and a dark-skinned man with a close-cropped beard and shockingly blue eyes steps out. He's wearing priest clothes. I'm assuming he's the guy. "And who might this be?" he asks with a mighty grin. I'd call it shit-eating if I wasn't trying to be a little less blasphemous.

"This is Mia," Ollie says and stands up to meet him. "The woman I told you about."

"Well, you do move fast." His voice is softer than I'd have expected but with a certain gravitas that makes you have to listen. I can see why he went into public speaking, though if he's as progressive as she makes him sound, I think his talents would be better spent in politics. "Do I have time to set things up, or do you want me to marry you two here and now?"

Olivia sputters. I can't help but picture her doing a spit take with blood instead of coffee, and I laugh like a slightly crazier woman than I actually am. "We're not getting married," she insists.

"Damn, and here I was preparing my vows," I say.

"I…you…what?" She flushes, her cheeks darkening almost imperceptibly, and her mouth dropping as she stares at me.

Father Gregory claps her on the back. "I like her." He takes a seat on a second bench near ours, leaving Olivia standing befuddled. "Are you trying to drag our friend into this century? Do you know how long it took me to convince her to get a cell phone? The internet was a quick sell, though. I just had to tell her she could shop while avoiding people."

"You know Italians. They love taking things slow, and she has all the time in the world to do so. I'm surprised you convinced her to get a phone at all."

She glowers at me. Apparently, she can't quite bring herself to do so to him. "I adapted fine, thank you. I'd love to see how you two would handle technology five hundred years from now."

"I'm afraid I'll be in heaven, so I'll already have whatever technology you'll receive and will have mastered it long before you even convince yourself to buy it," he replies, meeting my eyes with that same playful grin.

"I don't think there's technology in heaven."

"Who's the priest here?"

I can see why she likes him. "Come on, Ollie, sit down."

She does, begrudgingly, and I place a possessive hand on her thigh. Hey, she's making me go to church; I can make it fun.

"Ollie?" he asks. "I like that. It suits her."

"She wouldn't let me call her Liv."

"Yeah, I got that speech once."

With a groan, she turns to Father Gregory, her hand idly moving mine out of her lap. "We're here for an urgent reason, if you two are done making fun of me."

"I can take a break," I say.

"What is it, Olivia?" he asks.

"He's back."

The grin vanishes, and his eyes grow serious, his posture stiffening as he clears his throat. "Iago?"

"Yes."

"Well, fuck." Okay, coming here was completely worth it. "Do you need help getting out of the city? The country? A safe place to lie low? Any favors cashed in? I'm not letting him hurt you again."

"I appreciate that, Father, but no." She shudders, closing her eyes as she squeezes my hand. She hadn't taken it away after she moved my hand. "I'm not running anymore. I must stop him. He's hurting more people."

"Well, then, what can I do?"

We hadn't actually figured that much out yet. "He'll come after anyone close to me. That could include you. He's already shown that he knows about Mia. Last night, he broke in or more likely had someone else break in."

"Are you two okay?"

"We're fine. He just left us breakfast, but I need to figure out how he's doing it. If it's a human breaking in, I'll eat them, torture them for information, mind control them, whatever I have to do."

"Make sure you come for confession afterward."

"Of course." How are they even Catholic?

"You're okay with that?" I ask.

"She gave up killing, but she has to eat, and even the Bible is quite fond of war."

So he's more of an Old Testament kind of guy. But cool with gays. I don't get it. I wonder if he eats shrimp.

"I need you to get the word out. If anyone in your congregation knows anything, I need it. He's five-six, very pale, drinks blood, dark hair, sharp cheekbones and chin, a strong brow with a scar on the left side. He likely still has an Italian accent, but I haven't seen him in five hundred years, so despite having his image burned into my mind, I can't say what he may look or sound like now." She shifts uncomfortably, clearly disturbed by even picturing him.

I lace my fingers between hers. "We'll stop him."

"I'm not sure how much the description will help, but I'll find out anything I can. Do you want me to stay with you? Or find you a new place? I was in the army. I can handle myself."

Olivia gives a small smile and nods appreciatively. "I don't know. Maybe. I appreciate the offer, but right now, I want you to keep an eye out and to look after yourself."

"I'll be safe in the church."

She swallows, closing her eyes as a tear escapes them. "No, you won't. He can enter them."

His eyes narrow as he stares incredulously. "And yet you think your inability is a sign that God hates you? The man is a monster, and I don't mean that as the slur. I mean he is heartless, and from what little you've said, the vilest person I've ever heard of. It's not God's judgment. It's a weird quirk of your genetics."

"It sure doesn't feel like it."

"Be that as it may, I'm more convinced of it than ever. If you ever manage to die, I'll be sure to see you there."

She sniffles, but the corners of her mouth twitch slightly. That really meant a lot to her. I wish I could manage that. "Thank you. You have my cell phone number. Keep me abreast of anything you find out, and please try to stay underground."

"Because you think he wouldn't murder my congregation or the sisters instead?"

She falters, her gaze falling to the flowers nearby. "You're right. Let me know if anything happens."

"I will."

She rises. I guess we're done here. "Thank you, Father."

"You don't want to do confession?"

"I might die. I suppose I ought to." Really inspiring confidence, honey.

I move to leave, but Ollie's grip on my hand tightens. "Honey?"

"I don't want you out of my sight. I haven't done anything you don't know of. It's fine." She turns back to him and confesses biting some guy. Wow, I can't believe she'd do that to me. I have all this perfectly good blood inside me, and I'm not good enough. She goes into a bit more detail about last night, the carnage we saw, freezing up, and sharing a bed with an unmarried woman. He laughs that last one off and says that she's forgiven. I didn't think confession was quite that simple, but I've only seen it in movies.

"Is there anything you'd like to confess?" he asks me when they've finished.

"I'm good."

"Mia, please," Ollie says.

"I'm not Catholic."

"But—"

"We can't make her, Olivia," he says. "I know you're scared for her, but this gives you all the more reason to make sure she stays alive."

She looks down at me, pleadingly, for another moment but gives in. "Okay. Fine. Let's get going. We have some shopping to do."

That night, we head over to the Community Center. I'm starting to feel like a regular sidekick. Maybe I need a cape. After all, I can't *not* go with her. I won't let her face this alone. She needs me, and I'm not at all willing to go find some other girl to date. That'd take years. Besides, my life is on the line too, and at the moment, I would slightly prefer being alive over being dead. Especially if she'd end up blaming herself for it.

The parking lot is as empty as ever. We park and head to the old mall. "Vitaly again?" I ask.

"No. We don't need swords. I want something more practical."

I have my machete on my hip because I am rather lacking in natural weaponry, unlike some people. "I don't know how to use a gun."

"Well, I suppose I'll have to teach you."

"You can use a gun? Like a modern one. No black powder or flintlocks? Seriously?" I peer at her as we walk past the outer façade, trying to read her.

She smirks. "It's been a while, but the last time I practiced, I was still a pretty decent shot. They're a lot more accurate now."

"And there are guns that can kill vampires?"

"Incendiary rounds would be ideal. If the compressed versions actually worked, I'd want some grapeshot to take his head off, but for you, I'm thinking garlic. It won't hurt me too much if you miss, and it'll slow him down enough that we can take his head off without too much work."

I glare at her. "I wouldn't shoot you."

"Right. Says the woman who's never used a gun before."

"Well, if you're using incendiary rounds, you know fire kills humans too?"

"I won't miss." I hate how hot she looks when she's all cocky. It makes it hard to be mad at her.

"Wait, there're garlic bullets?"

"We'll dip them in garlic oil. They may even have some filled with it here. Or if you'd prefer, we could get you a tranq gun. That'd work just as well, if not better, though it could hit me too. Though it won't have the same stopping power for whoever's working for him, and it won't be quite as fast acting. Plus, if you put a bullet in his head, he'll have trouble functioning for a while. So make sure you don't shoot me in the head."

I said I'm willing to help her kill him or even to kill him myself, but this feels weird. We're literally premeditating murder here. I don't like it. I'm a fucking doctor, for Christ's sake. Damn it, I'm trying to stop that. "Whatever you think. I'll manage." I sigh, glancing at the various stalls we pass. I don't know how to feel. "Wait. Why does garlic work on him? You said it didn't work on you because you're Italian. He is too."

"Yeah, that was a joke."

"You lived in England for too long. I can never tell when you're joking."

"When I first moved to England, dry jokes weren't the standard. It was more making puns about sex and genitals. The dry humor was more of a thing in the 1800s."

"You didn't come over here until the 1900s."

"I'm aware."

I roll my eyes. I don't think I've ever actually been to this section of the bazaar. She leads me into an actual shop, not just a stall. No one uses the old storefronts except that human therapist. "This is different."

"Hey, Sven," she says, greeting the counter.

"Olivia, it's been too long," a male voice replies. I lean over the counter, but there's no one there. He's invisible? I've never had to deal with that before, other than…I try very hard not to think of that body. "May I help you?" I feel like the words are pointed at me, but it's tough to tell.

"Hi," I offer meekly.

"Mia, this is Sven. He's a nisse. Sven, this is Mia, my…" She hesitates, her eyes widening, but she quickly regains her composure. "Friend." That was good to see. I'm glad I'm not the only one jumping the gun there.

"It's a pleasure to meet you, Mia." A hand appears out of thin air a foot above the counter.

I shake it. "It's nice to meet you too, Sven."

The hand disappears and releases me. "What can I help you with? Need some new munitions? I think it's been a decade. Yes, not since the old Community Center, back when we were at that Quaker building. Finally go through all those bullets?"

"I went through them in a little over a year. I just haven't felt the need for a new gun in quite a while."

She already has a gun? "Why didn't you already have one that can kill vampires?" I ask.

The nisse doesn't say anything. I'm not sure if I've offended him or if he's simply staying out of the conversation.

She swallows, turning to admire a rifle that's prominently displayed on the counter. "I don't want to go home. I only have a pistol and a shotgun, and there are new ones I can get now."

I'm an idiot. He's broken into my place too, but that's not the same as him breaking into the home she's known for who knows how long. Maybe a century. Not that I've gotten to see it yet. Plus, he can personally break into her place but not mine. "Right. Sorry."

"It's okay."

"You're looking for a pistol and a shotgun?" Sven asks.

"Yes, for me, and as many incendiary rounds as I can get my hands on"—she glances over at me—"and for her, I think a pistol is the best choice. Maybe a tranq rifle as well. And we're going to need security cameras, motion detectors, perimeter alarms, maybe a few claymores, and I wouldn't say no to some C4. Blowing things up is far easier these days." That was weirdly hot. "You don't have a bullet that would hold garlic well, do you? I don't want to inject it with tranqs. Knocking him out would probably work better, but a garlic bullet in the brain would stop him for a long while."

"Expecting an assault?"

"Quite possibly."

"Then I'll set you up. I have quite a few vampire hunting items if you'd like to see those."

Is she up for that? She twitched from hearing the phrase "vampire hunting." How the hell is she going to look me in the eyes again if I'm the one who kills him? "Yes, that would be fantastic," she manages, the words coming out slowly and forced.

"All right. I have wooden bullets, but it sounds like that's out, silver bullets made from crosses—"

"He's immune to holy items. It'd be garlic, possibly wood, but I'd hate to test it now. Sunlight would help, though not fatally. Fire and beheading are the best options. If you have something that could chop his head off, that would be a delight."

So he can't handle the sun as well as she can? I swear, the only advantage he has over her is the one that hits the closest to home. "Something easy to use, preferably," I add.

"Ah, a greenhorn. You don't want to give her a shotgun?"

"I don't want to be lit on fire."

"You could douse some slugs in garlic."

She mulls that over, staring down at a crossbow. "Anything that comes premade?"

"For garlic? No, not really. A few things that you could put it in, but that's about it. Though if you want to take his head off, I do have this." He pulls out a strange item that resembles the crossbows but is metal and twice the size. "This thing will fling saw blades at a high enough speed to take anyone's head right off."

"Tempting. How's the kick?"

"Not bad at all, actually."

"I don't think so," she answers after a moment's consideration. "Any UV bullets?"

"Yeah, but to be honest, they're mostly a pile of crap. They won't stun most vampires any more than being shot would."

"Very well. Two nine millimeters, I think the Glock 19, incendiary rounds for them, and a bucket load of hollow points, two AA-12s, dragon's breath and slugs, and—"

"All the home security I have?"

"That's a start."

"All right. It sounds serious, so I'll get you the best equipment. Would you like help setting it all up?"

"That'd be great."

"It costs extra."

She smirks. "Come on, Sven. You know that's not an issue."

He doesn't say anything. Maybe he's nodding. I wonder if Ollie can see him. She seems to always be looking at exactly where his voice ends up coming from. "Immediate?" he finally asks.

"Yeah, just follow us back."

Now my apartment is better defended than most military bases. I'm never getting my security deposit back.

Chapter Thirteen

Amelia: Normal Life

"Where are you going?" Ollie asks, stirring from what may have been sleep.

"I have work." I toss the sheet at her face as I make my way to the bathroom.

"There's a psychopathic vampire hunting you, and you're going to go to work like it's any other day? You could've mentioned this last night."

"I told you I had to go to bed early."

"Mia," she says, out of the bed and a few feet from me, desperation clear in her eyes. "Please. Don't do this. It's a terrible idea."

"I can't call out. I have appointments, and besides, who knows how long we'll be dealing with this. I'm not putting my life on hold."

"You don't need to work. I can look after you."

I take a step toward her, glaring up at her towering form. She really is falling for me, isn't she? "I won't be your kept woman. You're rich, and you're welcome to buy me all the stuff you could possibly wish, but I like my job. It's one of the few things that gives my life meaning, and I won't let that asshole mess with my life. Until he decides to kill me or whatever else he's doing, I'm gonna keep going to work. Was there any action on the cameras last night? Is there any reason you think he'd attack today when he's shown that he's perfectly content biding his time and buying me groceries?"

She groans, her fangs showing in her annoyance. "No. I was watching them until pretty late, and every single sensor has alarms, and they're all still working fine." She checks an app on her phone. I guess you *can* teach an old dog new tricks. "But what if he's waiting for you to be alone?"

"You said he can't handle the sun very well. It doesn't seem likely that he'll attack me in the middle of the day."

"He can't break into houses either. He's not working alone." She hesitates, clearly considering whether she can convince me to stay home. I wonder if she considers using that vampire trick on me. I'd break up with her on the spot. Well, I'd break up with her as soon as I had free will again. "I'm coming with you."

"I don't think my boss would approve of that."

"I don't think he'd approve of your black-market operation after hours, but that doesn't seem to stop you. I can convince him that I'm supposed to be there. It won't even be an issue."

"Fine. Are you joining me in the shower?"

She falters, taking a step back. Do all old people take things this slowly? I figured her sharing my bed meant she'd be ready, but she's shown no sign of that. Maybe it's the constant threat of being murdered that makes her not in the mood. It kind of does it for me. "I don't sweat," she mutters, as if that's any real answer. "Let me know when you're ready to go. I'm going to watch through all of the recordings from last night."

"Sounds good." I close the door behind me and take my time getting ready. This will be a weird day.

❖

Work is as strange as I'd expected. After a quick question from my boss, Ollie is now seen as a normal part of the office, but I have to deal with her suspiciously eyeing every single customer that comes in. Who knows, maybe that little old lady with the twenty-year-old Himalayan is secretly in the employ of a centuries-old vampire. Surely her shaking arthritic hands are getting ready to wring my neck.

"Mr. Mittens's tumors are all benign," I explain. "He still seems to be in a lot of pain, though."

"He and me both," Mrs. Lakeson replies with a raspy chuckle. "I was hoping he could spend my last days with me. Do you think he can make it that much longer?"

This is the one part of my job I really hate. Looking after animals is easy—I can always understand what they want—but having to take their owners' feelings into account complicates everything. Normally, I would advise that he be put down to save him a lot of misery, but he probably doesn't have much longer left than her, and he may spare her some pain on her deathbed. If I could put them both down, it'd make things way easier. "I'm not sure." I don't think you're supposed to ask someone how long they have to live. I wonder if Ollie could make a cat a vampire.

"Would two months be too much torture for him?"

I stare at the shivering cat, the small lumps visible under his skin. "Probably not. Do you have people taking care of you?"

"Of course. My son is in the waiting room."

I can hear Ollie shift behind me. Which is odd, as she can move pretty silently. She must really be out of her mind with worry. I doubt this woman's son is him. "Make sure you bring Mr. Mittens back if he gets any worse. Otherwise, your son can take him in when you've"—I hesitate because it feels gross to say—"passed."

"Thank you, dear." She puts the cat back into his cage and manages to carry him on her own. She still seems strong. I wonder why she has so little time left. I'm sure Ollie would say that she's only acting and is actually a fiend pretending to be an old lady, and that's why she can carry the cat. Shapeshifter? Hag? I wonder what she'd go with for her claims. Maybe it's Baba Yaga. Of course she'd team up with Iago. It's the only way to find fresh children to eat these days.

I walk the Russian bogeywoman up to the counter, and she pays the receptionist before walking off with a young man. I turn back in time to see Olivia's eyes following them out the door. "You okay?" I ask. The waiting room is empty. The only other vet's door is closed, so she's likely with a client. I suppose I don't need to worry too much about us being overheard.

"It's not him."

"I figured."

"You seemed very uncomfortable with that woman. Scared about having to reach her age?"

"Why, you offering to prevent that?"

She shifts her feet, her gaze falling to the floor. I know part of her wants it. I'm sure that if we do actually end up in a serious relationship instead of being murdered, she'll want it a lot more.

"I'm not scared of growing old," I say. "I don't see it happening. Between my extracurricular hobbies"—hey, I'm not mentioning drugs at work—"and your old enemies, I figure I'm not likely to reach my forties, but I'd still rather only have the one lifespan. I was uncomfortable because I was forcing that cat to suffer needlessly to give her some extra comfort."

"Then why did you agree to it?"

"Because the cat could take it, and I'm not sure that she could take losing him. I've been treating Mr. Mittens for the last eight years, and I know how important he is to her. She was terrified when she found out he has tumors, and she's been very sick."

Ollie follows me back to my office, closing the door behind us before saying, "I'm surprised to hear you talking like that. You never seem to care that much about people."

It's true, but it still kind of hurts to hear. "As misanthropic as I can be, I'm still a doctor, hell, more of one than anyone else here. I actually work with clients who can talk back to me, other than just the occasional parrot. I don't like letting people hurt, especially when I have the means to prevent it."

"But preventing it required letting your patient hurt."

Grinding my teeth, I lean against the counter. "I'm aware."

An arm wraps around me, and I feel her lips press against the top of my head. "I'm sorry you had to do that. I'm understand acceptable losses, but I'd never wish having to make those sorts of decisions on anyone. If it provides you any comfort, I think you made the right choice."

"Thanks." I wipe at my eyes, leaning into her embrace. "It does." I stay there, enjoying her presence for a long while before I realize it's about time for my next appointment.

As soon as I'm told that they're here, I head out to grab Gary and his family. He's a little dachshund with recurrent gastrointestinal problems. As I lead them in, Ollie's eyes narrow at his owners. "Sorry, this is my intern, Olivia. She'll be watching. Silently."

"It's no problem," Gary's owner's mother says. "Hi, Olivia. I'm Sarah."

Ollie waves. Good, she's being silent.

I examine the dog, run a test, and find it's his usual issue. It's just best to be sure, particularly when it can lead to other problems and infections. "I'll write you a prescription for the normal medication. You know what to do."

"Can I give it to him this time, Mom?" the kid—Mikah—asks.

"Okay, honey," Sarah says. "You have to make sure you give it to him at the same time every day. How about right when you get home from school, before his walk?"

"After might be better," I add.

"Okay," he shouts, grinning ear to ear. As they leave, my *intern* glares after them. "How long have you known them?" she asks.

I shrug. "I think I've been seeing them for a little over a year."

"You're sure?"

"Yeah."

"Okay. If I was him, I'd want a fiend who can pass as a child. People trust them more. They can get through your defenses. Did the boy seem any different?"

I roll my eyes. "Nope."

"You're sure?"

"I'm sure."

Crossing her arms over her chest, she replies, "Okay. Keep an eye out for anything unusual. We can't trust anyone." She keeps this up for the rest of the day. It doesn't improve during my night shift.

❖

"Help!" a voice screams from the lobby. Christ, I'm glad everyone else is gone. I mean, jeez! Olivia and I dash out to find a pixie oozing blue blood from a nail stuck in her abdomen. She's dragged by two others, leaving a sparkly trail right through the lobby. The tiny creatures look almost like toys. It'd be comical if it wasn't so morbid. Cleaning that is gonna be a bitch.

Ollie scoops the fae out of the others' arms before either of them can object, standing between them and me, searching my eyes for guidance.

"The OR is back that way." I gesture behind us. "You two need to wait here."

"But—"

"Wait here. I promise, I'll let you know as soon as I have any information to give."

I wash up, throw on some gloves, and head into the OR. It seems like overkill, and likely infection won't kill a fairy, but I'll be damned if I'm going to be held responsible for germ warfare against the Fae. I also probably shouldn't call them fairies. I hear they don't like that. It's the only term I've ever heard of that's considered a slur by two completely different groups. Those poor gay changelings.

Olivia is already in there, and is, of course, not sterile. "Scrub up, or get out of my OR."

"But—"

"Now."

She glares and stares down at the injured woman. She must decide that she isn't a threat, as she walks out without a word and stands in the window to watch over me. I have the cutest guardian angel. "I'm going to apply a local anesthetic."

"Just take it out," the pixie pleads.

"It will hurt. I really think I should numb the area first. This seems risky."

"Please!"

She asked for it. "Okay." I pin her down with one hand and grip the nail with the other. It offers surprisingly little resistance and pops right out of her with a sickening slurp and a loud squelch. Blood splatters onto my disposable scrubs and mask. It smells strange. Not coppery like human blood. It's more of a sickly sweet scent, maybe lavender. If it wasn't so strong, it'd be pleasant.

I stare at what should be a gaping wound taking out most of her intestines and uterus as I try to sort out the next step, only to see that the wound already sealed. Other than the blood on her skin, she's in perfect condition. The rags she was wearing, however, are barely holding together and are stained blue from her blood. "Thank you." She shudders. Recovering from that big a wound must take a lot out of her.

"We have some bandannas if you need something new to wear." I considered offering her a surgical mask or hat, but they wouldn't hold together as well. We keep the bandannas for boarding dogs. A lot of them seem to love wearing them for some reason. Plus, they look adorable.

"Oh, yes, please," she squeals, sitting up on the metal table.

"Gimme a minute." I leave her in the operating room and fetch one from the back. When I return, her eyes light up, literally, and she flutters over to me, peering up. "This is for me?"

"Those rags won't last you much longer."

"Oh, thank you." She grabs it, tossing the rags on the floor and skillfully tucking the red, bone-covered bandanna in place to form a makeshift dress. "I love it!"

I throw the rags away and wipe down the table. I really need to make sure I have this place clean before I leave if I don't want anyone asking questions. "I'm glad." I take her up front, and one of her friends pulls a gold coin from a sack tied to her hip. It's small, barely bigger than a dime.

"Will this cover it?" she asks.

I'm not sure when Olivia joined us, but I find her hand on my wrist. "You can't take money from the fae."

"It's a fair trade," I answer. "Not a gift. Right?"

The bandanna pixie nods enthusiastically. "Oh yes, you've more than earned it. Though it may be too little."

I take the coin. "How about you clean up in here, and we'll call it even?"

"We can do that," she replies. Pixies aren't exactly known for their skills in cleaning, and these do nothing to counter that, but they do a good enough job that I'm not likely to have any probing questions in the morning, and they even take out the garbage.

"Thank you, again," she says.

Ollie stands next to me in the doorway as we watch them fly off. "All you did is take a nail out. Why would they possibly need a doctor for that?"

"None of them could have touched it. It's iron. Maybe there wasn't anyone else they could trust. I'm certainly not going to complain about getting more business."

She shrugs. "I suppose. You don't think they—"

"No, Ollie. Not everyone is working for Iago."

"But they could be. Anyone could be. We have no way of knowing."

I sigh. "No. We don't. That doesn't mean we have to treat every single client like they're the enemy. I saw the way you kept glaring at everyone."

"You don't know what he's capable of." She takes a step toward me, scared brown eyes meeting mine. "I'm terrified about what he might do to you. I have absolutely no idea who we can trust, and at any moment, he could attack. Excuse me for being a little cautious."

"Well this is my job." I step forward until my eyes are level with her chin. I glare, prodding her clavicle with my index finger. "I'm not letting you scare away customers. I said you could come, and in truth, I enjoyed the company, but I need to keep my clientele and maybe gain a few more."

"I'm sorry. I just don't want to lose you."

My anger diminishes somewhat at that, and I find myself smiling. "You won't. Play nice until they give you a reason not to. Then rip out their throats or whatever it is you would do. Far be it from me to decide how best for you to murder someone."

"I was thinking decapitation, but I didn't bring my sword."

"How restrained of you." God, what would people have thought? I know she could've magicked them to believe otherwise, but it doesn't look great for us to have a big scary woman with a sword in our lobby.

"Instead, I'd put a few incendiary rounds in the back of their heads."

"Make sure it doesn't go through and hit me."

Before she has the chance to come up with a witty retort, hoofbeats echo down the street, heading toward my hospital. "You have another appointment?"

"That wasn't an appointment either. I only have a nine o'clock with a nixie."

"Oh? For what?"

"Inner ear infection."

"That can't be fun underwater."

The sound grows closer, and we behold a rather horrifying sight. Something vaguely resembling a flayed centaur lumbers toward us, its single eye reflecting the streetlights, its massive maw showing sharp, fang-like teeth. Shit. It's a nuckelavee. I can't let it inside. Its breath could kill the couple dogs that are boarding.

Olivia's hand dips in her coat, doubtless gripping her new pistol, but I meet her eyes, pleading. Stop trying to scare away my customers. Sure, maybe he's working for Iago, or maybe he wants a skin transplant, I don't know.

"Hey," I call, waving at the creature.

"Good evening," it bellows back, its voice rough and hoarse; if I didn't make a pun of it, I'd be cowering in fear and standing downwind.

"What can I help you with?"

He trots up to the door, leering at us, and extends a sinewy hand. "You must be Dr. Sun. I've heard great things."

It takes everything in me not to pinch my nose. They smell even worse than I'd heard. I take the proffered limb. It's wet and not just from the water. It's so slimy. I wish I was still wearing my surgical garb. "It's nice to meet you. Mr...." I trail off, waiting for him to offer a name. I'm quite confident it's a him, as he didn't bother to cover up his skinless horse appendage.

"Caimbeulach," he says. That's a hell of a name.

"Mr. Caimbeulach," I attempt.

"I was hoping you could"—he hesitates, scratching at his neck, producing a puckering sound—"help me with my"—his voice grows quiet—"halitosis."

"Oh!" It's kind of a quirk of his species. Is there anything I can even do for that? "It's not really anything I'm experienced in, but I can certainly take a look. I assume you've tried mints."

"Of course I've tried them." He sounds like he wants to eat me, so I avoid any other obvious suggestions.

"It could be something to do with your gastrointestinal tract or kidneys." I barely know anything about the subject, but it would make sense. The question is, if it's something that his body produces naturally, can we cure it without issue? Assuming we can even get him inside. "Can you fit through the door?"

He eyes it, considering. He doesn't have depth perception, so I wonder if he can manage. "I'm not sure."

We don't have a portable X-ray machine. Maybe he could fit through the back, but the animals are boarded back there. "Ollie, would you take the dogs out of their cages and keep them in the lobby? I'm going to take him in through the freight door."

It takes the better part of half an hour to finagle him into the X-ray room, but I run some scans, and there doesn't seem to be anything unusual about his stomach other than that it's visible from the outside. "What do you eat?" I ask.

"Humans."

"That's probably not great for it. We're full of so many gross chemicals and things that may not react that well. Are you drinking enough water?"

He recoils in shock, almost kicking the X-ray machine over. That would've been fun to deal with. "Are you insane?"

"Have you ever actually tried it?"

"Well, no, but it repels me. I couldn't handle doing that."

There's a water cooler in the hallway, so I fetch him a paper cup. "Come on out here." I beckon. I would rather he not back up into the machine.

He approaches hesitantly, eyeing me. "I can't."

"Try."

He takes a few steps, his hooves clopping on the tile floor. "It's unnerving."

"I know, but you need to drink water if you want to fix your breath."

Finally closing the distance between us, he peers at the cup, before quickly snatching it with his massive hands. His eye tears up as he pulls it to his mouth, which has to be a full meter wide. "I don't think I can."

"Just try it." Worst that could happen is it kills him.

With one last shaky breath, he screws his eye shut and swallows the cup's worth in a single gulp. A few seconds pass as nothing happens, and he slowly lifts his eyelid, peering down at me. "I'm okay?"

"You seem to be."

"Huh." Staring in shock at the cup, he takes a step back.

"Try to drink eight glasses of water a day, and maybe lay off the humans. If the halitosis doesn't clear up in a few weeks, come back, and we'll try to figure it out."

"Okay," he stammers. "Thank you."

"It's no problem." I bill him there, not wanting to take him to the lobby where the dogs are sequestered. I didn't think that through. He pays up and heads off into the night to make his creepy way on his own. He left blood, and I don't even want to think about what else, all over the floor. Why couldn't the pixies have been my second patients of the night?

Chapter Fourteen

Amelia: My Girlfriend

I wake up to find Ollie's arm draped across me. I'm hardly going to complain, but this is a surprise. We've barely even cuddled, only enjoyed each other's presence. I hold on to her arm, pressing against her, feeling her coldness, her proximity. I hate getting sentimental, but I think I really like this girl.

She stirs but doesn't seem to wake. I risk disturbing her by resting my head on her chest and feel her arm wrap about my lower back. I guess this is happening.

I expect to feel her breathing, but instead, her chest is still. That will take some getting used to. I look up at her rapidly shifting eyelids, the slightly strained expression on her face, the sweat sticking her hair to her face. I guess that answers that question. Vampires *do* sweat. I knew they couldn't be that perfect.

I start to rise only to find her clutching tighter as she releases a shuddering breath. She wasn't even breathing a second ago, but now it's growing rapid. She twists and rolls over, yanking me with her and pulling me on top. Her breathing slows again, then stops. I don't even risk moving for a long moment, and simply rest my forehead against her back. Her skin is damp.

"Ollie?" I ask, slowly pulling back.

She releases me and rolls over again, taking up my side of the bed. Maybe she's waking up. Was it a bad dream? In lieu of an answer, she remains a silent corpse, having somehow stolen all of the pillows. Greedy slut.

I stand up and run a hand through my hair. Am I supposed to wake her? I guess she wasn't screaming or anything, but I don't know what her dreams are normally like. How do I not know what her dreams are like? Have I never seen her sleep?

I try to think back on the last couple days. This is the third time she's slept in my bed, and she even went to bed at the same time as me the other night, but I must've always fallen asleep before her and woken up after her. That's weird to think. I wonder if vampires need less sleep. Does she even need sleep at all?

I climb into the shower, and the hot water does little to stop my thoughts. I know she has PTSD, and I know how much both Iago and humans have done to fuck her up. I'm guessing that dream was something to that effect. Is that an every night kind of thing? She'd mentioned something of the sort before, but I hadn't realized it was this bad.

A knock rings out from the bathroom door. "It's open."

"Just making sure you're okay," she calls feebly, sounding like she's speaking to the ground.

"Oh, can you not cross running water?"

A quick giggle. "I absolutely can. I…you're in the shower."

"The centuries-old lesbian is embarrassed. Forgive me, I'd assumed it was nothing you hadn't seen before." I consider stepping out and seeing how she reacts, but there's still conditioner in my hair. And I suppose I'd also rather not rush the poor thing.

"I assure you, it's not," she manages, a faint hint of cockiness returning to her tone. "Didn't want to presume."

"Want to make breakfast? Maybe someone dropped it off again."

And now my doorknob's broken. At least, I assume that's what that sound of wrenching metal was. If it was the towel rack, I'd be able to see her.

"You okay?"

"Don't even joke about that. We don't want him breaking in here, remember?"

"It's not him. It's a henchman. And we do want that, actually, if you'll recall. It gives us information which we can use to track him down and figure out his plans. It's why we have cameras. And claymores." I guess the mines won't help get information, but they could still be effective in their own way.

"I'll make breakfast."

Maybe teasing her about the man who spent decades manipulating and abusing her isn't the best idea. Do I have any opiates left? Uppers would make me all the more anxious, and I'm not up for that, even if I might need it to stay awake today.

By the time I'm dried off and dressed, it's a little past six, and I head into the kitchen to find Olivia already dressed, going through the cupboards for something to make. "You didn't want a shower?"

"I'm fine."

"I mean, you got all sweaty."

"I don't sweat."

"Yes. You do."

She sighs, turning to me. "Do you want me to shower?"

I shrug. She doesn't stink or anything, but I assumed she'd want one. "Up to you."

When she finishes her shower, I'm still waiting for her in the kitchen.

"You look amazing," I say.

She rolls her eyes. "What time do you need to be at the office?"

"As long as I'm there by seven thirty, we'll be fine. Want to grab breakfast instead? I haven't had my favorite restaurant's peameal bacon in years. It's a little too far."

Ollie fixes me with a smirk as she works on her hair. "Are you only dating me for my car?"

"Well, now that you mention it…"

She bares her fangs.

"We can talk about it in the car." I grab my bag, and she acquiesces. As soon as the engine purrs to life, we're already on the road. "You don't need directions?"

"I looked it up. It's practically a straight shot from here. I don't think I'll get lost."

"All right." She could pretend it's harder to find. It makes me feel worse about my laziness for never going. "Did you sleep okay?" I ask, knowing the answer to it full well but wanting to know if she's up for talking about it.

"Not any worse than usual."

"It was nice waking up in your arms." I feel absolutely insane as soon as the words leave my mouth. What am I thinking? There's someone trying to kill me, and I'm not some lovestruck teen. I like her,

I do, but I didn't think I was that far gone. Can I throw myself out of the car now? "I mean, it was just a surprise. We haven't done anything like that before, and I didn't expect it. But I liked it. You smell good." Yes. That saved it. I don't sound even crazier.

"I hadn't realized I'd done that." Tucking a lock back behind her ear, she glances at me. It's not even six thirty, so the roads aren't exactly full of obstacles. "I'm sorry I've been so weird." With a heavy groan, she turns her gaze back to the road. "I know I must be sending incredibly confusing messages, climbing into your bed and refusing to even touch you."

"You want to protect me. I understand."

"I wish that's all it was." She apparently feels that this is an adequate explanation, as she says nothing to elaborate. I want to pry words from her, to drag out any explanation I can manage. To ask questions, to do something, but I know how scared she is. Hell, I'm utterly terrified. I don't date. Oh no, I'm cheating on drugs. I'm sorry, oxycodone, can you ever forgive me? She turns to me before we leave the car, looking like she wants to say something, but she shuts her mouth and doesn't say another word until we take our seats in the old-fashioned diner.

"What's good here?"

"Their omelet's pretty good, and I love their bacon. Nothing's too bad. I like their milkshakes."

Since we are in a bit of a hurry, Olivia waves the waitress over and we order two omelets, some peameal bacon, and a milkshake to split. "I wanted to," she finally says.

"Wanted to what?"

"Anything," she cries exasperatedly. "I thought maybe it wouldn't be that difficult. You're just one human—no offense—you shouldn't be that scary. I've slept with other human women without issue, and I've certainly killed more than my fair share. I didn't think it'd be that different with you. But it is."

"How so?" I take a sip of my water. I'm not sure how to take any of that.

She rolls her eyes, more dramatically than I feel is strictly necessary. "What do the kids call it these days? I haven't dated in a few centuries. I like you? I think I saw that on TV."

"Oh." Biting my lip, I turn my gaze down to the table. It's not like

I didn't know. We've both made our attraction clear. Hell, we've made out a few times. It's still nice to hear. "I like you too."

She rises, walks around the table, and gives me a quick peck on the lips before taking her seat again. "Now's just a terrible time for it."

"Personally, I'd rather have romance before I die than after. I guess." That didn't sound near nihilistic enough. Is my depressive episode ending early? Am I broken? I don't like it.

"Can we talk about it more tonight? I know it's not like it used to be, but it still feels strange being so blatant in public."

"You're the one who kissed me."

"Forgive an old fogey her occasional eccentricities."

"You better be really good in bed."

"I am."

My cheeks only slightly heat, and we make it through the rest of breakfast without any drama. Their bacon is as good as I remember, and the omelets and milkshake are absolutely perfect. I only have to make it through another day of work with Olivia staring over my shoulder the entire time before we can have that conversation. Wow. That sounds like hell.

❖

I collapse onto my couch, letting Ollie carry my bag. Super-strong girlfriends are useful that way. Wait, I mean dates. She's not my girlfriend. "Whose bright idea was it to put the centaur in the MRI machine?"

"Yours."

"It would've been easy if he'd held still."

"Of course," she says placatingly, setting my bag on the counter and giving some grapes and food mix to Harvey. "Did you miss us?"

"Miss us," he echoes, nuzzling her finger and grabbing a grape right out of her hand. "Grape!"

"That's right." She sits next to me, her fingers tapping a slow beat on her thigh. "So," she begins, cutting herself short to stare at her bird, then me again.

"You're rusty at this."

"Incredibly."

I smirk. It's nice being the one more accustomed to relationships for once. It's only been five years since my last serious one ended. "I'm enjoying dating you."

"I am as well. You're a very interesting woman."

"I'm not sure I deserve that." I lean back, staring at my fridge, willing a beer to come meet me. It doesn't work. I guess I'll have this conversation sober. I do my best to ignore the pills in my jacket pocket that could help with that. "I'm sorry we're both so terrible at this," I add with a wry chuckle.

"I'm not sure I'd be able to handle being with someone who wasn't."

And that's what we need to talk about. We can work our way up to it. I hesitantly reach out to her, meeting her eyes, searching for an answer to my unasked question. She doesn't give one, but she doesn't stop me either, so I drape my arm across her shoulders. "Is this too much?" I ask.

I can see how badly she wants to leap out of her skin, but she grabs my elbow before I can pull away and leans her head against me. I don't pull her closer, and she doesn't reach for any further contact, but it's something. "I'm such a coward," she says.

"No. You're not. You've just been through more than anyone should ever have to go through."

With a heavy sigh, she nods, and leans back against my arm, her eyes half-lidded. It's not exactly comfortable, but it's nice. It's the most intentional prolonged physical contact we've ever had. It reminds me of how good a kisser she is, but I don't want to push for more. I don't know why some things are harder than others, and I have absolutely no idea how to predict what would be which.

After long enough without her response, I say, "I don't want to put any pressure on you." This sounds ridiculous. I have no idea what I'm doing.

"It's not that," she insists. "I do want this."

"Want what?"

"You," she whispers. She turns to me, her cheek resting against my bicep. We both swallow audibly.

It's not every day you hear a fiend wants you, and they don't mean for dinner. "Like you want me in bed, or you want me…" I trail off, finding a lump in my throat. Just what is she asking?

Hesitantly, she reaches toward me, her fingers trembling as they brush my other shoulder. With a slight case of whiplash, I find her eyes mere inches from my own. God, I'd forgotten how beautiful they are. Scratch that first word. I'm working on it, I swear.

"Ollie—"

Her kiss silences me, our fingers intertwining. We kiss for so long that if I don't take in some air soon, I may suffocate, and she pulls away, her eyes locked on the floor, her fingers beating out an erratic rhythm on the back of my hand. "I don't know how to do this."

"I think you're pretty good at it."

She rolls her eyes but forces them to meet mine again. "I've not courted anyone since my late wife. I felt that I didn't have the right to. Not after what I'd done."

"That wasn't your fault."

She shrugs. Maybe someday, she'll believe me. "I know. But I still made vows to her, before God, to share my life with her."

"She died. Even the Bible is okay with people taking new wives after the previous one dies." And a bunch of awful things, but I won't get into any of the fun things I learned taking my cynical asshole courses. I know one story that would be a more relevant anecdote. "Take Job. He took a new wife after everything God put him through, and it was treated as a good thing. Hell, it was what he deserved. It was giving him a good life for all he'd gone through." And there were so many issues there. "Do the same for yourself. You've more than earned it." Wait, am I saying she should marry me? "But like, dating. I'm not ready to rush into anything just yet. I'm not the U-Haul type."

"What does that mean?"

Right. I'm dating a lesbian from before cars were even a thing. "Do you know what a U-Haul is?"

"It's like a moving van, right? I think I've seen them before."

"Well, there's a classic joke. What does a lesbian bring on a first date?"

She chuckles. "Oh. I get it. That does go with what I've heard, and what I've experienced from the handful of women I've been willing to fool around with."

"You gotta cut 'em loose." Are we horrible people?

"For once, I don't want that."

Swallowing a new lump in my throat, I yearn yet again for that beer. I'm almost desperate enough to go get it, but I'd have to stop looking into her eyes, and I'm not sure I could handle that right now. "Then what do you want? I mean me, you already said that, but like, what? I'm not running off to marry you before you sail off to war." I may have downloaded Othello to read while I was waiting for its villain to come murder me.

Biting her lip in an adorably bashful smile, she leans back. "I'm going about this all wrong. How about I order you dinner? Maybe it'll be easier to talk over food."

Part of me desperately wants to fight her. I need to insist that I want the answer now, that we can have the conversation and figure out what we want to be to each other, but most of me is a coward with commitment issues who hasn't had pizza in a week. "I have a menu on the counter from a local place. They're really good, and they deliver here." Maybe all of me is a pizza-loving coward, and that romantic part is only my imagination. It's certainly never been there before. Maybe I just feel like it should happen, or perhaps it's the adrenaline and fear from knowing that I could die at any moment.

While watching the beautiful woman in my kitchen order a couple pizzas and some breadsticks, however, I can't even pretend that that's true. I'm not a lovestruck teenager or anything so saccharine, but I like her, and I want her to be my…my…

"Should be here in twenty minutes," she announces, returning to the couch with a beer for me and a mug of warmed blood for her. "I put the kettle on. I hope you don't mind."

I stare at my beer, scratching into the thin blue label with my thumb. Fuck it. "Be my girlfriend."

Her eyes widen, and she coughs up some blood, trying to catch her breath. That should be more of a turnoff than it is. "What?"

"I like you. A lot. I might die any day now, so it's not like some long commitment. I want to be with you. Be my girlfriend."

She rubs a speck of red liquid off my cheek. I am trying very hard not to think about what it is and instead concentrate on her eyes. She nods.

"Yes?"

"Yes. I want it too, although I think girlfriend is an incredibly childish term."

"Womanfriend?"

She glares. "Partner."

Right. I shiver. Why is that word so much scarier? It should be less scary. Girlfriend only has two meanings; partner has dozens. We could be a law firm or going on a crime spree. It shouldn't sound that serious, but it does. I do my best to stop myself from clamming up and nod. She did it first, so it seems a sufficient response. I want this. I know I do. Why the hell is it this terrifying?

❖

Sleepy, full of pizza, and with a beautiful woman in my bed, I'm beginning to think that being her partner isn't as scary as I thought it'd be. It's not like we have to go antiquing or anything. I sigh, staring at her hair a couple feet from me. She tried to cuddle, and we made it a while, but it was still too much for her to sleep like that. I can't blame her. I toss and turn too much to want to sleep in someone's arms anyway.

Harvey squawks from the other room. "Shut up," I mutter under my breath. I don't want to wake up Olivia. He squawks again. Why are parrots such jerks?

Groaning, I drag myself from bed, wearing comfy flannel pajamas, to check on the noisy bird. I snatch my phone from its charger to avoid turning on any lights. We didn't lock him in his cage, so I'm not sure where he is, but it only takes a minute to locate him. He seems almost frantic, flapping, jumping, flying, squawking, and singing.

"Harvey?" I ask. Because of course, the bird can tell me what he wants. He's totally smart enough for that.

"Pretty," he replies. I guess that's gonna be my name forever. Or until one of us dies. I wonder who'll go first? Parrots tend to live fifty to seventy years, so he's getting up there, but I have a psychopath after me and a drug problem, so I'm probably well past my life expectancy. "Othello."

"No. You know she doesn't like that."

"Moor. Moor."

I roll my eyes. "Did you want something, or are you just feeling playful tonight?" I think Ollie would kill me if I gave him some oxy, but it'd calm him down.

"Othello."

"Okay. How about food. Do you want food? Carrot?"

"Carrot. No. Othello."

Whatever. I grab a couple of the remaining canned carrots from the fridge and drop them in his dish. "I'm going to bed. Some of us have work in the morning." With a final glare, I turn back to my bedroom and see movement in the corner of my eye. Everything goes black.

CHAPTER FIFTEEN

He's Back

I flee. I can still feel her blood pouring through me, caking my mouth, staining my hands. Guilt gnaws at me as I search for anyone else to blame. What have I become? Why would I do that to her? Why did she smell like food?

I shake my head, trying to still my mind. I expect to feel my heart beating in my chest but only feel this strange silent emptiness. It's like there's nothing there. How appropriate. Kill my love, and I kill my heart.

I have to turn myself in. I'll not have Desdemona's murder left unsolved, nor pretend that she vanished into the night. She deserves better than that. She's the best woman I've ever known, and I'll face my penance, no matter the cost. I did this, and I have to pay. Perhaps the executioner is free on the morrow.

I find myself outside, the dark night doing little to dampen my senses. There doesn't seem to be a soul around. Of course, Hector isn't making his rounds. I'll see him...Right, I suppose that Iago or Cassio will be the ones to see to that now. It seems unlikely that I'll keep command from my cell or the hangman's noose.

In vain, I attempt to compose myself. In a nearby pond, I check my reflection to find it lacking. Truly, it is queer to stare into a reflective surface and find myself not there. What am I? I'd thought I'd gone mad, but it must be something more. No human could simply not be there. Perhaps I truly am the son of the devil, as I've heard a few of the greener recruits insist when they believe I'm not listening. I splash some water on my face in the hope of ridding myself of her blood. It washes her scent away, and I find myself yearning for that familiar presence. It's as if she's died all over again.

The tears fall for a long while. I know I don't deserve them. After what I did, I have no right to mourn her, and yet I can't keep myself from doing so. I miss her.

Steeling myself, I search for Cassio's post. He's normally on watch at this time of night, but only halfway there do I remember that I'd stripped him of his charge at Iago's recommendation.

He had been insistent that Desdemona had committed adultery, almost as if he wanted it to be true. Now, I know, I did smell him on her, but it wasn't…I don't know how to describe it. The mere fact that I could identify a person by their smell brings me into a realm of language that I lack the words for. To put it crudely, she didn't smell like sex. He'd been to talk to her, as he had many times since I had him stripped of his title. He only wanted her help because she's the one person good enough to have believed him at his word, and for that crime, I murdered her.

The connection between the events finally begins to dawn on me. Zounds, am I slow! I cross myself, my mind racing. It burns. I deserve this.

But it isn't all my fault. I dealt the killing blow, this is true. I'm no better than Brutus, but I shall take my Cassius with me. I shall turn myself in, I shall face the executioner—I believe it's Marco of Venice, today—but I shall be Iago's executioner first. I shall end him for the lies he spread and the tangled web he weaved. I'll listen to no more of his words, for his mouth is that of a serpent, spreading nothing but lies. The time for discussion is well past. My blade is not at my side, but the armory is near, and none would dare stop their commander, even in my current state.

Anon, I'm equipped for battle against whatever beast my dear friend may be. Perhaps he's the monster he made me, or perhaps he's simply a witch. I suspect that without his head, the difference shall be one of speculation rather than of any practicality.

My fist thunders against his door. I shall have my satisfaction, and it will not wait for dawn. Emilia answers, uttering some cry of surprise and dismay as I shove past her, my weapon already drawn as I search for the merciless bastard who has taken everything from me.

"Othello?" he asks, scrambling from his bed, wrapping a robe about himself. As if this fiend has any modesty left to preserve.

"Iago," I growl back.

"What is this about?" he asks, his eyes locked behind me. He thinks he can protect Emilia from the truth. I'm afraid the truth comes for us all in time, and it is never sweet. I take a swing at his head, the blade moving faster than I thought possible. Perhaps this curse can be a gift in ending him. It's not only my senses. I'm stronger. Faster. Yes, I can use this.

A wicked smile flits across his face for the barest moment as he leaps away from me. "Emilia, get out of here!" he bellows. "I'll see to it that this freak does you no harm." I remember now. I remember him biting me. He did make me into this. Why? Now I recall that look of revulsion on his face. He'd come to call on me the previous night, and Desdemona had answered the door before I'd finished making myself decent. He found out my secret. He'd already found it agonizing being commanded by a Moor, but a Moorish woman living in sin with another woman? I suppose I should have no doubt as to why he'd attempt this treachery.

"A freak, am I?" I ask, not even bothering to deepen my voice. He knows the truth, and I'll soon hang. It hardly matters now. "What does that make you?" I ask, rage carrying my words with enough intensity that he recoils in fear. I was always the better fighter. I suspect that has not changed.

"Your better," he bellows back. He reaches for something behind him and comes out with a saber. "Oh, to think I groveled at your feet these past years. As if serving a blackamoor wasn't enough, you kept this treachery from me? Was I not your dearest friend, Othello? Did I not serve you faithfully all these years, Othello? When was my turn? When was it my time to stop being at the heel of a roach and have the chance to prove myself?" He steps toward me, managing a lunge that would have taken off an ordinary man's arm. I deflect it without the slightest effort as I circle around, putting the wall to my back and both Iago and Emilia before me. She didn't run.

"Thereby leaves any question I may have had. It's because of you that Desdemona is dead! You will pay for it."

"Ms. Desdemona is dead?" Emilia cries, looking between our maddened eyes for any semblance of truth. "But how? She can't be."

"Her freak of a husband—or is it wife—made sure of that."

"He deceived me for months and performed some dark magic on me. What have you done to me, Iago?" I told myself it didn't matter, that I didn't need to know, but it's all so strange. I just want answers.

"I've elevated you far beyond your station. Now, if you'll serve me, we can go back to our proper places, provided that you remember yours."

"I do."

He smirks, straightening, his weapon lowering. He thinks so little of me? That I would join the man who did this? Who led me to kill the only woman I'll ever love? I remember my place. The gallows. Right after him. I take one step toward him, lowering my own blade, and dash forward, bringing it up from belly to throat. It splits him open, covering us both in a shower of blood. I've done it. I've avenged you, Desdemona.

He stares down in shock. Blood loss shall claim him soon, and Emilia will run and tell the constables. It's better this way. "Basely done, Othello." What? He steps away, sauntering slowly but purposefully to Emilia as she looks on in shock. "You really are no better than your animal nature. I don't know why they thought you a suitable governor." His mouth opens wide, fangs protruding from his gums as he sets upon his wife, holding her in place, blood pouring down, staining her dress. After a few weak whimpers, the only sound in the room is the greedy gulps of the wicked monster. We're the same now, aren't we? Wife killers. Monsters. Damned.

I find my wits and move on him again. I could have saved her. Instead, I watched the blood pour out. Why? Was I too hungry again? At the last moment, he dashes out of the way, and the blade takes off Emilia's head. This strength will take some getting used to.

"Now, now, Othello. If you were hungry you could have told me. I'd have let you have your turn."

"You bastard."

Quicker than I can react, he's before me, his hand on my chin. How is he this much faster than me? "It seems you need training. Bianca!"

Jumping back from him, I feel something smash into my head. It feels like I've been run through the entirety of St Mark's Basilica, hitting each and every wall and ledge along the way. I don't even see stars. The world goes black around me. He's won.

I jerk awake, still feeling the throbbing in my head. As ever, it dissipates when I return to the waking world. I suppose if I must be haunted by dreams, I'm glad it's the one time I did the right thing. The one time I wasn't a coward. The last time I wasn't a coward. Loathing myself slightly more than usual, I sigh, and it turns into a yawn as I stretch. My hands meet both pillows, and I find the bed empty. "Mia?"

Would she have left for work without me? She certainly wanted to. Maybe I *have* been a little too demanding. "Mia?" I call again, louder this time. There're no sounds in the entire apartment save for an occasional squawk. I can't hear her breathing, her heartbeat. This isn't good.

As if in answer, the phone on the nearest nightstand buzzes loudly. That's not mine. "Hello?" I ask.

"Mia?" I recognize the voice. That man from her office, her direct superior, I believe. "Where are you? It's past nine."

Shit. Where is she? I've never tried mesmerizing someone when I couldn't see them, but it works over Skype. Maybe it'll work on the phone. "She called in sick last night. Do you not remember?"

"Of course I do. I must have forgotten to write it down. I've been such an asshole, blowing up her phone like that. Tell her I'm sorry, Olivia."

"Of course." He'd already been under my thrall the last few days. I wonder if it would work on someone who hadn't yet experienced my control. I may have the opportunity to find out, as I'm not sure I have enough favors to call in for this.

Before I give in to my fears, I throw myself out of bed and check every room. I listen, look, and smell for any sign of her, but she seems to be gone. Swallowing, I glance outside. My car's still there, so she didn't take it and go get groceries, and she doesn't seem the type to go for a run. Especially when she was supposed to be at work.

Amelia is missing, and there's one very obvious explanation for it. He has her.

I throw myself from the bed, toss some food in Harvey's cage, and lock him in, then search the apartment with every sense I can manage. If I can figure out how to sleuth with proprioception, I'll do that as well.

There's a missed call on my phone, but it's from Elizabeth. No ransom demand, then. It takes the better part of an hour, but I find a few footprints outside. I have to steady my breathing and blink away tears just to examine it. Men's size ten, so not too helpful—but I also find a broken lightbulb in the garbage. It wasn't there the previous night. It has to be a sign of a struggle. She was attacked. For an instant I can smell the thatch roof burning, but I find only an unburned stucco ceiling when I look up.

I take a few more deep breaths. I can worry later. Now I have to act. Whoever was in here was good. They left no other visual trace, and their scent is covered by a powerful cologne mixed with patchouli and I believe, deer urine. Assuming he made any effort to clean off afterward, it's going to take a lot of work to extract his scent from the other aromas.

Collapsing on a barstool at her counter, I throw my head into my hands. Okay, Olivia, Ollie, think. Right, we installed cameras. Christ…I cross myself. I'm stupid. I swear, it's been long enough. I should be used to the idea that technology can solve one's problems by now. Maybe I'll believe that when I start using my phone for directions. Change is hard.

I check the recordings and feel bile rising in my throat as I see a man snatch Mia from her kitchen. She doesn't even have the chance to fight back, but a plate is knocked off the counter. I fast-forward through the tape, looking for anything I can use. He parked in the blind spots of our cameras outside, and he was wearing gloves and a mask, except—there, right there. He had to adjust his mask after he picked her up. I pull it back, fractions of a second at a time, and find a clear image of his face from his nose down. Just an ordinary human. Of course he'd use one of them to hunt me. No, he doesn't know about the Hunt; he's just using what's practical. Don't let him get even more in your head, Ollie. I pause for a second, staring at the screen. I'd never called myself that before.

It can wait. This photo is far more pressing. It's not much, but if it's all I have, perhaps I can ask around. Other fiends make use of human mercenaries from time to time when absolutely necessary, and it seems unlikely that this one would be solely in Iago's employ. I need to inquire for more information at the Community Center.

With a renewed purpose, I throw on some proper clothes, strap my sword and pistol to my hips, and toss the shotgun and extra ammunition into a duffel bag. It's a little small, as she presumably did not intend to use it for this, but it will have to do. I *will* find my girlfriend. Damn it, now I'm saying it.

I make a few calls on the way over, but neither of my contacts have anything. If I want some useful information for insider trading or who's winning tonight's races, that they can give me, but apparently, finding Mia is a little too past their abilities. I shove my phone into my back pocket, grab the duffel bag from the passenger seat, and march inside, keeping an eye out for anyone suspicious.

Of course, it's 11:15 on a weekday, so anyone in here is suspicious. Most of the stands are empty, and the few shops have their shutters pulled down. I pray I won't have to wait until tonight to find anything out. He'll torture her like he did me. I'd sooner die than let that happen to her. Even if it means I have to face him.

"Sven!" I call near his store, checking for any sign of him. Damn it, I need someone who might know something. Who'd be better for that task than a paranoid nutter? Grumbling, I move to a nearby bakery stall. Unless I want to buy some cupcakes, no one seems to have anything helpful.

"Is everything all right?" one of the identical fauns asks me.

Fuck it, maybe the hellbound bastard likes baked goods. "Have you seen this man?" I ask, holding up a printout of his face. It took me longer than I'd care to admit to figure out her printer.

He shakes his head and turns to his partner.

"I'm afraid not, dear. Have you asked Carlos?"

I rack my brain for a Carlos. "No. Who?"

"I suppose you're not often here in the day. He does a lot of stock market stuff, helped us score the money to start this stand in a single night, but he'd probably have more info."

One doesn't need a license to start a stand here. It's a black market. Does he mean the money for enough ingredients? That's not that impressive from insider trading. My guy could've gotten them a real bakery in the same amount of time. "Could you point me to him?"

I follow his directions to find a short, dark-haired man. He looks human, though slightly too perfect, and smells faintly of the fae. "Changeling," I greet him. I have such great manners when I'm pissed.

"Vampire."

"Have you seen this man?" I hold up the photo. I need to be nicer.

If I piss off the closest thing to a lead I've found, I'm well beyond fucked. I won't let him take another woman from me. I can't. "Please. It's urgent."

"I have," he replies, grinning broadly.

Holy shit. "You have? Really? Oh, thank you. Tell me everything. What do you want for it?" I'll give anything. He can have my house, my companies, whatever he wants. I have to stop Iago.

"No need. I was already paid."

"What?"

"Yeah, this guy in the photo, he came to me and told me that if you ever came around asking about him, to give you this letter. I can't tell you anything more. I don't serve both sides if this is some sort of feud."

I bare my fangs. He just told me he was siding with Iago, and I will need some energy if I'm to walk right into a trap.

Outside, I wipe the changeling blood from my lips while I drop him to the ground—can't hurt anyone inside, that's against the rules. I finally read the note. It's an address, one not far from here. It doesn't say anything else. Wow, I was expecting taunting or some dramatic threat. Maybe he's mellowed in his old age. Pathetic whining sounds come from the pitiful excuse for a mortal who would dare side with that monstrosity as I head back to my car, leaving him to bleed on the ground.

❖

His hideout isn't the ostentatious castle I'd expected from his ego. It looks more like something an American doomsday prepper would have. There are no windows, and it's either quite small or largely underground. Either way, it has ornate double doors for the entrance. Only he would do that.

The doors fly off their hinges with a single kick. "You damnable coward!" I shout through the empty halls, causing a scurrying from deeper within the bunker. "I'll have your head, you pitiful, ignorant, utterly mad knave of a man."

A bullet tears into my shoulder. It hurts like a son of a bitch, but I do my best to ignore it. He's given away his position.

In an instant, I'm beside the man from the photograph, the man who hurt Mia. He's a mere human, as I thought. I tear him open, his blood filling me up. I hadn't bothered to take it all from the last idiot, but this one deserves to die.

He promptly does so.

The air stinks of betrayal and lies. Iago must be nearby. "Come out here, you murderous, manipulative son of a whore," I call, readying my sword in one hand and my pistol in the other. He'll burn. I'm done being his victim. I'm done letting him do as he will, hurting and manipulating people throughout the world. It won't happen again. I won't let it.

"Othello."

My vision goes red as I spin, my blade pointed right at his throat. "Iago." My voice is scarcely more than a snarl.

He pays the sword no mind. His features spread into a warm and genuine smile. "By God's wounds, man, it has been too long." He takes a step to the side, and I prepare to parry. Instead of striking, however, he claps me on the back and quickly dodges my riposte. "Oh, how I've missed you. I'm glad you're finally home."

Does he really need to take the Lord's name in vain? Hasn't he done enough? I cross myself with my gun hand. The pain grounds me as I force myself to concentrate. I'm here to kill him. He took her. He took both of them from me. He takes everything I love. Fuck, I need to focus. I try another swipe of my blade and don't land anywhere near him.

He giggles mischievously, sounding more like a ten-year-old in the midst of a prank than a sociopath carving a bloody swath through humankind. "Oh, Othello. Crossing yourself already. You always were the good Catholic girl. Of course, when I knew you, you were more of a good Catholic boy."

"Enough!" I swing at him, but he steps out of my weapon's path without the slightest difficulty.

"Very well, you can be Olivia now, if that's what you want."

"I want you to hand her over."

He cocks his head, narrowing his eyes as if he can't quite place his finger on who I'm referring to. "Her?" He places his hand on his chin as he stares up at the ceiling. "Oh, you mean your midnight snack. Of course she's yours. I simply assumed you were full after eating my man."

"She's not food."

"Oh, I beg to differ. Humans are food at most and toys at the least."

Another swing, another dodge. "Iago," I growl.

"But we have so much to catch up on. All these years, all this time, I've been waiting for you. I knew you'd come back to me—it was never in question—but I didn't expect you to be this resilient. You always were far stronger than Bianca, but women, and…what is the term now? Blacks? I think Moor went out of fashion a few centuries back. Well, they need a firm guiding hand."

He catches my blade in midair. That cocky grin I always loathed. He hasn't changed a bit. The lean, gaunt boy with his slick black hair and the attitude that the world owes him everything.

Since he's so busy holding my sword, I take the moment to fire a round right into his belly. He seems more stunned by the surprise than by the round igniting inside him. I take my chance and advance, cutting a black line across his chest and another one in his thigh, deep enough that the dark coagulated blood of his last victim oozes onto the floor. "I won't let you hurt her."

Laughter fills the room. He takes a step back, the only sign that he's at all worried as he grins at me, clapping his hands together. "Bravo, Othello…sorry, Olivia. You are doing so much better than I'd thought. Perhaps you truly do deserve your sacred place at my side."

"Go to hell." I raise the gun to fire a round into his head, but by the time I pull the trigger, he's already gone. His fist slams into my side, feeling not unlike being struck by a lance on the end of a freight train.

I stumble several paces to the side, having to move with the blow to avoid falling to the ground. My gun comes up as I spin, aiming at where he'd just been, only for my legs to fly out from under me at a kick from behind. The hand on my throat brings me the rest of the way to the ground. "You've grown soft, my dear friend," he says, his voice conversational. "I expected better of you. When we first fought, you nearly bested me. I knew I'd chosen right. And now…look at yourself. On your back, beneath me, where you've always belonged, unable to so much as put up a fight." He lets out a hiss, his hand touching the hole in his belly. "Perhaps I'll have you fetch me a victim when this is all through. Maybe that harlot I have locked up."

I bring my feet up in an arc, slamming them into his head, pushing off the ground as I swing my sword in a wide arc, nearly taking his hand.

He leaps back, that smirk still unmarred. "So protective of what's yours. I do know that feeling." He rushes in, ducking under my strike, his shoulder slamming into my stomach while he grabs my leg and hurls me against the nearest wall.

Before I can right myself again, he's on me, and all I can do is block his blows as they shower down on me. I pull the trigger, the bullet not even grazing him, but the sound startles him enough that I can attempt to stab him.

He steps to the side, dodging with ease. "What do you think this will gain you? You think you'll save her and be the hero? You're no hero. You're exactly the monster I made you. The sinful freak who killed her own wife."

An involuntary shudder runs through me. I want to say that he's wrong, that I'm not that, that I know better, but I don't. I can't. I'm not. Lunging forward, I shove my blade right for his atrophied heart. He catches it again. "I don't mean to offend, my dearest friend. I simply speak the truth. Oh, but I do marvel at you. The last year must have been eating you up, knowing that I was there, knowing that that which you desired most was so close, and yet you couldn't touch it. It must've been the sweetest suffering. Tell me about it, please. For old times' sake."

Bile rises in my throat. "What the fuck are you talking about?"

He blinks, his playful façade finally dropping as he peers into my eyes. "What do you mean?"

"'That which I desired most'? Are you talking about Mia? We didn't meet until a few weeks ago."

"No, not the girl!" he all but screams, stepping toward me, his eyes wide and panicked, his hand sliding through his hair. In another instant, he's composed again, sneering down at me. "You really don't know? Oh, I can't believe this. Did you at least see the messages at your favorite hunting ground before they shut it down? Not the one for hicks. The one where you find the vampire chasers."

I shake my head, staring down, barely able to even process that. He's been there this whole time. He's been watching me for who knows how long, and I never suspected a thing until Bianca showed up. I thought I was free. I thought I'd escaped. And he was right here. I'm even dumber than I thought. "Bianca really did escape, didn't she?"

"Of course. I had to make an example of her. I had to show what happens if you disobey me again."

I'm such a fool. "How long has it been?"

"Since we last saw each other? Oh, centuries." He smiles, realization dawning on his face. "Oh, how long have I been watching you? Waiting? Playing our game? It's been…" He purses his lips, doing the calculations in his head. "A little under three years. You did a good job getting away, but you knew it couldn't be forever. You belong to me, Olivia. You always have, and you always will."

I swallow, finding my throat dry despite the liters of blood I drank today. I scramble back, pressing against the wall.

"About a year ago, I decided that it was time to begin the game anew—after all, you wouldn't notice me if I didn't—so I gave your crucifix, along with a few pounds of other silver jewelry—mostly crosses—to a local butcher, with instructions to make sure to offer it free with every transaction. With your love of a proper Italian meal, I knew it wouldn't take long. I wanted to see your face when you saw it, but wouldn't you know it, the little moron went and sold it all to some wendigo. He had no right. I thought you'd at least seen it." He places his hand on his chest, collecting himself. "Well, I've dealt with him. He'll not double-cross anyone else."

"You're one to talk."

"I'd never betray you, Olivia. I simply had to remind you of where you belong. Your place is at my feet, serving me. Those fools in Venice had allowed you past your station, and when that happens, people begin to get unhealthy ideas. It's no wonder you'd have these perversions."

"I'm not—"

He swats my weapon away. I didn't even realize I'd swung. "You are. You're my depraved pet, but I'll fix you right up. Of course, you'll have to go back in chains until I can trust you. But before long, you'll be back where you belong, serving me."

There's no way to stop him. He's been watching me. He'll take everything from me. All this time, and I'm right back where it all started.

My sword doesn't swing. I stare at my hand. Nothing is stopping me. He doesn't have any power like this, even as the one who turned me. I'm not his slave. This isn't him stopping me. It's me. I'm so fucked up, I can't even rescue my girlfriend. I'm such a coward, I can't even kill the man who has made my life a living hell. My sword clatters harmlessly on the ground, tears falling to join it. I'm so pathetic. I'm so weak. I can't do it.

God, please forgive me.

Chapter Sixteen

Amelia: Escape

My head hurts. Holy fuck, it hurts. I screw my eyes shut and bury them behind my hands as the light pricks at my eyeballs. What happened? I swear I didn't drink this much last night. I had one beer. Maybe two. Probably two. "Ollie?" I ask. I don't want to risk uncovering my eyes again. This doesn't feel like my bed. Oh, shit. I'm kidnapped, aren't I?

"I'm afraid she's not here just yet," a voice says from somewhere off to the side. The slight sound sends me doubling over. "You may have a bit of a concussion. There's some ibuprofen and a water bottle on the floor in there. Don't worry, you weren't out for long. I wouldn't expect any serious damage."

"You," I manage. Holy shit. This is…him. This is the man my girlfriend is beyond terrified of. This is the crazy bastard who seemed more like a cartoon character than any semblance of a person in the play. I don't want to take drugs from this psycho, but I also really want this pain to stop. The one time I leave home without opiates.

"Yes, me. Tell me, what exactly do you believe you can offer our mutual friend? I knew it was only a matter of time, though I'll admit, the centuries it took was a surprise, but I knew eventually her perversions would return and she'd find another young woman to corrupt. But really, just go free. Forget about her. She was mine first, and she'll be mine for centuries after. You're a pathetic little bug in the road."

"She absolutely didn't corrupt me." Okay, speaking hurts. Fine, I'll take his damn pills. I find them on top of some metal bars and manage to screw off the cap and swallow a handful of them along with the entire bottle of water. Hopefully, he'll keep being such a gracious host and give me more later. And maybe a toilet. "And if anyone doesn't deserve her, I'd say it's you. All you can bring her is pain."

"Pain? Is that what she told you?" I hear metal groaning and risk opening my eyes to see a hand grasping the bars of my cage. Am I in a giant bird cage? Goddamn, this guy is needlessly dramatic. "I brought her truth, clarity, purpose. I led her, as her kind isn't meant to lead. Of course, none of your kind is, either."

"Are you being racist against Asian people or humans? I want to know why I should be offended."

He gasps, looking as genuinely offended as an old racist can manage, which is to say, a lot. "I would never. Your people brought us gunpowder. Where would we be without it? Now, humans…you're certainly more of a lowly insect fit only for being food."

"Ew, you eat insects?"

With a snarl, he rolls his eyes and flounces to the corner of the room, straightening the tie of his three-piece suit. "Well, clearly, you can't play nice. Perhaps I should have some fun while I wait for Othello. It's not like I've offered to return you. I can torture you until you beg to join our ranks. When I'm done, perhaps, if you swear to serve me, I'll allow you to spend eternity with her."

"Nah, I'm good. You can kill me."

"I believe I can make you change your mind."

I lie down in my cage, staring up at the little roost above me. There're no giant newspaper scraps. It's like he didn't even try. "Wake me when Olivia is here." I'm not brave. At all. This isn't me making some stand. But I have no desire to become a vampire, little desire to live in general, and I'm absolutely certain that Olivia would never forgive me for giving in to him. The only possible outcomes are Ollie rescuing me, me dying, or my pissing him off enough that he slips up. And people say depression isn't a superpower.

Groaning, he stomps toward me, fangs glinting in my peripheral vision. I wish the ibuprofen would kick in already. Snorting oxy would work a lot faster. "Have anything harder than ibuprofen? I'd be fine with Vicodin. Morphine would be amazing."

He stops short, staring. "What?"

"You're the one who gave me this headache. Least you could do is give me something that'll actually help with it."

"I gave you plenty."

"Some host you are. Thought you old Italians were supposed to be all proper." I sigh, trying to ham it up as much as he would. "Do you want Olivia finding out that you treated her partner like this?"

The cage shakes as his hands slam against it, his dark green eyes burning into me. I swallow, feeling a shiver run unbidden through my body. I did say I wasn't brave. "You want medication? It's been provided for you. Now, if I hear one more word from you, I shall flay you alive. I know how to make it take days. It won't be the pain or the blood loss or even infection that will get you. In the end, when you don't have enough skin to keep you warm, it'll be the hypothermia. You'll freeze to death with heat mere inches away."

"Don't…" I hesitate, averting my eyes, my voice dropping. "Don't make a girl promises."

Laughter fills the room. I hear the cage door open. His footsteps rattle the metal bars beneath me. Another step and he's standing over me. I can try to run, but I know how fast vampires are. No. There's no way out of this alive. He'll do whatever he wants with me now. All because I decided that pissing off the ancient serial killer was the best plan. I swear, if I didn't know better, I'd think I had a death wish. Oh. Right.

Well, I can make sure that whatever he pulls is fatal. I jump to my feet, ramming my head into his nose, using the momentum to hit hard enough that it should break.

Instead, I find myself flung to the wall of the cage, toppling it with the two of us still inside. I'm flung around as it rolls to a stop, but when I look up, he doesn't have so much as a hair out of place. If I make it out of this, I need to ask where he buys his gel. "I think I'd rather make you suffer in front of her."

Holy shit. I get to live? I'm getting out of this?

There's a flash of movement, and searing pain runs up my arm. All my nerves are firing, and I can't focus my vision enough to see what happened. Oh God. I blink away the light only for tears to block my vision. The pain won't go away. It's like my entire arm is being filled with acid.

"Perhaps she'll recognize this. I suppose this is rather like sending her your penis, if I understand right." I can barely hear his words as he climbs out of the toppled cage.

I blink away the last of my tears and manage to focus on the source of my pain. There's nothing there to see. My right hand is gone.

"You're a doctor or something of the sort, are you not?" He tosses in a few bandages and a lighter. "Take care of that. I can't have you dying of blood loss before Othello gets the chance to see you. Now, if you'll excuse me, I have some business to attend to. She should be here any minute."

His footsteps recede, but I don't look up. I can't draw my attention away from the blood. I know how to handle this. I've done it for fiends before, but it's going to be a lot harder doing it myself. With only one hand. And, of course, he took my right hand because why leave someone with their good hand? That'd just be polite.

For several seconds, I consider letting myself bleed out. It's not like I haven't considered it before. No more than a thousand or two times, but it's passed my mind. It's supposed to be a peaceful way to go. I could let it happen. I'd get to give him the finger one last time.

But then again, he now has that finger, and I'd like to take it back.

I try to think of how Ollie would react to finding my lifeless body after going through all the trouble of rescuing me. Goddamn it. Hey, I get that one for free; even she can't argue that I haven't earned it. I guess I don't have a choice. This is gonna hurt a lot.

I stare at the tools he gave me. Does he really think I can cauterize an amputation? That's not a thing. It wouldn't even help. I mean, I guess if a person didn't have bandages it could maybe work as a last-ditch effort, but most of what it would do is cause a lot more damage. Goddamn savages, what medicine were they practicing five hundred years ago?

Now, if he'd given me some scissors or a knife, that would actually be useful. I grab the bandages, unwrapping them the best I can with my teeth, ripping them in the process, but not enough to make a huge difference. The world is already starting to go gray. I'm bleeding out. I have to act fast. I pull it taut between my mouth and hand and, holding it in place between my teeth, wrap the bandage about my arm as tight as I can, cutting off blood flow. When the tourniquet is complete and I have a lot more bandage and no reliable way to cut it, I wrap it around my arm a few more times, covering the bloody stump, and tuck it in place. I need a way to secure it better. This is barely going to hold, but I don't have a better option.

The door is open. It came off in the fall. I can leave. If I can get back up. I push against the cage, trying to pull myself up, and fall right back down, letting the hard floor and the cage wall comfort my injuries. I don't have anything left in me, damn near including blood, so I promptly pass out.

❖

I'm getting really tired of passing out and waking up in a cage. I'm not that kinky. I try to pull myself to my feet but find that one of my hands is having trouble finding leverage.

Oh.

Right. That hand's gone. Shit. Clambering out of the cage, I find the room empty. I wonder how long it's been. Has Olivia come? Has he…is she okay?

I try to step away from the cage but stumble to my knees. I'm still pretty woozy. One more injury and I get a free sandwich, right? I've got my punch card somewhere.

On my third try, I manage to stand and take a few tentative steps. My legs seem to hold me. Thank fuck he didn't take one of them.

It feels kind of weird leaving this room. I'd been sure I would die in that cage. Being able to walk out without anyone contesting it seems almost wrong. The walls are all stone, but I can hear a heater buzzing away and see some vents. I'm not in an ancient castle or anything. It looks more like a bunker.

I wander as quietly and slowly as I can, listening for any signs of anyone else. Could they have killed each other? Don't be dead, Ollie. I've been through way too much today to lose my new partner too. I need a good two weeks with you. I think I deserve that much.

When I'm starting to give up hope and am beginning to think that I should focus on escaping rather than investigating, I hear voices. "Never betray," filters in from a few rooms away, and that sadist's voice is as clear as ever. He does love to hear himself talk.

Crouching low, moving as quietly as I can, I head toward the source of the sound. It takes long enough that I'm certain they'll have killed each other before I can ever reach them, but when I finally arrive, they're just standing there, talking like old friends. Ollie's sword is lying on the ground next to her, and her gun is shaking in her hand. Her lip is trembling. She's not talking to him at all. She's having a PTSD flashback. I'm so sorry, honey.

"I'll ask again. Join me, dear friend. You're all I've yearned for all these years. My life is simply not complete without you." He traces a finger along her hair, his eyes on her vacant stare.

Even in her stupor, she takes a step back.

Chuckling, he moves on her, pushing her against the wall. "I've asked you nicely. I've been patient. For centuries, I've waited for you to come to your senses. What possible reason do you have to play with these humans? I saw that plaything of yours. She's spirited, but she's a fool. How could such a being entertain you?"

His hand presses against the wall behind her, pinning her between him and it. "I thought that after the Hunt, you'd realize that this fascination is unhealthy. It's a sickness, Othello. These people, they'll never understand you. They're monsters." Shows how well he knows her. She hates humans. She just hates him more. "My Moor, please. You're better than this."

My eyes fall on the cavalry saber left on the ground several paces before them. I'm not sure if I can do this, especially one-handed, but it's the only option I have. I creep toward her, my every motion minute, so focused on being quiet that I can hear the blood pounding in my ears.

"What if I promise to let you keep your pet? I'll even—" He slaps himself in the forehead. "I forgot all about your present." He starts to turn. My heart stops. This is it. I made it through all of that, and I'm going to die one foot from her sword. "Oh, where did I put it?" He glances to the side and pats his pockets. "Oh, that's right. I left it all set up for you. Let me take you there." He starts to turn around as exaggeratedly as one can.

Fuck it. The second he sees me, I'm dead. No sense wasting time now. I break into a sprint, grabbing the sword as I run.

I'm too slow. Those cold green eyes lock onto me. "What have we here?"

He's going to rush me. Judging by the holes Ollie must have put in him, he'll just drain me in one go. At least it'll be quick.

Ollie taught me how to swing a blade, but I don't know how to fight, not really. I can hope that those wounds make him slow, but even then, he's still a vampire. I don't stand a chance. I'll have to take his head off in a single swing. If he so much as touches me, it's already over. Maybe if it was the gun instead of her sword, I'd stand a chance. But, oh well, it was nice knowing her.

He charges, and my life flashes before my eyes. Wow, I did a lot of drugs. I stand by it.

The second he takes his first step, I swing. As fast as vampires are, early is already too late. I'm going to die, but I can at least say that I tried. I wonder if Ollie was right about everything. If so, I guess I'll see her in hell. That'll be nice.

Blood splatters in my eyes. I blink. Nothing new hurts. I still hurt everywhere, but only to the same degree that I did before I fought a vampire in one-on-one combat. The bastard isn't standing in front of me, readying to strike. I know he's fast, but he can't just disappear. Can he? I look around for any sign of him. Maybe he dashed behind me, and his claws will rip out my heart any instant.

Instead, I find him crumpled in a heap at my feet, a line of blackish blood leading to what looks almost like a deflated soccer ball with a wig on it. Wow, that's his head. I did it. I saved the day. I wish Olivia looked like she'd been saved.

If she was catatonic before, she's something worse now. Her eyes are so wide, they look more like mirrors. She presses against the wall, staring between us, and I've no idea if she's seeing me or someone else. Oh. Shit. She's seeing a hunter.

"Stay back," she mutters, her voice faint and weak, nothing like the woman I've fallen for.

"Ollie, it's me."

She slides back, pressing into the corner.

"Ollie, please." I drop the bloody sword. That is not helping my credibility. I take a hesitant step toward her, and she looks like she wants to leap out of her skin. Instead, I hold my hands—well, hand and stump—up and sit a few feet away, as far as I can manage from the oozing blood of her old nemesis.

Tears thud on the hard ground beneath us. I think they're mostly hers.

I don't know how long we sit like that, but at some point, the distant vacant expression fades into one of familiarity and then one of pain. "You killed him," she says.

"I did."

Expressions war on her face. She's dating a vampire killer, she failed to get her revenge, freezing up instead, and she doubtless feels even more like a coward. Finally, it settles on concern as she stares at my hand. "Mia."

"I'm okay."

Hesitating for only a second, she flies across the few feet between us and wraps her arms about me. "I'm so sorry. Please, let me turn you. I swear, we can fix this. You need your hand."

"I have a spare."

"We don't have a spare doctor for fiends."

Grinding my teeth, I try to come up with a good response. It's probably been hours at this point, and I don't see a cooler or anything of the sort. I'm not sure my hand is still viable. "I don't want to be a vampire. I want to be a human, have a normal life, grow old, and then have the sweet embrace of death."

"You're dating a vampire, and you killed the villain of a Shakespearian tragedy, penned by said girlfriend. On top of that, you're a black-market doctor serving fiends. I think normal passed a long way back."

She's not wrong, but I don't want to give up my humanity. I'm not sure why exactly—it's not like I'm particularly attached to it—but I've always had it, and it never seemed worth trading in. "I can't."

"Please. Mia, please. Hell, you probably have an infection."

I glance at the reddened bandages clinging to my arm more from blood than from being tied on. "I'm probably okay."

"I won't do it without your permission. I won't do to you what that monster did to me, but please. Please let me save you. You did everything else. I need to do this. I can't have you die because of me. I can't have my cowardice and weakness kill another woman I love."

Given the seriousness of the situation, I let that slide. "Ollie, don't be ridiculous. None of this is your fault." I'm surprised to find that I mean it. Sure, Iago was doing this to get to her, but that doesn't mean it's her responsibility, and it certainly doesn't mean that she needed to abstain for the rest of her life on the off chance that this asshole would show up and ruin things. "This is Iago's fault." I stare at what was once my hand. "And you weren't a coward."

"I was. But that's mine to live with. I won't force anything on you." She sighs, taking my poor injured stump in one hand and my proper hand in the other. "I care immensely for you, Mia. Tell me, what do you want?" She walked it back? I'll try to forget she said it.

What do I want? I try to consider it. The adrenaline having faded, I'm in enough pain that it's hard to focus, let alone to answer existential questions. I have no real idea. I want to be human, but why? "I don't know. It feels like I should stay human, but I'm not sure what it's done for me."

"I promise you, being a vampire is no picnic either."

She has never made it sound great. At least I probably wouldn't have to give up garlic. Maybe I'd get lucky and have the same weaknesses as her. Avoiding church is easy. As I try to sort out my feelings, there are only two things that come to me. Two things I care about. Surprisingly, they're not uppers and downers. I swear, what have I become? "I want to be with you, and I want to be able to keep treating fiends and animals. I love my job. It means the world to me." Glaring at the stump, I shake my head. "I can't really keep doing that with one hand, can I?"

She shakes her head. "Probably not."

Fuck. Fine. "Turning me will let me keep working?"

"It should. It would take a lot to regrow your hand, but it should still be around here somewhere. I'm pretty sure that's what he was looking for right before you killed him. He wanted to taunt me with it. The sick bastard. We should check if it's on him, but I'm pretty sure he was only doing that for show and knew exactly where it was."

I guess that answers that. "If I let you turn me, do you promise to accept that you're not a coward? I mean, you did fight your greatest fear to save me."

"Yeah, and froze and had to be saved by you."

I wave my stump. "Minor detail. You still did it."

"Fine, I promise. Are you sure this is what you want?"

"Can we try finding the limb first? Maybe he put it on ice."

It doesn't take long to find that he left it out as part of a rather vulgar display in the next room. It is decidedly not on ice. Well, there goes that hope. "Will it still work like this?" I ask.

"It will."

"Okay. Fine. Turn me before I change my mind."

And that's how I die. On the bright side, I'm repopulating an endangered species. That makes me feel a little better.

Chapter Seventeen

He's Gone

Still shaking, I hold Mia's body to my chest. I can't believe I did this. Even with consent, turning another person feels wrong. I remember it being done to me. It's violating. It's disgusting. I'm ripping apart her humanity to keep her alive as the same twisted monster I am. But for her, I didn't even hesitate. What does this say about me? I was too much of a coward to face him, and now I'm too much of a coward to lose her.

A pang of guilt runs up my spine. I did promise, didn't I? I can't keep calling myself a coward. My fingers twine through her hair as I stare at her, her mouth red and sticky from my blood. "Mia," I mouth. Sometimes, it doesn't take. I've seen it happen once before, when Iago tried to turn another man to join his little pack. Our pack. Well, not anymore. He's really gone.

My gaze falls on the headless body a few feet away. I thought I'd feel more seeing that. Maybe a pain from the final loss of my old friend, maybe relief at finally gaining my freedom from my centuries-long torment, but now, seeing him as nothing more than a pitiful pile on the floor, it's barely even a side note. Perhaps I've just been through too much, or perhaps I'm simply too concerned for my partner. I can't believe the bastard cut off her hand. I can still feel something about that.

Said hand lies on the ground next to us. It's past the point where mortal doctors would be able to reattach it, but necrotic tissue is far less a concern when you're already dead. A few stitches and she'll be good as new, and even my limited medical abilities are enough to take care of that.

Since she is taking so much time to come back to life—I've seen it take well over eight hours where it's only been one now, but I'm more invested this time—I decide to take the time to sew her up. As I slowly remove the bandages, scared of hurting her, I take in a sharp breath. I'd expected something clean, precise, a cut, not this. It looks almost like it was torn off. Oh, my poor girl.

It will mend either way. I can't believe that demented bastard put her through that. It's all my fault. If I'd stayed away from her…I shake my head. She'll be okay. I can beat myself up when I'm done fixing her. The viciousness of the injury makes stitching more difficult than I'd anticipated, but I find a first aid kit in that mercenary's truck, and the actual sutures only take a few minutes. It's not good enough for medical work, but after she has a drink, it'll be fine.

I'm an idiot. I forgot to see about that. I drank everyone dry except for Iago, and his blood is all over the floor, but I don't want to leave her here while I go looking for some.

Pulling out my phone, I'm relieved to see it's almost evening. I shouldn't have near as much trouble finding someone now. I press a couple buttons, and a woman answers on the second ring. "Olivia?" I'd arranged regular deliveries years ago to make sure I had enough when I didn't feel up for going out, and the odd time I bought any extras, I always did it in person. I'm not sure when the last time I'd have called her is, but it certainly wasn't recently.

"Evening, Maria. I was wondering if I could have a rush order for delivery. O-positive if you have it." She might as well have her first taste be the best. "I can give you the GPS coordinates."

"Sure. Can I charge it to the usual card?"

"That would be no problem at all. Thank you so much. Oh, and a cooler with it. I don't have a fridge here."

"All right, just return it the next time you come by."

"Thank you. Seriously. You're a lifesaver." I can see why every fiend in the country ends up moving to Toronto. It's tough to beat this service.

Half an hour later, I meet her deliveryman at the door to this strange bunker. He doesn't ask any questions, and I don't give him any answers. You have to appreciate black-market confidentiality. I return to Mia's side and set the cooler beside me. Now I just have to wait.

❖

She sucks in a breath, gasping for air she no longer needs. Her panicked eyes stare up from my lap. Jolting upright at inhuman speed, she glances around. I remember how disorienting it was. I wish I'd had someone to walk me through it. "It's okay, Mia," I say, my voice quiet and soothing. Every sound will be amplified tenfold. It's deafening. "I'm here."

"Ollie." She snarls, hungry eyes locking on mine. I remember that feeling. I remember killing my wife for the life source inside her, how impossible fighting against it seemed.

I pull the blood from the cooler. Two bags should be enough. "This will help."

Her fangs sink into the plastic, causing an errant spray before she figures it out. I lick it off my hand. It would be better warm, but it's not a bad first meal.

She drains both bags before she attempts another word. "You didn't say how much it would hurt," she manages, her voice hoarse and distant.

"I'm sorry. I didn't keep that from you intentionally. I simply didn't think of it."

She nods, lying back down. "I can't believe I did this." Her hand flies up, almost hitting her face. The enhanced speed can take some getting used to. She stares at it, twitching her fingers, flexing them, watching their intricate movements. I think she pantomimes performing surgery, but I've never seen one performed upside down and without a patient. It's a strange sight.

"It looks like it works."

She nods, turning back to me. The hunger is gone from her eyes, but in its place sits fear. "Did I make the right choice?"

I wish I knew. "I don't think that's for me to say, but I'm glad you're alive."

With a weary sigh, she jumps to her feet and extends her hand. "Let's get out of here."

"You sure you're ready?"

"I was dead for the last few hours. I'd rather not have to stay here any longer. There's a dead guy rotting over there."

She has a point. I'm not too keen on being near Iago for a second longer either. Though it is quite nice being this solidly reminded that he's really gone. My suffering is finally over. Now I just need to deal with the whole "humans also being awful" thing. I should give her the talk. "Sure, let's head to my car."

Fortunately, the blood on us has dried, so it shouldn't get on my seats.

"Did you bring my pills?" she asks.

"I didn't. Sorry." Of course she'd want some after everything she went through. I should've seen about having them delivered when I was ordering the blood. I had more than long enough to come up with that.

She shrugs, setting her feet on my console.

"At least take your shoes off."

"Fine." She kicks them onto the floor.

"Mia, are you okay?"

She looks at me through half-lidded eyes. "It still hurts a lot, and it's taking some getting used to. It's like every organ in my body is shutting down. I could really use some painkillers."

Nodding, I turn the key and pull away. I can have her back at her apartment in around twenty minutes. Then she can relax and do whatever she needs to do to deal with this. I think a bath and some tea would do her a world of good, but it doesn't exactly sound like her cup of tea, to use a terrible pun. "I should probably tell you what to expect. Try to avoid the sun for now. It likely won't kill you instantly, but I'd much rather we wait and see how it affects you once you've had time to adapt. Same for garlic. Running water is a rare issue, but it can happen. Obviously, holy artifacts." I try to think of what else I might need to cover. I haven't given the basics in a long while.

"I think I had that all figured out." Is she mad at me? Does she feel like I pushed her into it?

"Okay." I risk a moment to glance at her. She's leaning against the window, watching the city pass by. I can't read her expression. She may be in a depressive phase, so I suppose that isn't too odd. "You'll need to drink blood. It doesn't have to be a lot or often. If you want to hunt,

I can show you how to do that without attracting attention, but I can also arrange weekly deliveries of enough that it shouldn't be an issue. Unless you're injured, usually a liter every two days is plenty."

"It feels weird."

"The blood?"

I see her nod out of the corner of my eye.

"It was cold. You should microwave it first, or you can let it sit in hot water for a while if you don't like how that tastes. Hunting also makes it taste better. The adrenaline gives it a nice kick, and since bars are one of the easier hunting grounds, it's intoxicating too."

"Great. I'll go feed on junkies."

"Mia..." I reach out to her, expecting my hand to be slapped away, but she lets me set it on her shoulder, showing no reaction as far as I can tell. "I promise, this isn't the end of the world." I shouldn't have acted like it was such a curse. It really isn't. Immortality is great. It's just that immortality and PTSD are a terrible combination.

"The alternative was having to give up one of the only things I care about. That would be worse. It doesn't mean I have to like it."

I nod, drawing my hand away and focusing on the road. I'm sure there's more to tell her, but hopefully, I'll have quite a while to do so, and that should be an adequate baseline. It's more than I had.

Risking another glance, I see a tear trailing down her cheek. I shouldn't have talked her into it. I should have let her be. Humans can live with one hand, and prosthetics have come a long way. Hell, maybe medical advances would have made her hand salvageable. No, that doesn't seem possible. I would have invested in it, and it would be commercially available at this point if it had shown any promise.

"I'm sorry," I mutter. I really am no better than him.

"You didn't do anything wrong."

"But—"

"It was a long day. I don't want to talk about it, okay? Just know that I'm not mad at you, and I'm still glad that I'm your girlfriend."

"Even after everything I put you through?"

"I already told you. That wasn't you. It was Iago."

My fears slightly assuaged, I decide not to fight her on it. I think she's earned a reprieve. She did save my life, after all. "Do you want me to stay at my place tonight?"

She sits up, staring, her mouth opening, then closing as if she's searching for words. "I wasn't going to ask that, but kind of. I want to see you. I want a little bit of time to myself if that's okay."

"I'm quite patient. You can have all the time you need." I pull up to the curb outside her apartment.

Her lips meet my cheek, and I turn into her in a heated but brief kiss. When she pulls away, her eyes are filled with tears, and her lips are trembling. "I promise, I'm not going anywhere. I just need some sleep. I'll call you in a couple days, okay?"

I nod, and she climbs out of my car. She continues standing there, staring. I roll the window down.

"You forgot Harvey."

Oh. Right. "Thanks."

❖

I pause the bake-off on television to answer my phone. Time for my therapy session. I'd slept through our last appointment as it completely slipped my mind, so I checked her schedule with Ashley and arranged for a new appointment tonight, now that I actually need it. "Hey, Elizabeth, sorry for missing yesterday."

"Do you have a good excuse?"

"For missing it? No. For not calling you back earlier? My archnemesis kidnapped my girlfriend, and I had to go rescue her."

"That's a pretty good reason. Dr. Sun's your girlfriend now?"

"That's the part you're taking notice of?"

She chuckles. "I figured I'd start with the good news. I'm really happy for you, assuming the rescue went well. I think she could be good for you. And you having to deal with a human all the time is great exposure therapy."

"About that…"

"She is okay, right? You said you had to rescue her. I assumed you'd succeeded. Oh, God, sorry, I'm such an ass. Is she okay? Please say she's okay."

That's a surprisingly difficult question. "She wasn't. Iago had cut—"

"Iago?"

"Yeah, I'm Othello. It's a long story. He cut her hand off, and the only way to save her was to turn her."

I can almost hear the gears turning in her head. I wonder if this explains a lot. "Is Iago the one who turned you?"

"Yeah."

"I take it you didn't choose that."

I almost shake my head, but I manage to mutter, "No."

"I'm sorry. That must have felt strange, turning someone else. It sounds like that was the start of a lot of trauma for you."

"It wasn't easy. I wish that I didn't have to do it, but she would've never been able to tolerate a life without her hand. And she actually asked for it. That helps a little."

"I'll tell you the same thing I tell my wife. You're not a monster. Whatever you've done in your past and whatever has happened to you, it doesn't change the person you are now. And, Olivia, I think that you're a good person. Clearly, Mia agrees with me."

"Wasn't I threatening to eat you a couple weeks ago?"

"Please, I've had worse threats from my receptionist."

She's a strange woman. "Well, I appreciate your faith in me." Faith. Now there's the key word. How am I to believe that I'm a good person when even my own faith damns me? Well, this is a therapy session, so I suppose I ought to talk about these feelings. "I don't know how well she'll handle this. At first, she seemed okay, but by the time I dropped her off at her apartment, she was crying, and it was pretty clear that something was massively wrong."

"Well, why don't you tell me what all happened? Maybe I can give some useful feedback."

I do so, catching Elizabeth up the best I can on the week's events, up to Mia killing Iago and my killing her.

"Well, fuck," she announces. She calls, "Hey, Ashley, do I have an appointment after this?" I can hear a faint "No" in the background. "I was gonna cancel it anyway unless it was an emergency. It sounds like you need me more right now. I take it Mia is what you're most concerned about?"

"I think so. Maybe. Fuck, I don't even know. For over the last century, I've been terrified of vampire hunters, and I had to watch the woman I…well, the woman I'm dating murder one. She saved me, and he needed to die, but it was rather traumatizing, especially considering that she was human at the time."

"How do you feel about that?"

"It's hard to find words for it." I stare at the swirl of frosting frozen on the television. "I'm glad he's dead. I wish I'd done it. At the time, I was so scared of her, I wasn't even seeing Mia, but every hunter I've ever dealt with. But it went away, and all I wanted was to be there for her. I think that, even if I'm not yet, I can be okay with it. I am incredibly fond of this girl."

"Well, that's good to hear."

It is. I'd been terrified that I wouldn't be able to handle it. I had so many other pressing issues that I didn't have the time to ponder it until now. "I wish that she didn't seem even more traumatized than I was."

"She had to kill someone. From what you said about her reaction to those bodies in the chapel—which I'm really glad he died for, by the way; I was married in there, so it's a bit personal for me—it sounds like she doesn't handle violence that well. She's a doctor, and she had to take a life. You're a soldier with hundreds of years of experience."

"Only a couple decades of actual experience."

"Nevertheless, it's a subject you're a lot more comfortable with. Think about it. What was your first kill like?"

I try to recall it. It has been well over five hundred years. "I can't say I remember. It was in battle, and it didn't leave that much of an impression on me. Or if it did, I've managed to forget it."

"Well, try to put yourself in her shoes. Think about how she must be feeling."

I try but find myself struggling. It came easy to me, and being a vampire only made it all the easier. Wait, my first kill as a vampire. Now, that traumatized me. It's not the same at all, but Desdemona was someone I thought I would never kill, and Mia thought that she would never kill at all. Okay, when I look at it like that, maybe I was being a little self-important thinking I was the reason she was upset. "She only had to kill him because I froze."

"She wouldn't want you to blame yourself."

"It doesn't change that I'm the one responsible. If I'd had the strength to do it myself, she wouldn't have had to. Oh, I'm such an idiot. I even told her that I'd teach her to hunt if she wanted. I'm supposed to be her partner. I should know her better than this."

"Everyone misses things like that sometimes."

I lean back on the couch, resting my free hand behind my head as I try to process this. No wonder she wouldn't want to be a vampire.

She's a killing machine now, when all she wanted to do was heal. A car honks outside, and Harvey honks back at it. "She said she wanted some space."

"That's probably for the best right now."

"Do you think I should apologize for offering to teach her to kill or wait until she's ready?" I am woefully inexperienced at relationships, and I'm pretty sure that sixteenth-century behavior isn't acceptable anymore. Not like I can send her a carrier pigeon. I roll my eyes at my own joke.

"I normally try to help my clients figure out their own answers, but on this one, I have to. She wants some space. Let her have it. Most likely, you'll be talking to her again before you know it."

"You're right. Thank you." I hold my hand up, and Harvey flutters onto it. I scratch his head, and he trills.

"Right, you have a parrot," she says after a moment. "Did you want to talk more about her, or are you ready to talk about him? I mean Iago, not the parrot."

"I thought I'd want to talk about how it feels weird to be with someone else after all these years refusing to love a new person, but I'm not sure I really need to."

"Oh?"

"It still feels weird, but I think Mia has gotten me to the point where I don't feel like I'm betraying Desdemona. I hate what I did to her, but I can accept that it was Iago's fault, and now she's been avenged. It wasn't by my hand, but it's something."

"I'm proud of you."

I snort. It's always weird hearing that sort of thing from a human. "So I guess I should talk about him."

"You'd mentioned the other cause of your PTSD, but you've gone into so little detail on this one. It sounds like he did a lot of harm to you."

"He did. He tortured me for years before I finally gave in and worked for him. He made me do so many horrible things."

"That doesn't make you—"

"I know. I can accept that I'm not a monster. It will take some getting used to, but I understand."

"Okay."

Harvey coos, rubbing his head against my finger. "It's going to take a lot of time to move past everything he did. I've been looking over my shoulder for the last five centuries, always on the lookout for him. Now he's gone. He'd been my best friend, my worst enemy, my abuser, and my nightmare."

"If you're thinking you miss him, I assure you, that's perfectly normal. People often feel nostalgia for even horrible things. You were used to the idea of him, and it's a strange change."

Miss him? I hate how that sounds, but it may be right. "I guess."

"I'm sorry."

Shrugging, I say, "It's okay. He's dead. I'm free."

"You are."

Grinding my teeth, I stare into Harvey's yellow-brown eyes. "Why don't I feel like it? I'm still ruled by my PTSD. It's why I couldn't save Mia, no matter how badly I wanted to. It's why I can't go out in public. Hell, I'm still ruled by this damn curse too. I can't even go to church."

I hear her take in a breath. "No one's free from everything, Olivia, but you still managed something. Like you said, you don't have to look over your shoulder anymore."

"Except for humans. They're almost always around."

"Unless you want to kill all of us, I think we'll have to keep working on that. You did manage to go to the mall not that long ago. If we keep making that kind of progress, who knows what you could manage."

Still won't get me in a church. "I suppose."

"Let yourself enjoy this victory. It's a more concrete one than most people ever get in therapy. One of the biggest triggers for your PTSD is now gone. Forever."

"Yeah." I let it sink in. She's right. Iago's gone. The source of so many of my nightmares, so many of my waking fears, is gone, and he's never coming back. I kicked his head like a football, and he couldn't do a thing about it. "If only he hadn't sold my mother's crucifix."

"When did he do that? You hadn't mentioned that part."

"Sounds like it was about a year ago. At the Community Center. He expected me to find it. Sold it to a butcher for some reason."

There's silence on the other end of the line for a long moment. I start to worry that she may have hung up. "It's not a little silver cross on a chain, is it?"

I blink. "Yes."

"Oh. I might be able to help with that if you're looking for it."

"What?"

"That butcher, Boris, my wife was his main supplier. We haven't seen him in a while. I assume Iago had something to do with that?"

"He killed him."

She sighs, and her chair creaks. After a long moment, she takes a deep breath, and says, "Well, he gave us a bunch of silver jewelry, including a cross that Abby used to wear, and I think a few of the other necklaces are crosses. I could bring them all into work so you can drop by and see if it's the right one. Though I'm not sure I can find all of them." She blows out a breath, the chair squeaking beneath her. "Tell you what, it's not like I can keep things really professional when I'm the only therapist in this community. Why don't you two come over for dinner? That way Mia can touch it, assuming she's capable, and you can check to see if it's the right one."

Huh. "That actually sounds amazing." Assuming Mia will still want to be with me. Watch her have no issue touching it. No one else seems to. It's only me that's damned. "Thank you, Elizabeth. That means a lot."

"Don't mention it."

We talk for a while longer, discussing Iago before moving back onto my normal issues and our exposure therapies. For the first time since I've started, I feel like it's worth fighting through. Things have changed so much. Maybe this can too.

Chapter Eighteen

Amelia: So, I'm a Monster Now

The warm water takes away a little of the sting. My hand is red, raw, bloody, and still a bit singed. Christ, she'd made it sound like going out in the sun would be nothing. I'm glad the running water doesn't hurt. I wrap a cloth around my yet again unusable hand and head over to the fridge. O-positive is the perfect chaser for a handful of oxy.

Even the skin regrowing hurts. I never thought being dead could be this painful. I wonder if it's anywhere near this bad when the death is permanent?

Collapsing onto the couch, I drape a foot over the armrest, recline against a throw pillow, and sip from the bag. I can already tell that my hand mended under the washcloth, but I keep it on for a few more minutes. It just takes some getting used to. Being immortal is weird.

It's a little past eleven, and I'm definitely not trying to go outside again. Being on fire may be the least pleasant thing I've ever experienced, and yesterday I had a concussion, my hand chopped off, and I died. I wonder what tomorrow will bring.

Some mindless show pops on the television as I finish the bottle of pills and let the bag of blood slip to the floor. It probably needs to be refrigerated, but I'll get to it later. It can't be that important, right? If my body can handle necrotic tissue, it can handle improperly stored blood.

The gunfight on the screen makes my mind go places I'd rather it not. I change the channel and sit through a few episodes of people shopping for absurdly expensive houses—probably the kind of things Ollie would buy—nodding off during the commercial breaks and probably a few other bits.

Several hours later, I wake up to find that the couples are no longer arguing over what house they want but over whether or not that is in fact their child. What would we do without daytime television?

A pill doesn't hit my tongue. I shake the bottle again, peering into it, hoping against hope that maybe it melted and stuck to the side. It wouldn't be the first time. Alas, I have no such luck. The sun is still high in the sky, so I'm not going anywhere. I may be out of painkillers.

I wake up again, the horror of my situation hitting me harder this time. Well, I can't have that. I'm in no mood to deal with the fact that I'm now a murderous monster. Drugs it is. I search every place I normally store them. There has to be some somewhere. I buy them all the time. I keep backups and backups for those. How are there not any in this drawer? Damn my new metabolism!

Of course I only have uppers. Normally, I need them more. I'm depressed more often than I'm manic, and they balance me out, but right now, if I try one, I'll end up staking myself or something. I need to be numb. I need to not feel a thing. There. That's it. I pry the little baggie from the bottom of my drawer where it stuck. Ollie helped me get this. It seems almost wrong to use it, but hey, beggars can't be choosers.

Injection is probably out, vampiric circulation being what it is, so I use the tin foil trick and am out like a light as soon as I've inhaled the entire thing. If I'd been human, it would've killed me. I kind of wish it had. Instead, I'm left dreamy, floating in my skin, the world outside barely even worthy of my notice.

So what? I killed someone. I betrayed every oath I've ever sworn, broke every principle I believed in, all because I like this girl. It hardly matters. It happened, and that's that.

I must've nodded off again as the sun is down. With some trepidation, I take a step outside and find that I don't burst into flames. That's a nice change of pace.

The Community Center is only a couple kilometers from here, so I grab some cash and head out for a walk. I need to not feel. I need to keep this high going. I can't take the alternative. I just can't. If I have to be blasted out of my mind forever, I guess I'll deal with that. My patients will be fine on their own.

The cool air feels nice on my skin, and the road seems surprisingly empty. I didn't think to check the time or grab my phone. It could be anywhere between eight and four, but it's dark and quiet, and I love it.

Was that… I turn, halting my momentum in an instant and crouching in a defensive stance on instinct. I swear I saw him. I shake my head. No. I killed him. He's not hunting me. He's not hunting anyone anymore, and it's all because of me. I took Ollie's sword, and I…I blink away tears. Right, drugs. I need drugs.

I try to focus on the walk, on the city, the smells, the sounds, anything that can block out the voices in my head. Anything that can make those empty eyes stop burrowing into me. I can hear cars a few streets away, shoes pounding on pavement as someone jogs. No, they're not jogging. I can smell their adrenaline. They're scared. They're running for their life.

Every fiber of my being wants to give chase. I can satisfy my hunger. I won't have to deal with that prepackaged crap. I can have fresh, delicious…human. I'm talking about hunting and eating a human. Pinning them to the wall and feeling the life leaving them as I swallow every last drop of blood in their veins. I'm a monster. I'm a murderer. I'm not even hungry, and I want to do it. What the fuck is wrong with me?

I run, putting every ounce of strength I can manage into my legs, feeling my body burn, my muscles fight back against me as they're pushed to their limits, and I find myself at the entrance to the Honeydale Mall in a matter of seconds. Claire is in today, so I can get my usual rates. Though, of course, that means I can't convince her replacement that my rates should be better.

"You look different," she says, looking me up and down.

"New haircut."

She sniffs the air, her snout twitching in my direction. "You're dead."

"Am I? Hadn't noticed."

"Mia, what happened?"

"Does it matter?"

"I just—"

"Drugs, please."

Before she can protest, I throw a wad of bills on the table and grab a handful of baggies, not even bothering with my normal pills. Clearly, oxy isn't enough for me. I need something stronger. I snatch a vial of morphine as well and bid her farewell.

That smell. It's amazing. Like a nice stew sitting on the stove, waiting for me. I find myself moving toward the slave auction but stop. I'm not killing anyone else. I can't. I'll kill myself first.

The second I'm home, I kill the thoughts and pass out. Maybe I'll feel better in the morning.

❖

I glare at the alarm. It's four a.m., but I need to make sure I get to work before the sun comes up. I want to stay home and keep myself dead to the world—appropriate—but the whole reason I went through this transformation that has ruined my tolerance was so I could keep my job, and I'm not likely to do that if I keep skipping.

I shower, do my best to kill the burned cocoa butter smell on me, and throw on a blouse and slacks, along with some sunglasses. I don't think they'll make a difference if the sun is out, and my pupils should be back to their normal size by now, but I'd rather not take the risk.

"You're here," David blurts when he wanders into the office and sees me already there, leaning against a wall, trying to avoid the sun filtering through the window.

"I am."

"You're feeling better?"

How do I even answer that question? Every second I spend with my full faculties is a second I want to end. I feel like a monster who can never make up for what I've done. "Much better." That about gets the point across.

When I make no effort to continue the small talk, he heads into his office, stopping to check in with another vet before settling in to do his paperwork. I do not envy that job. My first appointment isn't for a few more hours, so I sit in my office and wait. I can feel the narcotics burning a hole in my pocket. Hell, I can smell it. Along with every edible person and animal in this building. I could snort a little, and then maybe it wouldn't be quite as bad. With my new constitution, it's not like I would be out of it for long.

But doing heroin in the middle of my workplace is probably not the best plan, especially with my boss in the next room. I could always rip out his throat…fucking bloodlust. Does this ever go away? I pull out my phone, push a button, and stare at Olivia's name. It's a simple question. It's not unreasonable. She's the one who would know. But if I start talking to her, I'll want to talk to her about everything else, and then I'll want to see her, and I'm not ready for that. The last time I was with her, I murdered someone. I know it won't happen again...I hope. Who knows if she has any more enemies? What if it does happen again? Or if she goes out to hunt, and I decide to join her? How can I know that I won't do it? How can I live with myself?

A knock sounds at my door, and I shove my phone back in my pocket. "Come in."

"Hey, there're doughnuts in the lobby," Lisa, the other vet in today, says.

There's also sunlight in the lobby. We keep our windows uncovered to allow natural light in. It's supposed to make it look friendlier, more inviting, like someplace you'd trust with your pets. "Would you grab me one? I have a bit of a headache right now."

"Sure, no problem. You sure you're feeling well enough to be back? You don't look great."

"How well were you all managing without me?"

"I came in yesterday, so we were managing. I think Eric came in the other day. He wanted the overtime anyway. He's trying to buy a boat."

"He's been trying to buy a boat for the last five years."

"He has to have some excuse for when he gambles it all away."

Maybe I shouldn't judge anyone else's vices, the drug-abusing murder that I am. I clutch my head as if I'm in pain. "I'm fine. I just need some food."

"Right, a couple chocolates?"

I nod.

The door swings shut behind her, and I breathe out a sigh of relief. I've never been too keen on socializing with my coworkers, even when I'm not going through my own shit. Or maybe I was just always going through my own shit, as during my manic phases, I actually talked to them a good deal. Hell, I even brought in doughnuts myself a few times.

As if summoned by that thought, Lisa returns with a chocolate doughnut and a Boston cream. "They only had the one regular chocolate left. I hope this is okay."

"It's great. Thank you."

She hands them over and keeps standing in front of me. I assume she still wants to talk, but I'm just interested in burying my feelings in chocolate and opiates.

"Don't you have an appointment soon?"

She checks her phone and leans against my counter. "Not for another half hour. I'm trying to stay awake until my coffee kicks in."

She did save me from having to burn to dust in the sun. I suppose I can offer her my unpleasant company. "All right. What did you want to talk about?" I bite into the Boston cream and have to wipe some off my cheek. I'm not sure if it was overfilled or if it's from my not being used to my increased jaw strength.

Lisa shrugs. "I don't know." She pulls herself onto my counter and barely avoids hitting her head on a cabinet. "We haven't talked much in a few months. You see any good movies? Read something? New boyfriend?"

"New girlfriend."

"Oh." Her eyes widen as she stares from her perch. It reminds me a little of Harvey. I miss that annoying little fucker. "I had no idea. I'm sorry."

"It's fine. I've never said anything."

"Well, yeah, but I've known you for like eight years. I shouldn't make assumptions like that. What's your girlfriend like?"

This was a trap. I'm trying not to think about Ollie. Hell, I'm trying not to think about anything. "She's brilliant. She practically collects degrees," I find myself saying. Great, now I'm thinking about her.

"Wow."

"She's had a really rough life, but she's so strong." I see her face lying on the pillow before me, her muscles twitching and straining in a dream. I lean back, hitting my head. "I think I'm kind of falling for her."

"Aw!" She squeals, leaping from the counter and wrapping her arms around me. "I'm really happy for you. You always seem so sad. I'm glad you found someone."

Am I that obvious? "Thanks." Reluctantly, I pat her back a few times until she finally releases me.

"We could go on a double date sometime. I think my boyfriend may finally propose soon."

"Yeah, maybe." I guess that would be after dark.

Beaming, she plops back down with a little giggle. "How'd you two meet?"

She won't be in the system, and I don't know how nosy Lisa might get. What's a good lie that wouldn't make it sound like I keep this place running after hours off the books? "She was a friend of a friend, wanted to ask me some questions about her parrot."

"That's really cute."

"He's a good bird." I finish my first doughnut. Now I miss Ollie more, and I kind of want to eat Lisa to make her stop asking questions. I'm not sure this is helping.

"If she brings him in, will you introduce me?"

"Sure."

"Yay!"

Somehow, I make it through the conversation without killing her and deal with my various clients. At least the animals don't look like food. I'm not sure why that is. I know we can eat them, but it's only the humans I find myself watching the arteries of and smelling the air for their flavor.

Nevertheless, my teeth remain outside of anyone's throat, and I finish my appointments, dealing with each of the minor nuisances their pets have. When everyone else leaves, I'm tempted to close up. The sun won't be down for another hour, but I want to go home and get high.

Before I have the chance, the front door flies open. I find myself ready to fight and have to force myself to calm down. "Can I help you?" I ask, heading into the lobby to find a young man looking around nervously.

"Hi, you, um, you're the person I'm supposed to see, right? The one who deals with the…I mean, unless you're not. Do I have the wrong place?" His eyes fall over a few of the animal magazines in the waiting area. The sun is down enough that I can be in here, but I'd rather not try my luck outside yet.

He definitely doesn't smell human. "Do I work with fiends? Is that the question?"

"Well, yeah. That's a yes, then?"

"Yes."

He extends his hand, grinning broadly. "Hi, I'm Dennis. Ms. Rosseau-Lester recommended you. Does that, like, get her some special referral bonus?"

"Actually, it helps you. We made a deal for a slight discount since she sends so many over to me. What seems to be the problem?"

"Wait a second." He laughs, his smile going from toothy to fangy. "I know that smell. She didn't say you were a vampire. I thought you were human."

"I thought it'd be a nice change of pace."

"You're new." He pulls on my hand, tugging me into a hug. I shove him, but his mood seems unfazed. "I'm new too. I was only turned last year. We should hang out. We could make a club or something. Maybe we'd trade secrets, talk about our experiences, and all that. It'd be fun."

Am I that desperate that I'd be friends with this idiot? No. Absolutely not. "What was it you were saying brought you in today?"

"Oh." He gasps, letting out a hearty guffaw. "That's right. I ate someone who had, um, well…" He stammers, staring down at the ground. "AIDS."

"Okay?"

"Could you, like, test me? Make sure I didn't get it? Ms. Rosseau-Lester wasn't too sure if it'd be transmittable. She said it probably wouldn't, but that I should be tested to make sure."

"And when was this?"

"I saw her yesterday."

"No, the bite."

He smacks himself in the forehead. "Like three days ago."

"Did you tell her that? I'm pretty sure she's smarter than this."

"Well, she said I should see you in a few weeks. I figured sooner is better, right?"

I roll my eyes and resist snorting the rest of the opiates in my pocket. "It takes longer than three days to be detectable. Also, you're a vampire, so you're probably fine, and if not, drink some blood to heal up. But how about you come back in three weeks, and I'll run those tests. Even if you could get it, the antibodies haven't had time to develop yet."

"But that's so long."

"You're immortal. You're fine. I can almost guarantee you have nothing to worry about, as I've run blood work on vampires before, and nothing stays in there, but because you are this concerned, come back in about a month, and we'll run those tests to put your mind at ease. Okay?"

He nods. "Yeah. Okay. Since we don't have to do anything, want to hang out? We can talk about how you got turned. I'm a great listener."

For half a second, I almost consider it. "I'll see you in a month."

Sulking, he leaves me alone, and after another hour, I close up early. Sweet blissful oblivion awaits me at home, and I don't want to keep it waiting.

Chapter Nineteen

Three Weeks Later

"I've missed you. Can we talk tonight? Pick me up from work around ten?" I stare at the message on my phone. She really does still want to see me. I blink away sleep, chop up some carrots for Harvey, and take a shower. I wonder how she's doing now. I gave her the space she asked for, but I wish I could've been there for her. I know how terrifying this transformation can be. Well, she's a lot stronger than I am, so I'm sure she's fine.

Wearing a gray blazer, matching skirt, and a button-up blouse, I head through the open doors of her clinic. The door to her office is closed. I take a seat in the lobby, tapping the ground with my foot as I wait. I hate to admit how nervous I am. This woman must be special to stir such emotions in me. I had no issue being alone all these years, yet these last three weeks felt almost as long as three years. Not to say that's a terrible wait—three years is nothing for someone as old as I am—but it's still longer than three weeks should be.

"Hey, there," she says, flashing a quick smile as she walks a massive, furry four-legged creature to the counter. Is that a fucking bunyip? Glad she didn't piss it off. I prefer this block still being here. "Make sure you remember to brush your tusks too, okay?" she reminds the creature as it somehow hands over a hundred-dollar bill using its foot.

"I will. I don't want another infection." Her voice booms through the room. Her footsteps shake the chair beneath me when she leaves.

"Having fun?" I ask, pulling myself to my feet. Do I go in for a hug? I'm trying to see what she wants first, but I have really missed her.

Throwing her arms around me, she pulls me close, her lips brushing mine before she rests her head on my shoulder. "It's good to see you, Ollie. I'm sorry it's been too long."

When she pulls back, I can't help but notice how large her pupils look. "How have you been doing?"

She shrugs. "Buy me dinner? We can talk about it at my place, maybe? It hasn't been the same without you there."

With an enthusiastic nod, I slide my arm through hers and walk her to my car. "What are you feeling like?"

"Blood sausage?"

I quirk an eyebrow at her.

"I'm joking. How about pancakes?"

"Not like I had breakfast. Sure, sounds good." I open the door for her and drive the few kilometers there. It smells richly of syrup outside. I can't imagine how coagulated the blood of some of the people inside must be. We grab seats by a window, and I watch the night sky while Mia sorts out her thoughts.

With her lips pursed, she looks me up and down, an appreciative glint in her eye. "I want to say again that it wasn't anything to do with you. I do still want to be with you."

"I know." Well, I mostly knew. "I want that too." I wait, not asking any questions. She'll tell me what she wants me to know.

Mia smiles at the waitress and waits until she leaves with our orders to elaborate. "I killed someone."

"You hunted?"

"No. I can't. I mean, I killed Iago."

"You said it yourself, he was a monster." I want to comfort her, to convince her that she hasn't done anything wrong, but I know full well that I need to let her talk. She's had the time to figure things out, and my ill-informed additions won't help until I have the whole story. "Sorry."

"No, it's okay. You're right, he was, but it doesn't change that I'm the one that did it. And hell, now I'm a monster too."

I resist saying fiend. I suppose it's hardly offensive when she says it now.

"You know I never liked people, but I'm still a doctor. I never wanted to take a life. I wanted to help animals, and eventually, that turned into helping fiends as well. It shouldn't have ever involved killing."

"I'm sorry I made you do that."

Her hand snatches mine out of the air, squeezing it. "You didn't. Iago did. Like I said, I don't blame you. I just had a lot to process."

"And how have you been dealing with it?"

Those dilated pupils avoid my gaze. What would be strong enough to last this long on a vampire? "Same way I handle everything, but I have a much stronger tolerance now."

"That's not a sustainable solution—"

"I know!" She calms herself as a few stoned college students look in our direction. "I know it's not. But I can't even sleep at night. All I see is his face, a few feet away from his body, staring up at me. Every time I close my eyes, in every dream, in every face, it's right there. The only thing that quiets it at all, that makes me stop hearing his voice, stop killing him again and again and again, is being so high that I can't even think straight."

My heart breaks, and my grip on her hand tightens. I found this wonderful woman, and I turned her into me. A murderous, bloodthirsty, irreparably traumatized vampire. "I'm so sorry. I know that feeling. I deal with it every single day. In fact, you've actually helped me. Having you there when I woke up helped, sure, but you killed the source of half of my nightmares. I still see those hunters, all the time, but it's not like it was…it's my past haunting me now, not the eternal fear of it returning to my present."

She nods, taking a sip of water, blinking tears out of her eyes. "I know you know. I never wanted to understand what you go through, and now that I do, I don't know how you've put up with it for this long."

"Pets, mostly. It gives me something I need to look after. A reason that I can't give up and die."

"Huh. Well, maybe I should start looking after Harvey too."

"Mia?" I ask, not wanting to make any assumption from that sentence.

"I'm not saying we should U-Haul or anything, but I really liked sharing my place with you, especially since you actually cook and clean and do things that aren't drugging yourself up. Even when you're not on Ritalin, and that's more than I can say."

"My place is a lot farther from your work." I'm not sure if I'm trying to talk her out of it or saying we can stay at her place.

"I guess you'll have to drive me." She smirks. "I mean, on nights when I'm staying there."

"I suppose I will."

Plates of pancakes are set before us with hash browns on the side. She releases my hand, her fingers trailing along my wrist as she pulls away.

"Thank you," I say to the waitress. When she's gone, I say, "You know, you probably shouldn't keep all those drugs around Harvey. They could be bad for him, and you're his vet, so causing him to need more treatment must be unethical."

"I guess." She doesn't sound terribly convinced.

"Do you think you could handle not using them all the time?" In truth, it's not about Harvey, and she knows it. I didn't mind how she used them before because it was to keep her stable, and we all make sacrifices for that, but she's talking about turning off her emotions all the time. I'm a little jealous, but it's not healthy.

"I'm fine, Ollie."

"How much have you spent on drugs this week?"

Her eyes dance on the ceiling as she does the math in her head. "A couple grand. Like I said, this tolerance is ridiculous."

"And that doesn't sound like an issue?"

"Wouldn't be an issue if I wasn't a vampire."

"Mia—"

"Sorry. It's not your fault. I asked for this. It lets me work. I like working. I just hate dealing with being alive. Even more than usual."

"Will you try seeing Elizabeth? She's been a huge help to me, and I think it could do you a lot of good with processing everything. I'm here for you, whatever you need, and you know that I understand and am more than willing to listen, but you need more than that."

"You could go get a degree in therapy in a couple years. I believe in you. I have time. I'll wait."

"I have one, but I'm your girlfriend, and I'm not exactly impartial."

She shrugs, slathering syrup on her hotcakes and shoving a bite into her mouth, taking her time chewing so she doesn't have to acknowledge my point.

I wait and eat my own food.

"Can I still move in if I don't?"

She did mean that, then. With a sigh, I nod. "Yes. I want you to do it for you. I trust you, and I know that you'll try to look after yourself the best you can."

She scoffs at that. "Right." Another snorting laugh, and she adds, "I guess I can try to take care of myself if it means that much to you. I am stuck being alive for a while."

"A fate for which I am quite grateful."

"I'll see the fucking therapist," she grumbles, skewering another bite of pancakes. "But I'm still using drugs. The bipolar shit doesn't help."

"It's longer lasting, might be worth it with your new tolerance."

She chomps down on the pancakes hard enough to bite off the tongs of the fork. "I'll look into it."

"That's all I ask. Don't swallow that."

She spits out the metal, glares at it, and shakes her head. "After we finish up here, can we go grab my bags? I just want to be someplace where I wasn't knocked out and kidnapped."

I hadn't even thought of that. Why am I so bad at considering her trauma? I consider mine constantly. "Yeah, finish up your pancakes, and we'll go." I flag the waitress down for a new fork.

❖

"This is what you've been hiding from me," Mia marvels from the passenger seat, an actual emotion on her face as she takes in my estate. It's not as impressive as she seems convinced it is, but it's still a pretty large house, with a good bit of land. I do like my privacy. "I knew you were rich, but wow."

"Are you only dating me for my money?"

"If I was, I think I'd have pestered you for drug money the last few weeks."

I'd been wondering if that was going to come up. "Do you—"

"I can look after myself. I have a well paying job and a black-market operation, plus a good bit in savings. I promise I won't leech off you or anything."

"It wouldn't be the worst thing in the world."

"Please, you ate your last housewife." Her eyes widen, and she waves her hands in front of her. "Holy shit, I'm sorry. I wasn't…I didn't…"

Ignoring her, I climb out of the car. I know she didn't mean that. Just wasn't expecting it.

"Ollie, please, I'm so sorry." She hesitantly approaches me, reaching out slowly enough that I could avoid her without issue. I let her take my hand. "That was so stupid. I can't even offer an explanation."

"You're bitter and high and making shitty jokes?"

"That's a pretty good explanation."

I pull her hand to me, running my thumb along her knuckles. "Don't joke like that, please. Besides, I know you would never want to be a housewife. You love your work too much." It is why she became a vampire, after all.

She nods, leaning her head against my shoulder. "I'm still really sorry."

"I know. It's okay." I play my fingers through her hair, and I breathe in her scent. Maybe not the best first couple of hours, but it's good to have her back. "Want me to give you the tour?"

"Do we need a golf cart or something?"

"It's not that big."

"It's huge."

"Well, then, it's a good thing you're a vampire." Right, maybe we're both saying insensitive snarky things today. I hope it doesn't keep up. "Come on." I link my arm with hers and gesture for her to follow. We walk from the garage to the main house. "There's enough room for a second car if you want to get one."

"I don't actually know how to drive."

I can't help but laugh. "So you, who actually grew up when cars were a thing, can't drive?"

"I can't sail a ship either, and I'm sure you can do that."

"That doesn't tend to come up as often."

"I lived right by where I worked, and before that, I lived on campus in college. It's just never been an issue, and I never cared that much to learn. My parents were busy with work when most people would've been learning, and I was fine not knowing how. Besides, you really shouldn't drive when you're on drugs, and I like being high more than I like having reliable transportation."

I do not understand this woman. We're so different, even if we're both incredibly damaged. How is she the one I've fallen for? "I could teach you."

Eyeing me suspiciously, she purses her lips and shrugs. "If you want."

"Then maybe I wouldn't have to drop you off at work."

"See? I knew you'd try to get out of that."

I open the front door, unveiling the foyer and the faint smell of parrot. The ceiling is about ten feet high to make up for only having a single floor. "The kitchen's that way," I say as Harvey drops onto my shoulder.

"Tea?"

"Not right now, I'm showing Mia around."

"Pretty," he says, greeting her.

"Hey, Harvey. I missed you too," she says, scratching his head

He preens happily, stretching out against me. "Tea?"

"Give me a minute, Mia, while I put the kettle on." It only takes a few seconds, and Harvey hops on the counter to watch it boil.

"Tea!" he cheers.

We resume our tour, as I drag Mia past the living room. I'd forgotten how much of a mess it is. I've been spending a bit too much time watching television on the couch. I'm actually a bit behind on one of my classes right now. Her absence affected me more than I had realized. I haven't felt like this about anyone in centuries. I suppose that's why she's moving in. "Would you keep your apartment?" I ask, surprised by my own words.

She stares as if considering. I can see how desperately she wants to retreat, insist that she's not moving in, so of course she would, or maybe even run away again, but I think our separation was as hard on her as it was on me as she shakes her head. "I guess not. I'm on a month-to-month lease, so I could get out of it pretty easily. I thought we weren't U-Hauling, though."

"Do you want to? We seem pretty set on you moving in, even as we act like it's not the case, and quite frankly, I can't think of anything I'd like more than sharing my home with you. I promise, there's plenty of room for all your stuff."

"Keep bragging, why don't you?"

"Well, it's your place too."

She smirks as if trying out that idea for size. "It would be pretty cool to have a place like this."

"And the girlfriend?"

"I guess she's okay." She pulls me to her, more accustomed to her increased strength. She leans in to kiss me but catches herself. "I kinda promised myself that I wouldn't do this sort of thing."

"What sort of thing is that?"

"So many parts of this, but mostly the falling in love and moving in with someone, especially someone I've barely even known for two months."

"We've been through a lot in that time." Her words finally hit me. "Wait, you're in love with me?" I smirk, torn between how touched I am and my desire to tease the cynical woman for turning into a romantic.

"I didn't say that."

"Of course not. I must've misheard you."

"Fine, I'll move in."

"That's what I thought." I try to continue the tour, pointing out a room that she could take as her study, but find myself pinned to the wall.

"I think you can show me more in a little while."

"I have to fix the tea," I insist, giggling, not even attempting to push her off me.

Her lips meet my neck. "I'm sure I can finish you off once or twice before it boils."

❖

Several hours and a few dozen orgasms later, we lie tangled amongst Egyptian cotton sheets. It was the first time we'd done such a thing, but it wasn't some big unnerving emotional event either. Sex was never the issue for either of us, intimacy was. Wow, speaking of, I just realized I've never actually had a woman in this bed before. I tend not to let anyone come here. It's a nice change of pace. "That was amazing," I mutter, stretching and almost kicking her.

"It was pretty nice."

"See how much fun you can have actually feeling things?" I ask, reaching for my tea on the nightstand and finding it unpleasantly cold.

"I'm still high."

"Not like you were when I saw you earlier."

Groaning, she crawls up the bed until she's parallel with me. "It keeps me stable. Maybe I don't need it quite like I've been using it the last few weeks, but I can't just be sober."

"You used to use it to balance out your mood, but this isn't that."

"You could use it too. I know how haunted you are. Let me cope how I cope." She starts to sit up.

I grab her arm, meeting her eyes. "Okay. Sorry. You said you'll talk to Elizabeth about it. I'll try to drop it."

With a reluctant nod, she lies back down, her head resting on my pillow. We had quite a workout, and she falls asleep a few seconds later, her breathing stopping. A lot of young vampires are so used to breathing that they keep doing it consciously. Her body knows better when she's not controlling it.

I hear Harvey squawking as he tears apart one of his toys in his bedroom. I should buy him something new. I haven't in a little while. There was that interesting cube on Amazon that seemed different from the last few things I've bought him. He'd probably like that. I wrap an arm around Mia, holding her close while I contemplate online shopping. There are a few other things I should get too. She's moving in, and my place is only set up for one person. I know she has stuff to bring, so maybe we should go through all of that and go over what we'd need more of. More plates are always a good idea, and maybe a welcome present for her, like a nice bundle from a soap store.

She inhales sharply, bucking against me, her hand spasming on the sheet. "No," she whimpers, her breathing growing frantic.

"Mia?"

She tosses, elbowing me in the nose.

"I'm here." I place a hand on her arm as gently and comfortingly as I can. So this is what it's like being on the other side. I hope I never hurt her too badly in my sleep. My nose still stings. That was a good blow.

Another whimper and her eyes twitch rapidly as if she's looking around for something.

"It's okay, Mia. I've got you. You don't need to worry."

"Huh?" she asks, her eyelids fluttering open. "What?"

I plant a kiss on her forehead. "You were having a bad dream."

"Oh. Yeah. The usual one," she confirms, rubbing her eyes with her thumb and forefinger.

"I have some pills that are supposed to help with that."

"Or I could get high enough that I won't feel anything. I think that sounds much better."

"Mia, please. I've done this to myself for centuries. Doing that won't help. You still have the dreams even then, don't you?"

Her jaw clenches in annoyance. "It's not as bad."

"Well, all you're going to do is rob yourself of a lot of other emotions. Try my pills."

"You don't try them. I've never seen you take them."

Damn it. I didn't want to have this conversation. Ever, if I could help it. "They don't work for me."

"And you think they will for me?"

"It's worth trying, isn't it?"

She considers it, her annoyance slowly fading into concern. "On one condition." Her eyes stare into my very soul with a look so determined, I don't think I could possibly refuse.

"Name it."

"I'll try these pills if you'll give taking pills another chance and find something that works for you. Besides, then you won't beat me up in my sleep."

"You're one to talk. You have a hell of an elbow."

Contrition and pride war in her features, but she settles on a bemused smirk. "You'll do it?"

"Will you try bipolar meds instead of heroin?"

"I'll try bipolar meds *and* heroin," she offers.

"I want to have my girlfriend all the way here with me."

"I'm here," she insists.

I sit up, staring at the floor. I don't know how bad it's been, but I can't sit by when she's actively blocking herself off. For decades, I did the same, far more literally, and wouldn't allow myself any connection as a result. "I know what it's like to not want to feel anything, to not let yourself. I know exactly how incapable I was of being there for someone else. Maybe I'm selfish, but I'd like my partner to not go through that."

"Are you going to be weird if I still get high when I'm having a bad episode?"

"Hell, if I'm having one, I may join you."

"If it means I might get to see a high Ollie, I suppose you have yourself a deal. Do I need to see Liz for this part, or can we just try all of the pills?"

"Whatever works, I suppose."

"All right." She hops out of bed, stretching the arm she'd smacked me with. "Where are those pills?"

Her sleep still seems restless, and maybe it's just the placebo effect, but her dreams don't seem quite as violent. Maybe it helps. I've had no interest in trying medication again, especially after how the last time went, but if it gets her to do it, I suppose it's worth it. Maybe eventually, it'll even make a difference.

Chapter Twenty

Happily Ever After

The cabin is secluded in the middle of the woods. It's certainly not where I anticipated Elizabeth living, but it has a nice hominess to it. There's no doorbell, so I knock. Within a few seconds, the door swings open to reveal a wendigo towering over me, her dark fur neatly trimmed and the usual smell of death dampened and covered up with the smell of fresh flowers. "You must be Abby," I say, extending my hand.

Her massive fingers envelop mine as she shakes my hand. "I am. Liz has told me almost nothing about you, but it's nice to meet you. Olivia, right? And this must be Dr. Sun." Her voice is higher than I'd expected.

Mia waves. "Hi."

"Come on inside." She gestures for us to enter, her claws almost raking the opposite wall. "Liz is just finishing up dinner. I hope you don't mind vegetarian."

"You can eat vegetarian?" Mia asks, peering at Abigail. "I didn't think that was possible." Is she going to try to vivisect our host?

"I don't eat, but it's easier to be around food if it's not meat."

"Oh." Her eyes glint as she continues eyeing the specimen. I've heard about her, the wendigo who successfully swore off eating people. She's apparently a bit of a legend in that support group in the Community Center. I've never been, but I've heard good things about it. "And you're not having any health issues with that?"

"Just the perpetual starvation," she offers.

"Right. Sorry. Well, if there's anything I can do, feel free to pay my clinic a visit. Maybe we could run some tests and see if there'd be a way to suppress your appetite?"

"No shop talk," Elizabeth calls from the kitchen. "I'm sure Abby would be happy to try that out later, but as I'm seeing both of you as my clients, I'd rather we avoid any talk of work." We find her in the dining room setting a large salad bowl on the table along with some impressively sized mushroom burgers. "You have no idea how hard it's been to find a meat substitute that has the right feel for a burger. I hope you like it."

"I can imagine," I say. Meat wasn't as common for meals when I was growing up, but we also didn't have half a dozen alternatives to imitate the flavor. Live on sailor's biscuits for long enough, and you stop worrying about that sort of thing. Seeing Mia already picking up the food, I add, "Would you mind if I say grace first?"

"If you'd like," Elizabeth says. "But maybe try to skip the crossing yourself bit? I'd hate to see my client self-harming at my dinner table."

Mia doesn't tend to appreciate it either, but she's learned to stop trying to convince me to give it up. "Okay." I lead everyone in grace, to no one's joy, and Mia looks relieved when she can finally eat. She doesn't even get hungry, and she's immortal, so I'm not sure what could justify the impatience.

"It's delicious," Mia exclaims, staring in shock at her burger.

"You don't need to sound that surprised," Elizabeth says. "I've learned to be a much better cook over the last year. No place delivers out here."

"Sorry," Abby mutters.

"Honey, you know I don't mean it like that. Besides, you're more than worth it." She winks at her wife, helping herself to some of the salad.

Abby says, "So, Dr. Sun—"

"Mia is fine."

"Well, Mia, then." I've never seen a bashful wendigo. It's a little scary. "How're you adapting to your transformation? I know it's not the same, but I remember how rough going through mine was. It was only eight years ago, so it's still relatively fresh. I'm here to help if you need anything."

Might Mia just admit how traumatizing the whole thing was?

How desperately she didn't want to do it, but why she gave in? Maybe talk about how gross she thinks blood is? "It was okay," she says. "I've had Ollie helping me through it, and I was already familiar with the community, so most of it didn't come as a shock. I do catch fire in the sun, though. That was a pleasant surprise."

"Really?" Abby asks.

"You do?" I ask. "You said that it was bad, but I didn't realize it was quite like that. I expected something more like Iago's weakness. Oh, I'm sorry I wasn't there for you. That must've been terrifying."

"It's okay. You'd left some blood in my fridge, so it didn't end up being that bad. It just wasn't a fun thing to find out. But hey, it means that I'm not vulnerable to the same things as you, so I can look at that cross in a bit, and it probably won't hurt, right?"

"Yeah, hopefully," I say, still beating myself up. I chew some salad as I try to ease my conscience. She didn't want me there, and she would've called if she'd changed her mind. I did what she asked. I didn't do anything wrong, but it sure feels like I did.

"How'd you two meet?" Mia asks, moving the attention away from herself. She is never comfortable with it there for long.

"Grade school," Abby says with a light chuckle. "I honestly can't recall a time when I didn't know her."

"Oh, it wasn't after…" She trails off, gesturing toward Abby. I don't know how none of her clients have mauled her yet. She is the least tactful person I've ever known. Of course, with the temper I had when we met, I'm surprised I wasn't the one to do it. Well, I guess I *did* kill her.

"No, it wasn't after that," Elizabeth says quickly. "Though I don't think it would've stopped me." Her fingers interlace with her partner's skeletal ones. "She's my whole life. Plus, how cool is finding out that fiends are real? I would've been thrilled to go along with that no matter what." Her teeth show in a playful smile. "Oh, right, and she's the most caring person I've ever known and understands me in a way no one else could. Plus, the tongue."

Abby's black eyes roll at that. "Gee, Liz, you're so professional."

"I'm not at the office now. I can flirt with you."

"Love you too."

"That's really cute," I say, giving Mia's thigh an affectionate squeeze. I wonder if we'll ever end up anything like them. We still haven't said those words beyond her accidentally letting them slip when she moved in. And when I did as well, now that I think about it. "I'm happy for you."

"Yeah, me too," Mia adds, clearly realizing vivisection is off the table. "I was her vet when her parrot was sick. Not quite as touching a story as a lifelong romance."

"Well, Harvey's in love with you too, if that helps."

"It does a little."

"Harvey?" Abby asks.

"Her bird," Liz says. I suppose that hardly counts as breaking confidentiality. It's not like he's also her client. Though that would be interesting to see.

Abby nods, a finger tapping the table since she has no food to busy herself with. "I always thought parrots made the most interesting pets. I considered getting one, but I can't really anymore. Animals are all scared of me. I can't even pet a dog."

"I think I'd die," Mia says. Can I just not let her talk to Abby? "That sounds awful. I'm so sorry. Animals are the only thing that kept me going for most of my life." That's really not helping. "Do you know what it is that scares them? If it's because of how intimidating you look, I've known a lot of blind animals. We could go to the shelter and find you one? Hell, sometimes people leave abandoned animals with us, and I'm usually the one who drops them off since I'm the one who closes every night. Would you like me to get you one of them or check the shelter? I'm sure they would love having these woods to explore and run around in, and as gentle as you seem, if they aren't too scared of you initially, I think they'd adjust pretty quickly." Okay, she may have saved it.

"Liz, would that be okay?"

"Of course. You could take it hunting with you."

"Then, yeah, I'd love that."

Mia grins. "Oh, and don't worry, animals being scared of you is nothing to be too embarrassed by. I had to use that mind control trick on a cat the other day because it wouldn't stop freaking out over my undead ass."

"You learned it on your own?" I ask, genuinely impressed. "That's amazing. It took me years to sort out how to mesmerize people."

"It was either that or drug the cat, and ironically, I hate doing that if I can avoid it."

"Well, I'm still impressed." I bet she wouldn't have been able to pull it off if she was still high all the time. Influencing people requires a good deal of empathy with them in order to make them feel what you want, and that requires being able to feel. It's why it doesn't work so well when you're having a panic attack, as I've learned a few times.

"Would a blind dog be able to hunt?"

"A blind bloodhound probably could," Mia says after a moment's consideration. "Not sure how well they could hunt, but they mostly just go by scent, right? I'll look into it. Do you still want one if it can't?"

"Yeah, definitely."

"All right. Well, I'll let you know what I find out, and I'll tell you when we have any blind animals for adoption or anything else that might be easier to deal with for you."

"Thank you." Her jagged teeth show in a simultaneously terrifying and affable smile. "I really appreciate that."

We talk a bit more, and Mia manages to avoid making an ass of herself. I'm in awe of how much she's changed in the time that I've known her, but I suppose I couldn't exactly see me even going to a gathering like this just a few months ago. Maybe we really are good for each other, despite all of our issues.

"Do you think we could take a look at those necklaces?" I ask after we finish helping with the dishes.

"Of course," Liz says. "Abby, you found where we put them, right?"

"Yeah, the box is in the living room."

We meet her in there and find a box full of jewelry, most of it tangled together, a few crosses standing out, and a handful of rather handsome necklaces separated in their own corner, likely ones they wear. Merely looking at them hurts, but I move close, taking in the sight. Mine doesn't seem to be on the top, but there're enough there that it could be somewhere in the pile.

Mia steps up, putting her hand in the box. "Wait, are you sure you can?" I ask.

She shrugs.

"Does it hurt at all looking at them?"

"No, does it hurt you? Holy shit, it does?" She stares, looking more and more concerned as the implications dawn on her. "Then how can you handle going to church? Are you sure you even want me to get this necklace if it's only going to hurt you?"

"It's worth it. I'm sure. Please look."

With a quick nod, she picks up the first necklace, blissfully unharmed by it, and shows it to me, looking ready to throw it away if I catch fire or whatever she thinks it may do to me.

"I'm fine," I insist. I shouldn't have asked her. Now she's always going to worry about me.

She goes through a few crosses and crucifixes. They're all quite beautiful, but they're not… At the next one, my heart starts only so it can stop again. I lick my lips, trying to form words. It's been so long. Can that really be it? Taking a nervous step forward, I reach for it, but she rips it away from me before I can touch it. "Ollie!"

She's just worried about me. I can't be mad about that. "What does it say on the back?"

She turns it over and holds it up to her eye, blowing off some dust and rubbing it with her thumb. Her lips curl in a blissful smile. It can't be. Is it? "Olivia, my dearest daughter."

The world shimmers as I find tears in my eyes. It's my crucifix, the one my mother gave me when I was a child. All this time and I finally have it again. Even if I can't touch it, it's here, it's mine. My hand flies up to my mouth to stifle a sob. I can scarcely believe it's real.

"It's the right one?" Liz asks, setting a hand on my shoulder. "That's amazing."

Unable to form words, I only nod.

"It's yours."

"Thank you," Mia says for me, gripping my hand.

"Well, you are apparently getting my wife a puppy, so it's the least I can do."

I can't take my eyes off the cross, no matter how much it pains me. It's here. After all these years, it's really here. I find myself reaching for it but pull my hand back. "Ollie?" Mia asks, meeting my eyes. I try to find any words to reply with, but they seem to have all fled. "I know it hurts, honey, I'm sorry that you have to go through this." She seems to be searching my eyes for something, trying to decipher some clue. Her expression changes as if she's realized something. "You still feel damned, don't you? Like, even after all this, he doesn't forgive you."

It's not what I was thinking, but it's certainly true. As wonderful as having my mother's cross back feels, it hurts just as much and in as many ways. "Well, think about it. You made me. I'm a vampire because of you." Yeah, as if I needed that reminder. I know how she feels about it. "And I can touch it. Maybe that's a sign that God has forgiven you. You know I'm not the religious sort, but that sounds like how it goes. You went through all this, and you've more than made up for what you did, and now you have your cross back, and I can touch it for you. If he was ever mad at you, that must mean he's forgiven you."

The room swims. The dam breaks, and my tears fall free. I don't know if I believe what she's saying, but I love the idea. And it does sound like God.

As I'm still too emotional for words, Mia bids our farewells, thanks them for dinner, and does all of the normal activities one would expect after a dinner party, but all I can think about is that necklace. It's like my life has been taken back 511 years. For so long, it was his. He'd stolen it from me, but Mia killed him, and now she's gotten me back my crucifix. She even saved my soul.

Mia turns from the passenger's seat of the car to stare at me in shock. "What was that?"

It takes me a moment to realize what I'd said. "I love you."

I can see that flight instinct in the back of her mind, but she throws an arm around me, lays my head against her shoulder, and whispers, "I do too."

It's months before we manage to both intentionally say it, but there's no longer any suspense. We know it to be true. We have years of therapy and progress to make it through before we can be fully functional people, but together, we seem to have formed something of a functioning relationship. I think I can say without any question that I have the best vet in the whole world.

About the Author

Genevieve McCluer was born in California and grew up in numerous cities across the country. She studied criminal justice in college but, after a few years of that, moved her focus to writing. Her whole life, she's been obsessed with mythology, and she bases her stories in those myths.

She now lives in Arizona with her partner and cats, working away at far too many novels. In her free time she pesters the cats, plays video games, and attempts to be better at archery.

Books Available From Bold Strokes Books

Entangled by Melissa Brayden. Becca Crawford is the perfect person to head up the Jade Hotel, if only the captivating owner of the local vineyard would get on board with her plan and stop badmouthing the hotel to everyone in town. (978-1-63555-709-1)

First Do No Harm by Emily Smith. Pierce and Cassidy are about to discover that when it comes to love, sometimes you have to risk it all to have it all. (978-1-63555-699-5)

Kiss Me Every Day by Dena Blake. For Carly Jamison, wishing for a do-over with Wynn Evans was a long shot, actually getting one was a game changer. (978-1-63555-551-6)

Olivia by Genevieve McCluer. In this lesbian Shakespeare adaption with vampires, Olivia is a centuries-old vampire who must fight a strange figure from her past if she wants a chance at happiness. (978-1-63555-701-5)

One Woman's Treasure by Jean Copeland. Daphne's search for discarded antiques and treasures leads to an embarrassing misunderstanding and, ultimately, the opportunity for the romance of a lifetime with Nina. (978-1-63555-652-0)

Silver Ravens by Jane Fletcher. Lori has lost her girlfriend, her home, and her job. Things don't improve when she's kidnapped and taken to fairyland. (978-1-63555-631-5)

Still Not Over You by Jenny Frame, Carsen Taite, and Ali Vali. Old flames die hard in these tales of a second chance at love with the ex you're still not over. (978-1-63555-516-5)

Storm Lines by Jessica L. Webb. Devon is a psychologist who likes rules. Marley is a cop who doesn't. They don't always agree, but both fight to protect a girl immersed in a street drug ring. (978-1-63555-626-1)

The Politics of Love by Jen Jensen. Is it possible to love across the political divide in a hostile world? Conservative Shelley Whitmore and liberal Rand Thomas are about to find out. (978-1-63555-693-3)

All the Paths to You by Morgan Lee Miller. High school sweethearts Quinn Hughes and Kennedy Reed reconnect five years after they break up and realize that their chemistry is all but over. (978-1-63555-662-9)

Arrested Pleasures by Nanisi Barrett D'Arnuck. When charged with a crime she didn't commit, Katherine Lowe faces the question: Which is harder, going to prison or falling in love? (978-1-63555-684-1)

Bonded Love by Renee Roman. Carpenter Blaze Carter suffers an injury that shatters her dreams, and ER nurse Trinity Greene hopes to show her that sometimes love is worth fighting for. (978-1-63555-530-1)

Convergence by Jane C. Esther. With life as they know it on the line, can Aerin McLeary and Olivia Ando's love survive an otherworldly threat to humankind? (978-1-63555-488-5)

Coyote Blues by Karen F. Williams. Riley Dawson, psychotherapist and shape-shifter, has her world turned upside down when Fiona Bell, her one true love, returns. (978-1-63555-558-5)

Drawn by Carsen Taite. Will the clues lead Detective Claire Hanlon to the killer terrorizing Dallas, or will she merely lose her heart to person of interest urban artist Riley Flynn? (978-1-63555-644-5)

Lucky by Kris Bryant. Was Serena Evans's luck really about winning the lottery, or is she about to get even luckier in love? (978-1-63555-510-3)

The Last Days of Autumn by Donna K. Ford. Autumn and Caroline question the fairness of life, the cruelty of loss, and what it means to love as they navigate the complicated minefield of relationships, grief, and life-altering illness. (978-1-63555-672-8)

Three Alarm Response by Erin Dutton. In the midst of tragedy, can these first responders find love and healing? Three stories of courage, bravery, and passion. (978-1-63555-592-9)

Veterinary Partner by Nancy Wheelton. Callie and Lauren are determined to keep their hearts safe but find that taking a chance on love is the safest option of all. (978-1-63555-666-7)